Pierre Loti, E. P. Robbins

Into Morocco

Pierre Loti, E. P. Robbins

Into Morocco

ISBN/EAN: 9783742819901

Manufactured in Europe, USA, Canada, Australia, Japa

Cover: Foto ©Andreas Hilbeck / pixelio.de

Manufactured and distributed by brebook publishing software
(www.brebook.com)

Pierre Loti, E. P. Robbins

Into Morocco

INTO MOROCCO

BY

PIERRE LOTI,

AUTHOR OF "THE ROMANCE OF A SPAHI," "THE ROMANCE
OF A CHILD," ETC.

TRANSLATED BY

E. P. ROBINS.

ILLUSTRATED BY

BENJ. CONSTANT AND AIMÉ MAROT.

––––––––

CHICAGO AND NEW YORK:

RAND, McNALLY & COMPANY, PUBLISHERS.

1892.

This Book is dedicated to

MONSIEUR J. PATENÔTRE

French Minister to Morocco

with the grateful and affectionate respects of

THE AUTHOR.

PREFACE.

WHAT I have to say requires a few words of preface, for which I may be pardoned, as it is my first offence in that line.

I wish to say a few words of warning to the large number of people for whom my book was not written. No one need expect to find in it dissertations on the political condition of Morocco, on its future, or on what is to be done to bring it into harmony with the modern movement ; in the first place, these considerations have no interest for me, and then, what is more important, my reflections, to what small extent they have been carried, are directly opposed to common sense.

Circumstances gave me a close insight into the government of the country, and its court and harems, but I have been careful not to make my reflections public (while approving of everything in my inner consciousness), for fear of the brawlings that might arise among the witless. If the Moroccans, who received me so kindly, shall chance to read me, I trust that they will appreciate my discreet reserve.

Again, in these naked descriptions to which I have determined to limit myself, I am gravely suspected of partiality for this land of Islam, I, who through some inexplicable freak of heredity or of far remote pre-existence, have always felt myself half Arab at heart. The sound of the little African flutes, of the tam-tams and the iron castanets, awakens in me unfathomable memories, and charms me more than the most scientific harmony; the most trifling arabesque design over some ancient gateway that time and weather have almost obliterated—nay, even the simple whitewash, lying like a shroud on some old ruined wall—lull me into dreams of the mysterious past, and cause to vibrate within me I know not what hidden chord. Often at night, while lying in my tent, I have listened, absolutely carried away and thrilled through every fibre of my being, when some one of our camel-drivers chanced to strike upon his guitar a few notes that fell upon my ear, shrill and plaintive, like the tinkling of falling drops of water.

It is true that it is not very cheerful, this empire of the Moghreb, and I must admit heads fall there occasionally ; still, as far as I am concerned, I have met only with hospitality there. The people may be rather impenetrable, but they are smiling and courteous, even the common class. And whenever I in turn endeavored to say something nice, I received my thanks for it by that pretty Arab gesture, which consists in laying the hand on the heart and bowing, with a smile which discloses rows of pearly teeth.

As to his majesty, the Sultan, I am glad that he is handsome ; that he will have neither press nor parliament, roads nor railroads in his dominions ; that he rides splendid horses, and that he made me a present of a long, silver-mounted musket and a great sword inlaid with gold. I admire the lofty, serene, disdainful way he has in looking at outside contemporary agitations ; I agree with him in thinking that the faith of our fore-fathers, from which still spring martyrs and prophets, is a good thing to cling to, and a sweet consolation to man in his last moments. What boots it to take such pains to overturn everything, to understand and embrace so many innovations, since we must die; since some day, in sunlight or in shade, when, God alone can tell, we must give up the ghost? Nay, let us rather hold to the traditions of our fathers, which, by uniting us more closely with the generations that are gone and those that are to come, seem to lengthen out our own days. Let us live in a vague dream of eternity, careless of what earth has in store for us to-morrow ; let us suffer our

walls to crumble away beneath our burning summer sun, let us suffer the grass to grow on our
roofs, our cattle to rot where they fall. Regard-
less of all beside, let us grasp as they pass those
things which do not deceive : beautiful women, fine
horses, magnificent gardens and the perfume of
flowers.

Let those alone, then, accompany me in my travels who have sometime at evening felt a thrill
pass through them at the first plaintive notes of the
little Arab flutes accompanying the drums. They
are my comrades, they who have experienced that,
my comrades and my brothers ; let them mount
with me my broad-chested brown horse with flying
mane and tail, and I will be their guide over plains
carpeted with flowers, across solitary deserts of iris
and daffodils ; I will conduct them under the fierce
sun to the very depths of this immemorial country,
and will show them the dead cities there, whose re-
quiem is the murmur of unceasing prayers.

As for others, let them spare themselves the
trouble of commencing to read me ; they would not
understand, and my song would appear to them
monotonous and confused, the outcome of an empty
dream.

P. LOTI.

L. M. J. Viaud, known to the reading world under his nom de plume of "*Pierre Loti*," was born, in 1850, at Rochelle. The example of an elder brother seems to have strengthened the boy's inherent disposition toward a life of travel and adventure, and, at an early age, he entered the French navy, in which he now holds a rank corresponding to that of captain among us. He was thus afforded opportunities of visiting many places out of the beaten track, and the result has been the delightful volumes of impressions that have given him his well-deserved reputation. His recent contest with Zola, for a place among the "*Immortals*" of the French Academy, in which he scored a victory over the great novelist, is still fresh in the memory of all.

In 1889, the French government, finding that there were some old scores with the Sultan of Morocco that needed settling, determined to send an embassy to that potentate. M. Patenôtre (the same who is to succeed M. Roustan in the French legation at Washington) was intrusted with the mission, and invited Loti to make one of his suite. Had it been a question of visiting any civilized *country, the writer would have spurned the offer ; but Morocco, the land of darkness and mystery, that was another thing ; he accepted, and gave us another of his pleasant books, " Au Maroc."*

The reader who expects to find in Loti tables of distances, political disquisitions, or essays on commerce and trade statistics, will be disappointed, for these subjects, and all allied to them, he holds in supreme contempt.   He states his creed very explicitly in his introduction to " Morocco."   Notwithstanding this apparent inattention to detail, however, it will be found that he is a close observer, otherwise he could not give such vivid and faithful pictures of the scenes that he describes..   He not only sees, but feels; and when, to this faculty, there is added a poetic imagination and an equaled power of word-painting, it is not surprising that his books are considered very charming reading.   It is doubtful if there is any other traveler who has the power to impress his reader as he does with a sense of verisimilitude ; his word-pictures are so warm, so glowing, that one feels they must be true.   Let the reader who is disposed to mount with him his " brown, broad-chested horse, with flying mane and tail," decide how faithfully he keeps the promise with which he concludes his preface to the present volume.

M. Loti's wanderings have led him to almost every quarter of the globe, and he has given us books whose scenes are laid in the South-Pacific,

Japan, and Eastern Asia, Northern Africa, and his own sunny land of France. His more recent works — "Le Roman d'un Enfant," and "Le Livre de la Pitié et de la Mort,"—are introspective, and rather melancholy, not to say sombre, in their tone. It is to be hoped that before he finally assumes his seat at the domestic fireside he will give us some more of his delightful "impressions de voyage."

E. P. ROBINS.

October, 1891.

INTO MOROCCO.

I.

Mᴀʀᴄʜ 26th, 1889.

FROM the southern coast of Spain, from Algésiras and Gibraltar, can be seen across the strait, Tangier the White. This Moroccan city, posted like a sentinel upon the northernmost point of Africa, is quite near our Europe; the mail-boats reach it in three or four hours, and every winter it is visited by many tourists. It has become very common-place, and the Sultan of Morocco partially abandons it to foreign visitors and ceases to interest himself in it, looking upon it as an infidel city. Seen from the deck of the approaching steamer, it has a cheerful, gay appearance, with its villas in the European style standing among their gardens; still, it has a foreign look, and remains more

1760

Mussulman in appearance than our Algerian cities, with its walls of snowy white, its crenellated *Casbah* and its minarets covered with old earthen plates.

It is singular to note how much more striking is the effect produced by arriving here, than that produced by arriving at any other of the African ports of the Mediterranean. In spite of the tourists who land with me, in spite of the few French signs that are displayed here and there in front of the hotels and bazaars, as I step onto the wharf of Tangier to-day under the bright noon-day sun, I feel somehow as if I had suddenly taken a step backward through past centuries. How remote we are, all at once, from Spain, where we were only this morning; from the railroad, from the speedy and comfortable steamboat, from the very time in which we had thought we were living ! Something like a winding sheet seems to have been dropped behind us, deadening the sounds of elsewhere, checking the currents of modern life ; the old, old winding sheet of Islam, which will no doubt enshroud us more and more closely in a few days, when we shall have advanced more deeply into this gloomy country, but which already produces a sensible effect on imaginations fresh from European contact.

* * *

Two guards, Selim and Kaddour, in the service of our minister, looking like characters from the Bible, in their long flowing woolen robes, are awaiting us at the wharf in order to conduct us to the French legation. Gravely they walk before us, with their staves driving from our path the small jackasses that here supply the place of trucks and drays, which are totally unknown. We climb upward to the city along a sort of narrow pathway, between crenellated walls, which rise in steps, one above the other, white and melancholy as snow-banks. Those whom we meet, robed in white also, like the walls, drag their slippered feet noiselessly through the dust with majestic unconcern, and it is easy to see, simply by their way of walking, that they have nothing in common with the activities of our age.

We have to cross the main street, where we notice a few Spanish shops, some French or English signs, and among the multitude of bournouses, alas! some gentlemen in cork hats and some pretty young lady travellers bearing upon their cheeks the mark where the sun has kissed them. But no matter; Tangier is Arab still, even in the quarter devoted to trade. And farther on, as we approach the French legation, where hospitality is extended to me, there commences the labyrinth of little narrow streets, where the houses are buried under successive coats of whitewash that have been applied and renewed from remote times.

II.

AT sunset of the day of our arrival, I proceed to pay my initial visit to our travelling camp, which is being made ready for us out yonder on a lonely elevation beyond the walls, overlooking Tangier. It is a small migratory city, complete in itself, already set up and inhabited by our Arab escort ; around it our horses, our camels and our bat-mules, tethered with long cords, are grazing on the short, sweet grass ; it is all like a tribe on the move, a *douar ;* a Bedouin odor is prevalent through it all, and mournful songs, sung in falsetto, and the twanging of guitars are heard proceeding from the tents of the camel-drivers. The whole, men, material and cattle, was provided by the Sultan for the comfort of our minister. I satisfy myself with a long look at these persons and things, with whom we must be familiar and live, who are soon to penetrate with us into this unknown land.

The falling night and the cold wind, which, as is always the case, springs up with the fading light, increase the feeling of remoteness from home which impressed me when I first touched the soil of Morocco.

The western sky is of a clear dark blue, verging into a pale, extremely cold yellow ; Tangier, visible down below me in the distance, resembles a hap-hazard collection of stone-blocks upon a mountain side ; as it grows darker, its white tones change to tints of a cold steely blue ; beyond stretches the dark blue of the sea ; still beyond, like a phantom of slate gray, rise the shores of Spain, of Europe, with which this country, it seems, has as little intercourse as possible. Seen from here, this portion of our own world, which I left behind me so few hours ago, seems to have suddenly retreated to an immeasurable distance.

On my way back to Tangier I pass through the place of the *Grande Marché*, lying a little above the city, outside the old crenellated walls and the ancient ogival gateways. It is almost dark. Covering the ground for the space of about a hundred square métres is a mass of brown objects that move uneasily ; kneeling camels, making ready for their night's rest, interspersed promiscuously with Bedouins and bales of merchandise ; caravans, that over blind and dangerous roads have perhaps started from the confines

of the desert, aiming to reach this place, where
old Africa ends, facing the shores of Europe, at
the gateway of our modern civilization. The
hoarse sound of human voices and the grunting
of animals arise from the confused masses that
cover the place. A negro fortune-teller is singing softly and beating his drum in front of a little fire, which flares up and casts its yellow light
upon the persons who squat around it in a circle.
The night air grows cooler and cooler and sends
forth damp exhalations. The stars shine out in
the clear depths of the sky. And now a great
Arab pipe sets up its wailing lament, drowning
all other sounds in its s' rill yelping tones . . . .
Ah! I had almost forgotten that sound ; how
many years it is since it last pierced my ears !
It makes me shiver, and now I receive a very
vivid, a very striking impression of Africa ; such
an impression as one only receives the day of
landing, such as one does not have on succeeding days, when the faculty of comparison has become blunted by contact with novelty.

It keeps it up, does the pipe, with increasing
fury, its monotonous, ear-splitting melody, and I
rein in my horse that I may hear the better ; it
seems to me that the air it is playing is the
hymn of by-gone times, the hymn of the dead
past. For a moment I feel a strange pleasure in

reflecting that as yet I am only on the sill, at the gateway that has been profaned by the footsteps of the world, of this empire of the Moghreb into which I am soon to penetrate ; that Fez, our destination, lies far away beneath the consuming sun, deep-buried in the bosom of this inanimate, close-walled country, where life is now the same that it was a thousand years ago.

III.

APRIL 3rd.

EIGHT days have passed in preparations and delay.

During the week spent at Tangier we have been bustling about, very busy in inspecting tents and in testing and selecting horses and mules. And many times have we climbed the hill out yonder, where our camp has been steadily waxing in size as objects, animate and inanimate, poured into it ; always standing, as it does, facing the distant shores of Europe.

At length it has been definitely decided that we set out to-morrow morning.

Yesterday and to-day the vicinity of the French legation is like a port where emigrants are embarking, or a town given over to pillage. The little white, winding streets are filled with great bales and boxes by the hundred, all covered with Morocco carpets striped with many colors, and secured by cords made of rushes.

IV.

APRIL 4th.

TO guard our countless packages our people have slept in the street, bundled up in their bournouses and their heads buried in their hoods (*capuchons*), looking like so many shapeless heaps of gray wool. At break of day, all shake off their uncomfortable torpor, awake and are on foot. At first the uncertain calls and the hesitating steps of people between sleeping and waking, soon to be succeeded by shouts and fierce disputes. The harshness and the deep-drawn aspirates of the Arab tongue, moreover, as it is used by the common people, might induce one to believe that they were overwhelming each other with abuse. All the usual morning sounds, such as the crowing of cocks, the neighing of horses, the braying of mules and the grunting of camels in the nearby caravansery are drowned in this grand concert of disturbance, which increases continually in volume. Before sunrise it has reached an infernal height; shrill cries, such as we hear from monkeys, a wild pandemonium fit to curdle one's blood. In my half awake condition, I should imagine, were I not familiar with their African splutter, that there was a fight going on under my windows, and that, too, of the fiercest kind; that they were killing and eating each other. As it is, I just say to myself: "Our cattle are coming up and our muleteers are commencing to load them."

It is no small matter, it is true, to load a hundred headstrong mules and stupid camels in these little streets that are scant two métres wide. There is no place for the animals to turn, and they snort in their distress; some of the cases are too large, and are caught in the angles of the walls; there are encounters, collisions, and kicks.

Along about eight o'clock, the tumult is at its height. Seen from the terraces of the legation, as far as the eye can reach, all is an inextricable confusion of men and beasts, all giving tongue at the very top of their voice. Besides the bat-mules, there are those of our Arab escort, equipped with harness of a thousand colors, with high-peaked saddles on their backs and saddle-cloths of red, blue or yellow cloth, hanging down like skirts. The brown-faced, white-robed horse-men are already in the saddle, their long, thin muskets slung behind their backs. The whole train, which is to precede us under the conduct of a Cadi sent by the Sultan, gradually and with difficulty puts itself in motion, man by man ; by dint of many a shout and blow, they all melt away in the direction of the city gates, and finally leave the little streets around us clear.

Then comes the turn of the beggars—and they are plentiful in Tangier; the halt, the lame, the blind with bleeding holes where eyes should be, mad men, idiots ; all flock to the legation to say good-by. Observant of custom, the minister appears upon the door-sill and throws out handfuls of small silver money, so as to deserve the prayers which are to bring good luck to our caravan.

* * *

One o'clock of the afternoon is the hour fixed for our departure. The rendezvous is appointed at the place of the *Grand-Marché*, the spot where, on the evening of my landing, I first heard the never-to-be-forgotten music of the Arab pipes. The great, muddy, stony esplanade lies overhanging the city, its dimensions extending far in every direction. Here the surface of the ground is constantly concealed by a layer of kneeling camels, and the behooded, becloaked crowd, where a reddish earth color predominates, swarms and stirs with the activity of an ant hill. All which is arriving from, and all which is departing for, the far regions beyond the desert, assemble and are confounded upon this place. Here, from morning to night, the drum rattles and the flute wails, and fortune-tellers, fire-eaters and snake-charmers ply their trade.

To-day the usual bustle and turmoil is increased by the formation of our caravan. Before noon, under the bright sunlight, the first of our horsemen begin to make their appearance; our guard of honor, the headmen, and the Sultan's standard-bearer, who is to march at the head of our column during the entire journey.

It is high market in the place; hundreds of camels, mangy and repulsive, are kneeling in the dust, stretching their long, hairless necks to right and left with snake-like undulations, and swarms of peasants and paupers in gray bournous and brown tunics move about confusedly among the reclining animals. It is an immense confusion, all of one same dead neutral tint, serving admirably as a foil to the white city, overtopped by its green minarets, and the deep blue Mediterranean, as they lie basking in the splendid light. The oriental coloring of our horsemen, too, stands out more boldly against this dull background; their pink, orange or yellow caftans, their saddle-cloths of red stuff, or of velvet of many shades. Our embassy is composed of fifteen persons, of whom seven are officers, and the uniforms add their gold and color to increase the diversity of the picture. We are accompanied by five *chasseurs d'Afrique* in their blue cloaks. In addition to all this, almost the entire European colony has come out on horseback to see us off; there are the foreign ministers, the attachés of the legation, the painters, and good-natured people of all sorts. And here comes, too, the Pacha of Tangier, to see us as far as the verge of his dominions; a venerable, white-bearded man he is, with a head like a prophet, clothed in white from head to foot and mounted on a white mule with red trappings, which is led by the bridle by four attendants. Any one beholding us might take us for a cavalcade taken from some theatrical spectacle.

Let us turn in our saddles and bid a last farewell to Tangier the White, whose terraces lie far beneath us, sloping down the mountain-side to the sea; let us not forget, too, to say farewell to those bluish mountains that are visible across the strait, for they are in Andalusia, the extreme southern point of Europe, so soon to fade away from our view. One o'clock has come, the hour appointed for us to march. The red standard of the Sultan, which is to be our guide to Fez, is shaken out to the breeze, surmounted by its

brass globe ; the drums and flutes of the mountebanks serve for martial music, and so our column
is off, very gay and brilliant, even if somewhat
disorderly.

Our horses are feeling good, too, and dance
along the sandy roads of the suburbs as they are
wont to do at the start of an expedition. Our
way at first lies between rows of European villas
and hotels, where some good-looking lady tourists
have congregated under the shade of their para-
sols to see us pass. We really might almost
think we were in Algeria, at some review or
other military ceremony, were it not that the
terrible condition of the roads and the entire absence of wheeled vehicles give to the approaches
of Tangier a strange and unusual appearance.

All our surroundings, however, quickly
change their aspect. After riding four or
five hundred métres, the aloe-bordered avenue
which we have been following all at once dries
up, so to speak ; disappears among the fields
and is seen no more. There is never a road in
Morocco in any place whatsoever. There are goat
tracks that have been widenened and deepened
by the passage of caravans, and one is at liberty
to ford the rivers wherever fancy may dictate.

To-day these pathways are in horrible condition. The soil, saturated by the winter's rains, gives way everywhere beneath our horses' feet, and the poor beasts sink deep into the yielding quagmire of black mud.

One by one the friends who have accompanied us so far leave us and turn their horses' heads towards home, after a warm shake of the hand and many a wish for a safe journey. Tangier, too, has at last disappeared behind the lonely hills. Soon we are abandoned to ourselves. to follow the red standard of the Sultan, which we shall have to do during a ride of some twelve days, alone in this wild, silent land, where the sun pours down floods of light.

V.

TIME, eight o'clock on the evening of the same day. Place, under my tent, by the light of a lantern, in some spot or other where we have pitched our camp for the night. Left suddenly quite to myself in the midst of the deepest silence, calm after the turmoil and excitement of the day and resting peacefully upon my little camp-bed, I take pleasure in reflecting upon the great regions that stretch away around us, where there are no roads, no houses, no protection from the weather, no inhabitants.

The rain beats against the tight-stretched canvas, which is my walls and roof, and I hear the whistling of the wind. The weather, which was so fine at our departure, took a change for the worse as night came on.

We made but a short stage of it on this first day; only some twelve or thirteen miles. Before daylight left us we could discern our little travelling city standing waiting for us, cheerful and hospitable, all white among the green solitude. It was started off in good season this morning, reached its destination, was unpacked and set up, and the two flags of France and Morocco were flying over it in fraternal union when we came up. There is a Cadi who is responsible for the tents, whose duty it is to attend to the pitching of the camp at night and the breaking of it in the morning. The sites are always selected in advance, close to rivers or springs, and as far as possible on dry ground where there is good grazing for the animals.

* * *

My bed, which is very light, is comfortably arranged on my two boxes, so as to be sufficiently elevated above the floor, out of reach of the ants and crickets; my saddle serves as a pillow, and I am wrapped in a coverlet of Morocco wool, striped with orange and green, which keeps me warm and comfortable, while the cool night wind blows in on me loaded with the health-bearing odor of grass and wild flowers. Over my head the roof is shaped like a great umbrella; it is white, the seams are ornamented with blue lace and finished off with gores of red leather. Surrounding it, like one of those moveable canvases which serve to enclose a circus tent or a merry-go-round, a *tarabieh* is fastened, that is to say, a sort of little circular wall of white duck, set off in the same way with blue lace and red gores, and kept in place by stakes driven into the ground. All the tents in Morocco used by chiefs and by persons of the higher class are constructed on this model. There would be room enough for five or six beds like mine, but the Sultan in his munificence has alloted to each of us a separate dwelling.

For a floor I have the short, close turf embroidered with the blooms of a minute variety of iris; it makes a beautiful, sweet-scented carpet, in the midst of which three or four marigolds, springing here and there, stand out like small rosettes of gold.

My companions and our Arab escort are doubtless doing as I have done: they have gone to bed and are preparing for sleep; throughout the camp no sound of man is to be heard.

And whiie I am revelling in this restful silence,
in these fresh odors, and this pure bracing air,
behold ! I chance to cast my eyes upon an article by Huysmans in a review that I happen to
have brought with me, descriptive of the delights
of a sleeping-car ; the sooty smoke of the lamps,
the crowding and the bad smells of the contracted berths ; above all, the charms of the neighbor
overhead, a fat, flabby, wheezy gentleman of fifty,
with charms dangling from his watch-chain, glass
in eye and cigar in mouth. My feeling of supreme content increases with the certainty that
this neighbor of Huysmans is too far away to
trouble me. The portrait of the self-important,
elderly gentleman of our time, travelling express,
is sketched with a master hand. In my delight
at knowing that this kind of a character does not
as yet favor Morocco with his presence, I am
conscious of a dawning feeling of gratitude
toward the Sultan of Fez, for that he will have
no sleeping-cars in his empire, and that he does
not interfere with the wild by-ways where we
can gallop our horses in the open air.

At midnight the hail is beating on the ground
outside and my canvas walls are shaken by a
sharp squall of wind. Then a confused sound

is heard of approaching voices, and some one carries a lantern around my abode ; the forms of those without are reproduced on the tightly-drawn canvas as gigantic arabesques, as if in a transparency. It is the officer of the guard with his men, coming with mallets to drive my tent-pegs, for fear lest the wind should carry away my house.

It seems that when the Sultan is travelling with his great tent, which requires sixty mules for its transportation, if the wind gets high during the night the mallets are not called into requisition, lest the noise disturb the slumbers of the master and the pretty ladies of the harem. But a regiment is routed out and seated in a circle around the ambulatory palace and there remains until daylight, holding in its many hands the ropes which keep the walls in place. The story was told me to-day by a gentleman who was for a long time an inmate of his majesty's household, as we were trotting along side by side; this squall puts me in mind of it ; —and so I commit myself again to slumber, to dream of this court of Fez, where so many mysterious veiled beauties dwell in seclusion behind the envious walls.

* * *

About two o'clock in the morning we are again aroused from our slumbers ; horses are snorting, hoofs thundering over the plain, Arabs shouting. Our animals have stampeded and broken loose, maddened by some indefinable terror. I hope that they will take another direction than mine, and not come and entangle themselves in the ropes and upset my tent ; that would be no end of a nuisance, with the rain pouring down as it does.

Praise be to Allah ! the mad hunt takes another direction and is soon swallowed up in the surrounding darkness. Then I hear our men bringing back the fugitives, and peace is restored —silence—sleep.

VI.

APRIL 5th.

AT six o'clock, broad daylight, the bugle of one of our chasseurs d'Afrique sounds for reveille. We must be quick in turning out and getting into our clothes ; already the Arabs are in my abode to pull it down—my white duck house that got such a soaking in last night's rain. The work is done in less time than it takes to tell it ; the wind coöperating, the canvas rises, flutters an instant with a noise like the sail of a ship going about, then falls flat upon the wet grass; I fasten my spurs and finish the other details of my toilette in the open air. The little flowers which slept under my roof-tree will have their liberty again, will again enjoy the refreshing showers, and again will be consigned to solitude.

All our camp is dismantled in the same manner, is folded up, is tied in packages secured with many thongs, and is loaded on the backs of the kicking mules and grunting camels. Forward! Camp is broken.

* * *

Our horses are in great spirits at the start; they dance, whinny, amuse themselves with a pretense of attack and defence.

Our second day's march commences among mountains covered with thickets of holm-oak, with heather and daffodils. You scarcely ever see a tree in Morocco, but as if to atone for this, there are the grand tranquil lines of the virgin landscape, unbroken by roads, houses or fences. The country is uncultivated, left to lie almost in its primitive state, but it appears to be wonderfully fertile. Here and there you will see a few fields of wheat or barley, to which it has not been deemed necessary to give the rectangular form which obtains with us, and which present the appearance of meadows of a tender green. How restful to the eye is this, after our petty French system of farming, the land cut up and parceled out in squares like a checker-board. Before this time, in other lands, I have felt what a comfort it is to live where space is free and where the title to land rests in no one ; there it seems that the horizon extends immeasurably further, that the field of vision is infinitely enlarged, and that the far-stretching landscape has no bounds.

Drawn in relief against the tranquil green distance that keeps unrolling itself before us, some fifty métres or so in advance of the main body, our advance guard is constantly to be seen, the guides whom we follow as they un-interruptedly recede before us ; three horse-men riding abreast. The middle one is a tall old negro of majestic carriage, in pink cloth caftan and bournous and turban of snowy white, carry-ing high aloft the standard of the Sultan, the red silk standard with its globe of brass ; those at his side, negroes as well and similarly dressed, holding in their hands their long muskets, the bright barrels of which gleam out against the bluish background of the mountains and the plains.

* * *

About ten o'clock, beneath a sky as gray as ever and in the midst of a country that has lost nothing of its verdure and its wildness, we are conscious of a motionless array of men on horseback, drawn up in line to receive us. We are about to change from one territory to another, and all the men of the tribe which we are approaching are under arms, their chief at their head, to receive us. As is customary upon the passage of an embassy. they will escort us through their country, and our late companions will return to Tangier whence they came.

As we look upon them at rest and at a distance, what a strange set of cavaliers they are ! Perched on their lean little horses, on their high peaked saddles that are almost like easy-chairs, they look like so many old women shrouded in long, white veils, or like old black-faced dolls, or old mummies. They carry long, thin sticks covered with shining tin—but these are the barrels of their muskets—their heads are all done up in muslin and their bournouses hang down over their horses like shawls.

We draw near, and quickly, at a word of command given in hoarse tones, the whole array scatters like a swarm of bees, horses curveting, arms jingling, men shouting. Under the spur their steeds rear, leap, gallop like frightened gazelles, mane and tail flying in the wind, clearing rocks and great stones at a bound. At the same instant the old dolls have been restored to life ; they, too, have become superb ; they are metamorphosed into tall, active men, with fine keen faces, standing erect in their great silver-plated stirrups. The white bournouses, which but lately made them look ridiculous, now fly open and stream behind them in the wind with the most exquisite grace, revealing beneath robes of red, orange and green cloth, and saddles with housings of pink, yellow and blue silk embroidered in gold. And the fine symmetrical arms of the men, of the color of light bronze, emerge from the wide sleeves that are turned back as far as the shoulder, brandishing in the air in their headlong course the heavy bronze muskets which, in their hands, seem no heavier than reeds. It is a first welcoming fantasia,* given in our honor. As soon as it is concluded, the chief who played the part of leader comes forward to our minister and extends his hand. We say farewell to our companions of yesterday, who withdraw, and under the escort of our new hosts we continue our journey.

---

* Fantasia—an exhibition of Arab hard riding.

VII.

I REMEMBER travelling all the afternoon of this day over interminable sandy plains, covered with fern, very like our *landes* in the south of France. These plains, extending as far as the eye could reach, were of a bright, soft green, the tender green of early April. One thin ray of sunshine fell on them persistently just at the spot where we chanced to be, as if the light were following us, while all around us the grand mountain horizons, over which the black clouds were hanging low, melted into the sky in ominous, oppressive darkness. The sunlight, filtered through the misty curtain, gave a pale effect of silver plated with gold, and it was an unexpected sight to find these African plains so clouded and so fresh.

As we rode along, our horses' hoofs, crushing the stalks and leaves, brought out very perceptibly the delicate odor of the ferns, and this recalled to my mind the fine June mornings of the country of my birth, and the coming to market of the hampers of cherries. (In Saintonge cherries are always packed for transportation in fern-leaves, hence the two odors are always inseparable in my mind).

Every five minutes, on both sides of our

column, bands of Arab horsemen, going like the wind in a direction opposite to ours, would meet us. The sound of their horse's tread was scarcely to be heard on the sand or the vegetation ; the only warning that we would receive of their approach was a faint clank of arms and the noise of their bournouses as the wind took them ; it was more like a squall singing through the rigging of a ship, or the noise made by the flight of a large flock of birds. We would find difficulty in getting out of their way, so as to avoid being run down by them. And at the moment of meeting us, they would utter a hoarse cry and then fire a blank cartridge from their long muskets, enveloping us in the smoke. These fleeting visions, these warlike nightmares in their swift flight, thus continued appearing incessantly to our right or to our left.

It was only toward evening that there was a cessation of these fantasias. The country around us took on a still more beautiful green and might almost be said to be wooded ; there were clumps of olive-trees, and the dwarf palms were so old and tall as almost to reach the dignity of trees. Here and there hamlets were seen on the hillsides, their walls of beaten clay and roofed with gray thatch, the whole surrounded and almost concealed by hedges of cactus of dark green, bordering on blue.   And from these formidable enclosures, all bristling with needle-like thorns, women, clad in ragged robes of gray wool, came forth at our approach to do us honor with cries of "you! you! you! you!" uttered in shrill, piercing tones like those of martins as they circle through the air of a calm summer's evening.   Then we left this inhabited region behind us, and after fording two or three streams, down in a fresh green level, we saw our men just completing the work of setting up our camp.   Our horses whinnied with pleasure at the sight.

*   *   *

Our little city never changes; it is always laid out on one unvarying plan, as if it were carried about in its entirety on rollers. Each of us as he comes up, goes straight to his own abode, which always occupies the same position relatively to the others ; there he finds his bed, his traps and his Moroccan carpet laid over the primeval carpet of grass and flowers. We travel with all the comforts of a tribe of nomads, with nothing to trouble us, only having to enjoy the free air, the motion and the limitless space.

Our fifteen tents are arranged in a true circle, enclosing a sort of place, or inner pasture ground where our horses graze. Each one is like the other, the central pole surmounted by a great ball of copper and the outside of the walls decorated with rows of arabesques in dark blue, contrasting boldly with the prevailing white. (These arabesques are made of pieces of cloth cut out and sewed on; they are of one unvarying, extremely ancient design, dating back to remote antiquity : the same that the Arabs carve in stone on the top of the walls of their mosques, that they embroider on the border of their silk curtains, that they employ in decorating their pottery ware; they are also to be seen on the panelling of the Alcazar and the Alhambra.)

The tents of the camel-drivers, the muleteers and the guards form a second circle outside of and surrounding our own. They are smaller and more pointed than ours, of an uniform grayish color, and arranged in a less orderly manner. They form a quarter that is purely Arab in character, where our pack-animals are tied and from whence the sound of strange weird music is heard issuing in the watches of the nigh

** * **

The appearance of the *mouna* is always the most noteworthy event of the conclusion of our day's journey; it generally appears about twilight, accompanied by a long procession, and is deposited on the ground before our minister's tent. I must be pardoned for using this Arab word, but it has no equivalent in French : it is the tithe, or contribution, that our character of embassy gives us the right of levying on the different tribes along our route. Were it not for this *mouna*, which is ordered a long time ahead and frequently brought from a great distance, we should be liable to die of starvation in this country where there are no markets, no inns, scarcely even a village, where the land is a wilderness.

Our *mouna* this evening is of royal abundance. In the fading daylight we see a line of sedate, white-robed men advancing in the midst of our camp ; their handsome chief, a man of noble bearing, marches with stately step at their head. As we catch sight of them, our minister withdraws within his tent, so as to receive them at his threshold, in accordance with the dictates of Oriental etiquette. The first ten men bear great jars filled with butter made of the milk of sheep, then come jars of milk and baskets of eggs, round wicker baskets containing live chickens tied together by the paws, four mules laden with loaves of bread, oranges and melons ; finally twelve sheep, which men drag along by the horns, and which are reluctant to enter the camp,

poor things, as if foreseeing that there is something evil in store for them. There is sufficient
to feed ten caravans like ours, but it would be
fatal to our dignity to decline any part of it.
Then, too, the guards and muleteers are waiting
for their share with the greediness of their wild
nature; all night long they will make good
cheer, they will have enough left over for to-morrow, and there will be enough of the fragments
to feed the stray dogs and the jackals. Such is
the custom that has prevailed for ages; in the
camp of an ambassador there must be an uninterrupted feast.

*　*　*

All fall to upon the quarry the moment the
minister has returned thanks to the givers, which
he does by a simple movement of the head, as is
fitting in the case of a very great lord. At a sign
our people come forward; the bread, the butter,
the eggs are divided up and carried off in the
folds of the bournous, in hoods, in baskets of
grass, in the pack-saddles of the mules. The
sheep are taken behind the cooking tents to an
evil-looking little nook that we seem to carry
with us in our travels day by day, and they have
to be dragged there forcibly, for they understand
what is awaiting them and struggle and hang back.
There, by the expiring daylight, with scarcely

light to see, they are slaughtered with a blunt knife ; the ground is always bloody in that little nook. The chickens, too, are killed there by dozens, the head being only partially separated from the body so that they may flutter for a long time and drain themselves of their blood. Then fires are everywhere lighted for the Pantagruelian Bedouin cooking ; little yellow flames run flickering here and there over the piles of dry branches, bringing out sharply groups of camels and mules that before were invisible in the darkness, or the forms of the tall, white-robed, ghost-like Arabs. In the midst of the wild country, which extends around us on every side in an immense circle and which appears darker and darker than ever now that the fires are lighted, we might be taken for a camp of gypsies engaged in an orgy.

The weather continues overcast and very dark; it is almost cold. We are in a region of pasture land and marshes. And while the preparations for the feast are going on, the frogs simultaneously commence their nightly concert in all directions, even in the remote distance, an eternal music which has been performed in all ages and in all lands.

** * **

About eight o'clock, just as we are finishing dinner under the great tent which does duty as our common dining-room, some one informs the minister that a heifer has been sacrificed to him out-doors there, at the doorway of his tent, and we take a lantern and go out to learn who has offered the sacrifice and the reason of it.

It is a custom in Morocco thus to sacrifice animals at the feet of great men as they pass on their journeys when there is a boon to be requested. The victim must die a lingering death, parting with its blood drop by drop. If the great man is disposed to look with favor upon the petition, he accepts the offering and directs his servants to remove the carcass to be cooked and eaten ; in the contrary case he continues his journey without turning his head, and the rejected offering is left to the ravens. It seems that sometimes when the Sultan is travelling, the road which he has followed may be traced by the dead bodies of animals.

The heifer, still alive, lies before the minis-ter's tent, across his doorway ; it is breathing heavily, with wide extended nostrils ; the light of the lantern shines upon the blood which runs from its throat and collects in a pool upon the grass. And there are the supplicants, three women, embracing with their arms the flag-staff which bears the standard of France.

They belong to the neighboring tribe. During the first few moments of the repast with which our guards were gluttonously appeasing their hunger, under cover of night, they succeeded in penetrating among our tents without being perceived; then, when efforts were made to drive them out, they attached themselves to the flag-staff, as if its protection secured them from danger of attack, and no one dared to remove them forcibly. They brought with them four or five little young ones, clinging to their garments or suspended from their necks. In the darkness, and with their veils down, it is impossible to tell whether they are young and pretty, or old and ugly, while their forms are effectually concealed by their loose flowing robes, hanging suspended from their shoulders, where they are fastened by great plates of gleaming silver. The interpreter comes up and more lanterns are brought, which bring out in sharper relief the group of white-clad forms around the beast which lies drawing its last breath upon the ground.

They are the three wives of a chief of the neighborhood. For certain misdeeds, unnecessary to mention here, their husband was im-

prisoned at Tangier some two years ago, at the
instance of the French legation; and now
they would like to have the new French minister, as an act of mercy upon his accession,
intercede with the Sultan of Fez to give the
prisoner his liberty.

He may be very guilty, this chief; whether
he is or not I won't pretend to say; but his
wives might move a heart of stone. The minister is of the same opinion, so far as I can see,
and, although he will not formally commit himself at the moment, their cause seems to me in
a fair way for a favorable decision.

VIII.

April 6th.

ABOUT five or six o'clock in the morning,
before reveille sounds, I raise the flap of
my tent and look out; the first early view of the
surrounding country produces an unexpected
impression.

A sky of uniform darkness overhangs all the
broad green country in which we are; great plains
stretch away, covered with irises, with dwarf
palms, with daffodils, and here and there with
great tufts of daisies, so thick that they look like
drifts of snow; all wet and heavy with rain or

dew. In the distance, this vivid green becomes
darker beneath the heavy, low-hanging clouds;
it turns to a dark gray, and finally, off toward
the horizon, it gradually shades off into the
black of the mountains and the sky : a cheerless
dawn to look upon, in a spot that lies lost in the
midst of an immense primeval country.

The servants have been early astir, and the
mules, ready saddled, stand crowded against each
other, sleeping on their feet, while their high-
peaked saddles, covered with red cloth, form
brilliant splashes of color on the neutral tints,
the grays and blacks, of the background. There
they stand, motionless, as if they had been made
ready for some fairy spectacle for which there
are no spectators. One by one our guards
awake and come from their tents, stretching
their long brown arms, their robes and their veils
always giving them the appearance of lean old
women, or gigantic gypsies.

The supplicants of last evening, they, too, are
still there! In spite of the drenching rain, it
seems that they have spent the night cowering in
front of the minister's tent. Their numbers have
even increased this morning : old women, young
women, the captive's entire family, no doubt, and
poor little babies, hooded after the Bedouin
fashion, sleeping in their mother's bosom, be-

numbed with cold. Near them, on the wet grass, at the spot where they slaughtered the heifer, is a great stain of blood, that the rain has not washed away. I approach the group; an old tatooed woman, who tells me she is the chief's mother, seizes the skirt of my cloak and kisses it. From this moment, I feel that they have entirely gained me over to their side, and I promise them my intercession at the proper time.

How gloomy this place is under such surroundings; how melancholy and mysterious! How white our tents stand out against the dark background!

IX.

OFF we go at a gallop in the cold morning wind, like a fantasia, riding nearly all abreast, pell-mell, climbing a hill. A very pretty sight it is, too, to see our bright uniforms and the gay bournouses relieved against the bright green of the hill-side. No one knows what idea has taken possession of the three old negro images who lead us that they should rush the standard of the Sultan forward at such a pace, but our horses are fresh and willing to follow, and we are not going to hold them in. And it is good to awake to this hurly-burly, to the rapid motion, to the jingling of arms, and to the excitement of the race through the pure air that no one had ever breathed before and that fills full our lungs.   The bat-mules, which had first shown an inclination to keep with us, are soon left behind; a dozen or so of them, loaded with our stores, go down and roll over and over ; then there are shouts and shrieks from the Arabs; the muleteers hurry up, bournous streaming in the wind ; like birds of prey they fall in clouds upon each unlucky animal, to raise it, reload it, beat it.   In our headlong course we catch only vague glimpses of these scenes, and then lose them from sight again.   Besides, it is no affair of ours, nor do we let it bother us at all ; the baggage is sure to come up all safe at the end, and the chief is responsible for it all.   So we keep on, straight ahead ; in the wind, through the rain, which is commencing to streak the sky, let us keep to the gait of our wild Arab race.

When we stop in our headlong course, the rain is falling in torrents and the wind is piping its lament in our ears.   We are on high, broken ground, in a sandy country, covered with a sparse growth of bracken; before us the undulating plain stretches away in sandy knolls as far as the eye can carry. The sand is of a golden yellow and very fine; we trot over it as noiselessly as we would over the tan-bark track of a riding school. The bracken predominates, but intermingled with it are daffodils, lavender, and quantities of a white flower that closely resembles a large species of eglantine. Drenched as they are by the rain, all these plants are delightfully fresh and exhale the sweetest perfumes beneath the rapid beat of our horses hoofs.

For the succeeding two hours, we traverse a more cheerless country, stony and seamed with many a ravine, with much of the sweet-scented furze, covered with yellow flowers, and a few hawthorns here and there; this is in turn succeeded by a region of wild little valleys, each one exactly like the other, and all equally destitute of any trace of human habitation. The sky grows blacker and blacker, the wind shrieks more loudly over the heath and the rain beats in our faces. It reminds one of old-time Brittany, before the days of church-spires and way-side images; of pre-historic Brittany as it might appear in the spring time.

Our three old ebony images, the advance guard, have drawn the pointed hoods of their cloaks up over their ears; towering erect upon their small steeds, their bournouses spread out behind in order to protect their horses' croups, they resemble so many baboons, when thus seen from behind—conical shaped baboons, broad at base and terminating in a sharp point. And the red standard, too, which was brand new when we took our departure, now hangs draggled around its staff, an object pitiable to look upon.

* * *

It seems that we are about to change tribes and enter upon the territory of El-Araïch, for down below there, on the crest of the hill, are a hundred horsemen awaiting us. They are an odd looking troup as seen through the blinding rain ; all robed in white with their hoods down, their thin-barreled muskets held erect, they neither speak nor stir. It is striking to see them thus, motionless as so many mummies, when we know that in an instant the very madness of motion will seize upon them, and that we shall see them striving to outstrip the wind in their headlong course, while horses' manes and tails, gay bournouses and disheveled turbans will be streaming in the air like pennons.

From among the horsemen as they stand thus hooded and mummy-like, their chief advances to the front in order to give his hand to the minister. His face is regularly beautiful, sweet and mystical like that of a holy prophet. He wears a pink cloth caftan and a double bournous of white and blue, the one draped over the other; his steed is a dapple gray, caparisoned with green embroidered with gold. His lieutenant, who rides at his side, contrasts with him by having a cruel face, a thin, little, hooked nose like a hawk. He wears a capuchin brown caftan and a slate-colored bournous, and bestrides a yellow horse with blue trappings. Such is the effect of light in this country, that even in this gloomy, rainy weather, these combinations of color produce an effect that no costume could attain to under our European sky.

In spite of the rain we all have to assist at the great fantasia of welcome. As one man the horsemen throw back their hoods and put spurs to their horses, which bound forward madly, heads up. Allah ! with neighing of horses and shouts of men, the race has commenced, draperies stream in the wind and muskets circle in the air. Three-fourths of the guns miss fire beneath the torrents of rain, and the chief overwhelms us with excuses, explaining that the powder is wet. But it is very fine and very animating notwithstanding, perhaps even more so than it would be under a clear sky : the mad horsemen, the stinging rain and the black clouds, all driven by the wind in one eddying vortex.

In this new escort, which is to accompany us until to-morrow, there are to be seen looking out from beneath their turbans more than one pair of very savage eyes.

*   *   *

A halt is called of two hours for breakfast on a hill-top where, by some extraordinary chance, a village has been built. (It is owing to these noonday halts that each day the tents and baggage reach the end of the day's route before we do, and that we always find our camp pitched and ready for us upon our arrival.) Our people hastily set up the great dining tent, which, an exception to the rest, always travels at the same gait we do, keeping close in our rear. As the weather is cool, they also light a great fire of leaves and twigs of the dwarf palm, which exhales a balsamic odor and gives out a cloud of smoke.

The village here, like those we saw yesterday, is composed of little gray thatched huts, concealed behind hedges of aloes or of great bluish cactus. Close at hand stands a date-palm, its top swaying on its slender stem high above the ground, the first that we have met since our departure. There is also the tomb of some holy marabout of great repute for piety in the surrounding country, and a white flag flying over it serves to tell the lone traveler and the passing caravan that it is well for them to stop and leave a few pieces of money as an offering at the shrine of the holy man. (In Morocco there are many of these sacred tombs with their white flag, even in the most desolate regions, and the infrequent passer-by leaves his gift there, which is almost always respected by the robbers.)

While we were breakfasting on what was left of last night's *mouna*, it cleared off with a celerity known only to Africa; the sky swept clear of its clouds, took on again its magnificent transparency of blue, and the sun came out dazzling.

In this treeless country the eye is capable of ranging over immense distances ; moreover there is scarcely ever a house or a village to break this great green or brown monotony, so that the eye accustoms itself to search the extreme limits of the horizon, and, as on the broad expanse of the ocean, to discover at a glance anything out of the common, anything indicative of life or movement, even at distances where, in our country, objects would be entirely undistinguishable. If on some desert hillside, blue in the distance, we see some white points, if they are motionless, we

say they are stones ; if they move, we say they
are sheep. A collection of reddish points indicates a herd of cattle. Finally, a long brownish
train that keeps advancing with an incessantly
undulating, slowly creeping movement, is, our
eyes at once tell us, a caravan, in which we might
even discern the camels following each other in
file and sleepily swaying their long necks from
side to side.

An object, singular from its associations, that
has followed us from Tangier, and that we have
become accustomed to look for, sometimes
ahead of us, sometimes behind, is the electric
boat, of some twenty feet in length, which we
are transporting as a gift to the Sultan. It is
enclosed in a wooden box painted of a grayish
color, so that it is not unlike a great block of
granite, and it advances with difficulty, over
mountains, across valleys, on the shoulders of
some forty Arabs. We are familiar with similar scenes in the Egyptian bass-reliefs, where
we see enormous burthens like this carried by
men with white turbans and bare legs.

*   *

Our encampment to-night is at a place called
Tlata-Raïssana, where it seems that a great fair
is held every month for the sale of slaves and

cattle. To-day, however, the place is a desert. It stands on the bank of a fresh water stream, among mountains that are covered by such an uniform growth of bracken that they would seem to have been upholstered in cloth of a beautiful green color. As is always the case, our tents are surrounded by flowers, but none of them are the flowers of France; in this particular nook, abounding in furze, species grow that are unknown in our territories; extremely sweet, all of them, and some of them of remarkable color.

Fantasias are racketing around the camp all the evening; until the going down of the sun nothing is heard but the thundering of horses' hoofs, the cries of the Arabs, and the report of fire-arms.

* * *

About seven o'clock the *mouna* makes its appearance in camp with the customary cere-monial. But it will not answer; only eight sheep and the rest of it in proportion. It is not sufficient for an embassy; we must refuse it in order to maintain the dignity of the flag. And this refusal constitutes a diplomatic inci-dent, which would have serious effects for the chief of the region, should the affair come to the ears of the Sultan. The handsome chief in the pink robe affects surprise and consternation; he lays it all on the shoulders of the subordinate chiefs, who in turn shift the responsibility upon some other people, and these last fall upon the innocent shepherds and give them a sound beating. The whole thing, however, was nothing more nor less than a plot arranged among them all to see how far they could go with us ; a suitable *mouna* was all prepared in case of need, and concealed in a ravine a little way off. After supper, a new procession appears by the light of the moon, bearing sixteen sheep, a goodly number of chickens, loaves of bread and jars of butter. The chiefs, apprehensive of what the minister may say, wait silently around his tent in the majesty of their long white bournouses.

The new *mouna* is all that it should be, is accepted, and so there is an end to the incident.

———

X.

SUNDAY, APRIL 7th.

UNDER a dark and lowering sky we crossed the first of the surrounding mountain ranges, clad in their smooth coats of bracken, and came out on vast solitudes white with daffodils in flower. Here and there a great gladiolus, or a tuft of violet colored iris, relieve the monotony of this great flower garden by their lively hues. And thus it continues as far as the eye can reach. Now and then a stork sails slowly overhead, beating the air with wings of black and white—or crows, or sometimes an eagle.

The rain hangs on. Not a living thing to be seen this morning ; not a group of laborers, not a train of asses, not a caravan. Finally a camel, with her young one, that has been lying hid by our path, comes up and watches us with interest as we pass by. The young camel, which cannot have been long in this world, I think, is so thin of neck and so small of head that any one a little way off would take him for a four-footed ostrich. In his astonishment at sight of us, in his youthful and timid gracefulness, he comes near to being pretty.

Rain, rain, torrents of rain. Our three old negro images, the advance guard, have drawn their hoods up under their eyes until more than ever they are like pointed baboons. The silk standard, which the middle image always carries upright as if it was a wax candle, is nothing but a colorless rag, torn by the wind. Water streams from our clothing. The Sultan's boat, still reminding us of the passage of the Egyptians, gets forward with the greatest difficulty, the feet of its forty bearers sinking deep into the soaked ground at every step they take.

After two hours spent thus in this meadow of daffodils, we notice something that resembles a very long crack winding through the plain, something which can be nothing else than a river running between deep banks. It is the Oued M'cazen, reputed to be difficult of passage, and on its bank there is a group that bodes no good; loaded mules by hundreds, camels, horsemen, footmen, all evidently halted there because the river is not fordable. What then are we to do?

The Oued, swollen by the rains, is angry and rapid, and rolls its turbid waters with a sullen roar; moreover, it is evidently very deep. It runs between lofty, vertical banks of clay that have been soaked by the rain until they have become slippery and dangerous. With our European ideas of travelling, it would seem to be physically impossible to pass over our men, tents and baggage without a bridge. The chiefs think differently, however, and the attempt is to be made, sending the heavy freight over first.

First our laboring men promptly divest themselves of their bournouses, disclosing their tawny forms, and plunging into the cold, seething waters, ascertain that the depth is a scant two mètres. With a little effort then on our part the crossing may be effected.

We will make the initial attempt with some of the mules that are lightly loaded. By dint of many blows they make the passage, swimming to the middle of the stream, struggling an instant against the current which carries them away, then quickly regaining their footing in the mud of the opposite shore with loads intact, although thoroughly soaked in the muddy water.

But as our ambassadorial dignity will not permit us to remove our clothing, how are we to pass? And our camp beds? And our fine gold embroidered uniforms, which are to figure in our presentation to the Sultan? A little troop of horsemen gallop up and signal us from the top of the opposite bank. We are safe. It is a certain Chaouch, of Kazar-el-Kébir (a town that lies in our route), who comes to our assistance with a numerous fol-

lowing, bringing a "mahadia" that he has hastily constructed for our behoof. (A mahadia is a
great mass of reeds, compactly bound together
with cords so as to float.) Two by two we shall
embark on this improvised raft, we shall be
hauled across by a cord, and our baggage and
camp equipage will follow in the same way, as
dry as if in a ferry boat.

As to the rest of our following, every one
must swim for it, man and beast, and that quickly. The headmen rush to and fro, shout, call to
each other in tones to split their throats, always
using those hoarse aspirations which would lead
one to believe they were suffocating with rage.
" Ha ! Caïd Rhaâ ! " " Ha ! Caïd Abder Han-
an ! " " Ha ! Caïd Kadour ! " And right and left
they ply their sticks upon those who hesitate to
make the plunge into the chill water. Resigned-
ly the handsome Arab horsemen undress, then
strip their horses and remount, holding their
steeds in the grasp of their sinewy legs as in
the grasp of a vise of bronze. On their heads,
done up in a monumental bundle, they place
their caftans and their bournouses, and still above
this their high-backed saddles and their trappings of state, and to keep all in place they raise
their arms, like the handles of a Greek amphora.
Next all these multi-colored scaffoldings are seen

advancing resolutely in the direction of the river, each one having for base that uncertain object, a rearing, restive horse, hanging down along the flanks of which are two bare legs; and all these men, burdened as they are, deprived of the assistance of their hands, urge their horses down the slippery and almost vertical bank by the mere pressure of the knee against the flank. The horses whinny with fear; they slide down, like a man on skates or like one descending a toboggan slide, some on their feet, some on their haunches; and plastered with the slimy mud, with a tremendous splash, they tumble into the waters of the Oued, where they breast the strong current and scramble up the opposite bank like so many goats.

Among them are some who stumble and, failing to recover themselves, go down; some of the horsemen, embarrassed by the weight of their fine bournouses and their heavy saddles, take a header in the river. Loaded mules are caught in the viscous mud and struggle frantically; they are extricated by dint of shouts and blows, horribly galled by their girths and pack-saddles, their flesh raw and bleeding. Our tents, so white but a short time since, are dragged through the mud. It is a strange spectacle that we behold beneath this leaden sky, in the midst of the grassy plain upon these banks of grayish clay, the bustling activity of a hundred horses and horsemen of all shades of color, of as many mules, camels, bearers and laborers. We might be taken for a tribe of emigrants that some sudden accident has put to rout.

Now the situation is complicated by a drove of cattle crossing the stream by swimming, in a direction opposite to ours. They are cattle with a mind of their own, and would much rather have remained on the far shore, but the Arabs who have charge of them resist this inclination, swimming with one arm and beating their charges with the other, twisting their tails to force them onward, or dragging them forward by their horns.

Toward the end the clay banks, worn by so many descents, have become as smooth as looking glasses. Then the scene becomes wilder still, the hurly-burly greater, the shouts louder and more furious; a confused mass of terrified animals, naked men, baggage of every description, red saddles and packages wrapped in envelopes of every color of the rainbow. It is a scene such as must have been witnessed at the time of the invasion of the armies of the prophet. A great picture of ancient Africa, admirable for life and color, is this which we behold among these solitary plains, under this clouded sky.

At length, after shouts and blows innumerable, the transit is successfully accomplished, and we are all on the far bank with our baggage, without loss of life or property. Our bedding and camp equipage are soaked with water and smeared with mud, our panting mules are sadly galled; as for ourselves we are only drenched with rain.

The desert of daffodils and iris begins again; for an hour we journey on through the monotonous landscape, lying silent and gloomy beneath the falling rain. Our band is increased by the people of Kazar-el-Kébir, who come to meet us under the leadership of Chaouch; about a dozen mounted Arabs and as many long-haired Jews with great gold rings in their ears, mounted on asses, two by two. Kazar-el-Kébir, which will be our halting place to-night, is the only city between Tangier and Fez, and Chaouch, a fine looking Arab with a purple bournous, is our consular agent there. If it is asked why we require a consular agent at Kazar-el-Kébir, the answer is that we have French "protégés" there—some twenty of them—as we have at Tangier and at Tetuan. In most of the Mussulman cities of Turkey, Syria and Egypt, we have these "protégés"; that is to say, people upon whom it is not permitted to lay hand unless with the consent given of our legation.   In Morocco, I never knew why, most all our protégés are Jews.

So we jog onward across the flower enameled plain.   Innumerable swallows skimming along the ground, flit between our horses' legs.   Now and then we come across a flock of sheep.   The shepherd or shepherdess is a little heap of grey wool, ending in a pointed hood, squatting among the grass in the rain.   As we pass, the bournous sits up and finally rises erect on foot, to enjoy the astonishing spectacle of our march past. Then there is to be seen, beneath the rags, the half naked, lithe and yellow form of a child ; almost in every case the face is intelligent and prepossessing, with very white teeth and big black eyes.

Toward evening we enter a cultivated region. The country is uninteresting, reminding one of the plains of la Beauce, but on a very much larger scale, without houses or fences ; great fields of Indian corn and interminable fields of barley.   The rich, black soil must be wonderfully fertile.   What a granary of abundance this Morocco might be made !

On an elevation which closes in our view in front, we behold something unexpected, a spectacle to which our eyes have not been accustomed for some time past—a crowd of human beings.

It is the population of Kazar-el-Kébir, come out to meet us, that now sways back and forth against the grey background of sky, all draped in their grey bournouses. Some are on foot, some are mounted, all are hooded, and they stand like rows of pointed shades. Already we hear the beating of the tambourines and the squeaking of the pipes.

As soon as we are near enough, all the long muskets, loaded with powder only, are discharged toward us, while the musicians, in mad crescendo, emit their most ear-splitting strains. Then the whole array, by a flank movement, surrounds us, and, penetrating our lines, the two bands are mingled in one confused mass, the horses crowding against and biting one another. The bold riders trot their horses, the footmen use their legs and run, their bournouses streaming in the wind, to avoid being ridden down. There are quantities of children on asses, two or three sometimes mounted on one beast, as if a skewer were run through them—a comical sight. There are old men with crutches who still have not lost the faculty of running; there are beggars and idiots, and holy men singing their sacred songs. And the tambourinists, who are on foot, beat their instruments madly, frightening our horses. And the pipers, who are mounted on

mules and whose cheeks are distended like the
bag of a bag-pipe, their eye-balls starting from
their sockets, blow, blow to burst a blood-vessel,
urging on their wayward beasts by kicks from
their bare heels ; one of them, a rotund little
fellow with a big head and an enormous stomach,
mounted on a diminutive ass, might have sat for
the picture of old Silenus. He sticks persistently at my side, pouring into my ear the yelping notes of his pipe, sad as the voice of a jackal.
In drawling, mournful falsetto, the men shout at
the top of their voice: "Hou! May Allah
grant victory to our Sultan Muley Hassan !
Hou !"

Excited and uneasy, our horses dance to the
music of the tambourines, keeping time to the
rhythm, and thus we journey on toward Kazar-
el-Kébir in an intoxication of sound, deafened
by the strange music.

Little by little Kazar, at first only dimly seen
through the rain, reveals itself to our view.
Placed in the middle of a plain fertile as the
promised land, it is surrounded by groves of
olive trees and magnificent green orange trees.
It is not white, like the towns of the Arabs, but
a neutral, dark tint is the prevailing one, and

its fifteen or twenty minarets, of a dark brown color, might be taken for the church spires of our northern cities, so that, beneath this cloudy sky and across these flooded plains, we might think we were entering a Flemish town. It requires the few palm trees that are swaying gracefully on their lofty stems down yonder to produce in us the impression of Africa. This impression, however, soon becomes firmly fixed in our minds, as we approach the crumbling old ramparts and look upon the exquisite ogive arches of the gateway, with their surrounding arabesques.

We find our poor little camp going upon a hillside, about two hundred mètres from the walls, in an abandoned cemetery where the ancient tombs are covered over with golden-yellow lichens. Tents, bedding, baggage are lying on the grass, soaking in the rain. A troupe of mountebanks, unpacking their effects in a snow-storm, could not afford a more mournful spectacle.

In addition to the *mouna* which is obligatory, we were this evening furnished, as a compliment, with several dishes ready cooked and hot. It is, moreover, the first appearance in our camp of a utensil with which, we are told,

we shall become better acquainted at the banquets of Fez : a huge round box, surmounted
by a covering, or I should rather say roof, of
conical form and tapering up to a sharp point,
constructed of esparto grass and gaily decorated
in colors. At banquets of ceremony, the dishes
must always be presented under this covering,
brought in on the heads of the servants. As it
is growing dark, ten solemn persons approach,
decked with this extraordinary head-dress, their
naked arms extended upward to keep it in position
giving the effect of handles of a jug ; and without uttering a word, each deposits his burthen
upon the grass, before the minister's tent. Beneath the covering of esparto there are earthen
vessels filled with edibles heaped up in pyramids ; a sweetened cous-couss, a salted cous-
couss surmounted by a preparation of chicken,
a roasted sheep, a pile of those highly spiced
little cakes known in Morocco as "Gazelle's
Shoes."

And so we eat of all these dishes this evening, under our tent ; our modest little table is
invisible beneath the huge trenchers ; it is like
a supper with Pantagruel. With what we leave
unconsumed, our people will keep up the feast
until daylight ; to-morrow there will not remain
a crumb of these heaps of victuals. No one can

imagine the gourmandizing capacity of the Arabs, in general so abstemious, when fate has selected them to be an escort to an embassy.

XI.

MONDAY, APRIL 8th.

THE bugle does not sound reveille this morning in our camp, which means that the rain has made us prisoners and that the river of Kazar-el-Kébir (the Oued Leucoutz) is, as we had reason to fear, unfordable. We arise later than usual, having slept under a wet tent, over the wet ground, between wet coverings.

Already the sound of the pipes and tambourines is heard, and all the morning our camp is surrounded by a miscellaneous crowd of musicians, mountebanks and buffoons. Poverty stricken people, men and women, also come to gather up from the mud of the cemetery such chicken's claws and half-gnawed bones as they can find, the débris of our last night's orgy.

After breakfast, when the rain holds up a little, we mount and ride to take a look at the ford, that impracticable ford of the river. Under escort of our guards, and preceded always by the red standard, we advance toward the city, which we shall have to traverse in the direction of its greatest length. (Notwithstanding the indisputable warmth of our reception, notwithstanding presents and smiling looks, we follow the advice of those who are wise, which is, never to stir out without an escort, and never to trust one's self alone more than a hundred yards away from the tents; this, moreover, is recommended to us by the Sultan himself, who fears that his Christian guests may suffer by the misconduct of some fanatics.)

The road leading to the city is a sewer of liquid mud, beset with great stones and the decaying carcasses of cattle. We push forward at a gallop, notwithstanding, since such is the custom; this gait is always taken in Morocco, even over by-roads where, with us, one would even be afraid to lead a horse at a walk by the bridle.

Outside the walls which are still standing, hidden among the cactus, the tall reeds and the wild oats, there are many ruins of the old ramparts, dating back to I know not what indeterminate epoch. Kazar-el-Kébir, of which so little is known at present, has a most involved history. In old times, it was from here that the expeditions of the holy war for the conquest of Spain set forth; some centuries later, after the fall of Granada, the city, after having been taken and retaken, destroyed and rebuilt an incalculable number of times, fell into the hands of the Portuguese, and about three hundred years later, as one of the results of the "Battle of the three Emperors," it finally assumed its present status as part of the empire of Morocco. Since that time it has been dozing and gradually wasting away among its delightful gardens.

We make an entry through a series of ancient arched gateways, always splashing through pools of sticky mud, which spouts up beneath our horses' hoofs and makes great blotches on the walls. Among these rain-washed ruins, all to-day is dark and threatening. Every little, narrow, winding street is a sewer, a filthy gutter where horrid stenches are stirred up as we pass. Nothing animated to be seen, save people covered with their gray-white hoods, clothed in gray rags, their bare legs yellow and plastered with mud. They get out of our way and take refuge in doorways to avoid the mud thrown by our horses' feet, and look at us with indifference; their features, generally fine, bear an indefinable sombre and close-set expression; their minds are given over to following the thread of a dream of their ancient religion, to us entirely incomprehensible. It is very evident that these people are not the same as those who came to meet us yesterday with music in the fields; I don't know whence they who gave us that welcome could have come, but these are scarcely curious enough to turn their heads to look at us.

* * *

It is easily to be seen that this city was never built by the Arabs; it is not white, and its sloping roofs are covered with tiles. The buildings are of a dark gray, concealed in spots by patches of yellow lichen, and the whole gives an impression of extreme antiquity in decay. The Portuguese were the builders, and the Arabs, when they came in, found all as it is now, except that here and there they have cut through their inimitable ogives and their portals rich in lace-work carving. They have also erected their mosques, their great square towers where prayers are chanted, and the lofty minarets, roosting places for the motionless storks. But as white-wash would not hold without a glaze on these foreign built walls, the original color has been allowed to remain undisturbed.

In the bazaar, which is roofed over and extremely dark, the passages are so narrow that our horses catch against the booths. The merchants, in white robes and white turbans, squatting in their narrow shops, have no apparent connection

with the commerce of this world, and do not
seem to care for customers. Their stock in trade
consists chiefly of manufactured leather in various forms, ornamented horse-trappings, and
highly colored articles made of esparto grass,
which hang from the beams in all directions
like charms at the end of a watch-chain, and are
shaken by the wind.

Then comes the Jews' quarter, as large at least
as that of the Arabs. Here we might imagine
ourselves to be in Turkey, in Syria or in Egypt
equally as in Morocco ; in all Mussulman countries the Jews are alike ; their faces, their dress,
their houses are copied, as near as may be, from
invariable models.

We leave the city by other archways, which,
though falling into ruin, are still enchanting by
their beauty of form and by the airy grace of the
carved work that enframes them. And before
us is the river, the Oued Leucoutz, (the old Leu-
cus of the Romans). It is broader than the one
which we passed yesterday, and the banks are
higher ; its muddy stream rolls rapidly by with
an ugly roar. Some of our people undress and
dive to ascertain its depth ; three to four métres!
Nothing can be done to-day. It seems that there
is an old ferry boat somewhere in the neighborhood, and it is to be repaired and brought

hither without delay. We will return to the
city where we have invitations to two collations, one at Chaouch's and the other at the
house of a certain *scherif*, whose father was
court-jester and favorite of a Sultan before the
present one.

The receptions at the two houses do not differ
greatly from each other. Dismounting in front
of the little scalloped gateway, cut deep into the
lofty crumbling wall and so narrow that it scarcely
seems to open at all, we are introduced into the
interior court, which is collonaded, and paved
and wainscotted in mosaic. First we are
sprinkled with rose-water from long-necked vessels of silver ; the attendants dash it in our faces
as if it was a scourge ; next pieces of a very ex-
pensive East Indian wood are lighted in a censer
to honor us, producing a dense odoriferous
smoke ; then we are offered " Gazelle's shoes "
on immense plates, and tea in tiny cups, as in
China. The tea is made in silver samovars on
the floor, and is very sweet and highly spiced with
mint, anise seed and cinnnamon. Coffee is
hardly ever taken in Morocco ; tea at all times
and in all places. England supplies it, as well
as the samovars in which it is made and the cups
in which it is drunk. English ships throw these
goods in large quantities into the open ports,

whence caravans distribute them to the remotest regions of Moghreb.

The reception of the Scherif, the court jester's son, however, seemed to me a little the finer of the two, as did also his house, his old tumble-down dwelling, rich in mosaics and resplendent with whitewash. There is something about his personality that is strange and attractive. Over his wild and intelligent features there plays a constant expression of mystic meaning; whenever a compliment is paid him, he folds his hands upon his breast after the manner of the pictures of the early saints and lowers his head with the smile of a young girl.

I linger with him upon the terrace on his house-top, which is as large as a public square and fissured and cut up by sun and storm; its rough places have all been made smooth by the coats of whitewash that have been accumulating for centuries; it is surrounded by a crenellated wall in which are cut narrow loop-holes so as to give an outlook while the observer remains unseen. It is the highest terrace in the city, of which it overlooks every quarter; only the stern old towers of the mosques, with their motionless storks, rise higher in the air. Although not in accordance with custom, he tells me that he passes the greater part of his time here, and especially the summer evenings. He was expelled from Fez for political reasons while he was still a child, and has no hope of ever being recalled from this residence of Kazar-el-Kébir which the Sultan has assigned him as his place of exile. He devotes his time to the study of science and philosophy, such, no doubt, as they were taught in the middle ages, from rare old Arabic manuscripts, where divination and alchemy hold an important place.

There are three of us walking gravely up and down the lofty terrace ; the Scherif, robed all in white, Chaouch in a long violet caftan, and myself, who in some way feel uncomfortable in thus inflicting a blemish upon this immemorial picture, which, were it not for me, might be dated back to the year 1000 or 1200. I reflect upon the depths of tranquility and mysticism which must distinguish the ideas and feelings of this scherif from those of a monsieur fresh from the boulevard ; I try to picture in my mind what may be his cloistered life, his dreams, his hopes, and I envy him the summer evenings that he tells me of, passed in looking down upon all the other terraces of the dead city, in listening to the chanting of prayers, in trying to fathom the distant wilderness of the plain and the surrounding mountains, and in watching the caravans as they creep along the narrow roads where wheels have never passed.

On our return to the camp, splashed from head to foot with the stinking mud of the gutters and by-ways, we find our tents more than ever beset by the rag-tag of Kazar. There is the whole array of fortune-tellers and legless beggars who have dragged themselves hither through the mud on their stumps, in the hope of gathering in their small harvest of bronze *floucs* (petty coins with the impress of Solomon's seal, about seven of which go to a sou). There are old women, too, half naked, down on their four paws under our mules, scratching the ground with their long claws and picking up the unconsumed grains of oats and barley.

XII.

TUESDAY, APRIL 9th.

THERE was heavy rain and a high wind during the whole night. There is not a dry thread under our tents. Once more reveille sounds beneath a lowering sky. We mount, however, resolved to cross the river and continue our journey at all risks. We shall again have to pass through Kazar, with our entire escort of camels and mules ; again we shall have to pass the scalloped gateway, wind among the dark and tortuous lanes, and stir up the vile filth of the gutters as our horses splash through them.

At the exit-gate on the far side of the city, an old woman who thinks that we will not understand her words begs from us while pretending to pray for the success of our journey, and, as she stretches out her hand to receive our alms, she howls : " God's curse be on your religion ! Curses ! Curses on you ! " She rocks back and forth, keeping time to the rhythm of her words, just like an old pauper saying her prayers, and her shrill, mocking voice rises louder and louder, following us as we pass on beyond her.

We make a long circuit among gardens and

orchards, in order to reach the river at a more convenient point, where the boat, which has been put in repair, awaits us.   What wonderful gardens !   The orange groves, perfuming the air around, and the palm trees, and the great cacti, large as trees almost, with their blue-green leaves ; and the red geraniums, and the pome-granates, and the figs, and the olive trees ; all clad in the beautiful, fresh green livery of spring, the tender green of April.   In the redundant exuberance of this vegetation, we find European plants intermingled with those of Africa ; among the aloes there are the tall blue borage covered with a profusion of blossoms, the acanthus, its green leaves specked with white and growing in clumps to the height of eight or ten feet ; the hemlocks and the fennels rise above our horses' heads, and the old walls are clothed with bind-weed and periwinkles.

As we turn and look over the tops of the trees, we behold the gray towers of the mosques growing dim in the distance; in this enchanted grove their summits, which seem to rear them-selves in order to give us a parting glance, serve to strengthen in our minds the stern, cheerless impression which we have received of Islam. And the bridle-paths along which we pursue our way are filthy cesspools, of which nothing in our country can give an idea ; our horses sink above their knees in a kind of slab-broth ; every now and then they stumble over the skull of an ox or the carcass of a dead dog, and at every step, flop, flop, the black mud spurts over us in great streams.

Orioles and finches are singing loudly among the branches, and storks come and perch on one foot in the tree-tops to see us pass. Here and there, giving access to these shady retreats, are ancient, narrow ogive gateways, surrounded with their carvings of scallops and stalactites, exquisite even in their mouldering decay, beneath their shroud of whitewash, with their crowns of trailing roses or red geraniums. Over all the orange trees lift their great masses of white blooms and fill all the surrounding air with their delicious perfume.

The stream of the Leucoutz rolls along no less rapidly than yesterday ; the river seems even to have increased in volume. The boat, however, has been patched up and is here, and we will cross in instalments, as at Oued M' Kazan, leaving most of our people and all our animals to swim over. A crowd has followed us out of the city, especially the Jewish portion, who have no feeling against us. The summit of the bank is soon crowded with human heads peering above the rushes, while the children climb the trees in order to get a better view. Then the drama begins; our escort starts a row which, moderate at first, increases rapidly, and becoming general, assumes a pitch of frenzy.

In order to load the boat, which has to make a countless number of trips, these shouts and blows and fisticuffs cannot be dispensed with. And at last when the work is finished and the boat is loaded with its animate and inanimate cargo and the chief, by dint of furious imprecations, has succeeded in getting it pushed away from the shore, all the men who are in it, apparently from the necessity of exercising their lungs, strike up a prolonged howl of another description, in unison this time; something like a shout of triumph, as if to say: " We are off, we are afloat ! "

The horses hang back ; they cannot see the fun of taking a plunge into the cold, swift stream. The camels, too, wave their long necks, and grunt and groan. Above all, the mules, who are by nature headstrong, will none of it. Sometimes eight or ten Arabs will fall upon a single obstinate brute, who throws back his ears, brays and kicks, his back all raw and bloody where it has been galled by the pack-saddle. The blows fall thick and fast on the poor beast's ribs, which resound under the clubs like a drum.

On the far bank, escorted by a hundred horsemen, with sword by side and musket on shoulder, we re-form our long column among the luxuriant wheat and barley, which carpet the earth with a green so vivid as to seem unnatural. We trample the beautiful vegetation under foot, but that matters little in Morocco, where there is plenty and to spare ; wheat brings three francs a quintal, and every one looks upon it as an article of no importance ; if people only knew enough to store away the harvests at the proper season, there would be no starving ones in Morocco, and the poor old women would not have to come and pick up the grain spilled by the mules, as I saw them do yesterday. The sun has come out scorching ; the weather has changed sharply to stifling heat, under a sky with great blue rifts in it. Kazar-el-Kébir recedes in the distance, with its orange groves, its delightful gardens, its mud, its stinks and its sweet odors.

About noon we again find ourselves in a wild solitary region, and the breakfast-tent is set up in a charming spot that is absolutely redolent with perfume. It is at the bottom of a fresh green valley that has no name, where springs are gushing on every side from among moss-covered rocks, and where cool clear little brooks meander among the myosotis, the cresses and the water anemones. The sky, now entirely blue, is wonderfully clear ; it brings to mind our noontides of the month of June at mowing time. There is still a dearth of trees, but this is atoned for by the carpet of flowers ; as far as the eye can reach, the plain is an incomparable medley of color; but the expression " carpet of flowers," has been so abused by application to ordinary meadows that it loses its force here. There are belts that are absolutely pink with great broad mallows; patches white as snow with daisies ; broad stripes of resplendent yellow where the buttercups are. Never in any bed, nor in any artificial basket in an English garden, have I seen such a luxuriance of flowers, such a crowding together of those of the same species, producing a combination of such brilliant colors. The Arabs must have drawn their inspiration from their lonely prairies when they designed their high grade carpets, variegated with such fresh and striking shades of color, which are manufactured at R'bat and Mogador. The hills, where the ground is drier, are decked out in a different dress ; that is where the wild lavender grows, the plants of which are so thick and bloom so to the exclusion of all other flowers that the ground is absolutely of a violet color, of a sort of ash-colored, grayish violet ; the hills appear to be covered with plush of a very subdued tint, and the contrast with the blazing display of the plains is singular. When the lavender plants are crushed beneath our feet, a strong and healthy odor is disengaged from the broken stalks, and fills our garments and pervades the air. And there are thousands upon thousands of butterflies, beetles and flies and every sort of little things with wings, which are flying about, buzzing and getting drunk on the light and the sweet smells. In our paler lands, or in tropical countries where the heat is enervating, there is nothing that can equal the bright splendor of such a springtime.

At the commencement of our afternoon's march we come again upon the region of the white daffodils, and they remain with us until evening.

About ten o'clock we leave the territory of El-Araïch and enter upon that of Sèfiann. As in every case, two or three hundred horsemen are awaiting us on the boundary of the new tribe, drawn up in line, their muskets erect and glittering in the sun. As soon as they are sighted, the men who have escorted us from Kazar gallop forward and form in line facing them, whereupon we defile between the two columns, and as we pass them the men wheel to right and left, the two ranks close up, are united and follow in our train.

The spot where this manœuvre takes place is, as usual, gay with flowers; flowery as the most wonderful garden. Here and there the tall red gladiolus and the great violet iris are seen among the stalks of the daffodils. Our horses are breast high in flowers; we might extend our arms and pluck great bunches of them without dismounting. And the entire plain answers to this description; no vestige anywhere of human life, surrounded at the horizon by a belt of wild-looking mountains. The long stalks of these flowers give a faint sound as we pass, like the rustling of silk.

The sky is overcast again, but only with a light haze, a web of light fleecy clouds of a delicate gray, which seem to have mounted high into the ether. After the dark, heavy, low-lying clouds, which for days poured down upon our heads their never ceasing showers, it is delightful to ride beneath this reposeful dome, which transmits to us a softened light and still leaves the horizon clear and distinct. The distant hues of the great garden in which we are journeying this evening have all the delicacy of an Eden.

There are incessant fantasias all along our route, which last for two hours yet. First all the horsemen dash forward, two or three hundred at once, and a strange spectacle they present as seen from the rear, their hoods running up to an acute point and their white forms beneath their streaming bournouses; from where we are we cannot see their horses, which are lost to sight among the tall grass and flowers, so that it is difficult to account for these long-veiled gentry, flying with the speed of a dream ; and then this subdued spring sky and all these white robes among the white flowers produce an indefinable impression of religious ceremonial, of " Month of Mary." Suddenly they turn back, all together; then the bronzed faces of the men, and the wild heads of the horses, and the gaudy colors of robes and saddles, all become visible. At a hoarse command given by their chief they return and bear down upon us at the top of their infernal galop—Brrr! .... Brrr! They pass on both sides of our column, standing up erect in their stirrups, giving free rein to their excited steeds, twirling their muskets in the air, their long bare arms escaping from their bournouses, which float upon the wind. And each man of every squad shouts his war-cry, fires his weapon and throws it up and catches it with one hand in his rapid course. We have scarcely time to glance at them when others follow close on their heels, then more, and still more of them, like the unending processions that we see in a theatre. Brrr! .... Brrr! .... they pass with a noise like thunder, always with the same hoarse cries, with the same sound of the daffo-dils broken and crushed as if under the breath of a white squall.

* * *

These men of Sèfiann are by far the hand-somest and the most numerous of all the tribes that we have encountered since we left Tangier. Our encampment to-night will be near the resi-dence of their chief, Ben-Aouda by name, whose little stronghold we can see down yonder in the flowering desert, surrounded by a grove of orange trees. Our tents are already pitched there, in a circle as usual, upon an elevated plain, a sort of esplanade overlooking the un-inhabited wastes, where the grass grows thick and fine. A hedge of prickly-pears, as high as trees, surrounds the camp like the enclosure of a park.

Ben-Aouda's *mouna* is magnificent; it is laid at the feet of the minister by the usual array of grave, white-robed Bedouins. There are twenty sheep, countless chickens, jars containing a thousand and one things, a loaf of sugar for each of us, and, bringing up the rear, four great bundles of wood for our fires. (In this country where there are no trees, this gift of wood is quite a royal one.) And as if this was too little, along toward eight o'clock we see another procession advancing slowly and silently in the bright, blue moonlight; other fifty white shrouded figures, bearing on their heads those great objects in esparto grass that I have already mentioned, which resemble nothing so much as little pointed turrets; in them are fifty dishes of cous-couss, piled up in pyramids, all cooked and ready, hot and hot. So sleepy that I can scarcely keep my eyes open, I am about to retreat to my tent when this concluding tableau of the day falls upon my sight, as if seen indistinctly through a veil; the fifty dishes of cous-couss placed upon the grass in a perfect circle, we in the center; around them the fifty bearers, forming a second circle, in position as if to join hands and dance a reel, but always maintaining their

imperturbable gravity in their long white garments; still beyond, our white tents, forming a
third and more remote circle, and beyond that,
surrounding and enwrapping all, the grand horizon, dim and blue in the far distance. And exactly above us in the center of the heavens, the
moon, a pale ghostlike kind of moon, with a
great white halo around it, seems to be the reflection in the sky of all these round things on
earth.

I am lulled to sleep by the song of the guards,
who have orders to be more than usually on the
alert to-night against nocturnal attacks. As the
sound of their voices dies away and is lost in the
silence of the untenanted plain, there come back
in response the low cries of the jackals, the first
that we have heard since our entry into Morocco;
not very much to speak of, is it? Only two or
three low stifled cries, as if to say; we are here;
but there is something so mysteriously mournful
in it that we feel the very marrow chilled in our
bones at the announcement of their presence.

Beneath the tents sleep, while asserting its
full power over us, is still not heavy; it is very
restful and still checkered with dreams; dreams
which are rather the furtive recollection of

physical sensations and very incomplete, such as the dreams of animals must be. Brrr! there is a sound like the faint echo of a flight of Arab horsemen meeting you in the night, or perhaps you have the impression of flying over the ground on a gallop, the recollection and the consequence of some scamper that you have had during the day, or the arm quickly stiffens itself in the instinctive motion of holding up a stumbling horse. While these confused memories of animal life are passing through your brain, the cool pure air from out-doors is blowing in upon you, and the night's slumbers, commencing very early, generally end with the break of early day.

XIII.

WEDNESDAY, APRIL 10th.

I AM am awakened by cries, fearful cries at my very bedside, a kind of rattling that seems to proceed from the windpipe of some unclean thing that is bursting with rage. It is already day, alas! and soon the bugle will sound, for I can see the dark forms of those outside my tent reproduced in shadow on the canvas, through which the golden light is streaming. The rays of the rising sun also produce for my benefit a profile of the brute that is uttering these villanous cries ; a long, long neck which writhes back and forth like a snake, a small flat head with pendant lips : a camel ! I had recognized him at once by the sound of his horrid voice. Some fool of a camel who is either restive or in trouble. I follow the movements of the shadow on the tent wall with extreme uneasiness. Ah ! It is all over, the mischief is done ; he has got his feet tangled in my tent ropes and now he is plunging and crying louder than ever, shaking the whole edifice, which will certainly tumble about my ears. At last the driver comes running up with his call : "Ts ! Ts ! Ts !" (This is what they say to the camels when they want to quiet them, and the brutes generally yield to the argument.) Again : "Ts ! Ts ! Ts !" He quiets down and goes his way. My tent is safe, and I snatch a few moments more sleep.

Loud and gay, the bugle for reveille ! Our customary hurried toilette follows, then breakfast on black bread and mouna butter, full of red cows' hairs and all uncleanness. While this is going on, the camp is dismantled, then the call for boots and saddles, and away !

Our flowery carpet this morning consists at first of large blue volubilis, interspersed with red anemones. Then come sandy plains, where only

a few scorched, dwarfed daffodils are to be seen;
yellowish expanses which commence to take on ?
Saharan aspect.

We are approaching a place called Seguedla,
where every Wednesday a great market is held,
even more resorted to than that of Tlata-Raïs-
sona, by which we passed day before yesterday ;
it is visited, it seems, by people within a circuit
of eight or ten leagues.   In the distance, in fact,
in the midst of this landscape where there are
no villages, no houses, no trees, down yonder in
the distance, two or three low hills are seen, covered with a coating of grayish objects which look
like heaps of stones, but which have motion and
emit a murmuring sound : it is a dense and compact throng, ten thousand people, may be, all
clad in long gray robes and cowls lowered upon
their necks ; a closely compacted crowd of one
uniform neutral tint, such as the pebbles of the
brook, or dry bones, might be. We are reminded
of those primitive gatherings, composed of nomads to whom it is indifferent whether they be
here or there ; of those multitudes which followed the prophets through the deserts of Ju-
dea or of Arabia.

Our approach is signaled from a distance ;
forthwith the assemblage is stirred by a great
movement and a murmur of curiosity arises from

the throng ; all the yellowish points which top the bundles of gray wool and stand for human faces are turned in our direction. Then, with an outburst of irresistible curiosity, the entire mass wavers, breaks, runs, and finally throws itself upon our horses and surrounds us. We have great difficulty in advancing, and our Arab guards only succeed by dint of repeated blows of sticks, straps and butts of muskets in driving off this mob, which opens for our passage with shrieks and howls. We are now in the very centre of the turmoil ; interspersed among the human beings, who scarcely trouble themselves to move to make way for us, are kneeling camels and sleeping mules, which do not trouble themselves to move at all. There are all sorts of ridiculous commodities exposed upon the ground on rush-mats ; there is an infinite number of small, low tents, beneath which spices, saffron, jujube, and dyes for the wool of sheep and for ladies' finger-nails are offered for sale; there are repulsive butcher-shops, in front of which, on wooden frameworks, hang the carcasses of animals that have been stripped of their skins, together with dark and malodorous refuse of every description, the lungs and entrails of beasts; there are also horses and cattle for sale on the hoof, and slaves are auctioned off to the highest bidder.

In every direction are heard the little bells of
the water-sellers, who carry their merchandise
on their backs in great leathern bottles on which
the hair still remains, and who give every one a
chance to drink from the same glass at the cost
of a *flouc* (the seventh of a sou). And old women, with scarcely a rag to their back, display
those scraps of white cloth attached to long
staves, which in Morocco serve as the badge of
mendicity.

The chiefs who are responsible for our safety
charge us to keep close together and not to separate from one another by so much as a horse's
length. They doubtless have their reasons for
this, but there does not seem to be any ill-will in
the curiosity about us. It is even true that when
the first outbreak of the tumult has quieted down,
some women having struck up their shrill "you!
you! you!" in our honor, the cry at once spreads
and runs like a train of lighted gunpowder into
the remote parts of the market. "You! you!
you!" As we draw off, the whole excited mul-
t.tude join in the piercing, persistent chorus,
which grows fainter and fainter as we recede,
like the cries that we hear from the locusts when
they are warmed by the July sun.

We soon lose sight of the thousands of bournouses and human faces behind the undulations

of this uneven sandy plain. We again enter upon a lonely country. The landscape becomes more and more level, and the lofty mountains among which our line of march lay during the first few days stretch away far in our rear, and the horizon to our front becomes more and more monotonous.

Spirited fantasias continue to pass, tempest-like, on the flanks of our column, with wild cries and discharges of musketry, the rider's bournouses and the manes and tails of the horses streaming behind them. We scarcely pay them any attention now, except to get out of their way when we hear them coming. And yet they are even more astounding than before; the display would not be unworthy of a first class circus. Men pass us with the speed of a flash, standing erect upon their saddles, or standing on their heads with their legs waving in the air, like circus-riders practising in the open country; two horsemen make for each other at a mad gallop, and, as they meet, without drawing rein or coming in collision, exchange muskets and give each other a kiss. An old gray-bearded chief proudly calls our attention to a squad of twelve horsemen who charge down on us abreast, and such handsome fellows they are! They are his twelve sons. He wants us to tell the minister of it, and that the whole world should know how blessed he is.

We come to a river which we pass by fording; it is the boundary of the territory of Séfiann. We are about to enter the lands of the tribe of Béni-Malek, whose chief is awaiting us with two hundred horsemen on the far bank of the stream. He is the Caid Abassi, one of the Sultan's prime favorites, an old man with an extremely intelligent and diplomatic countenance, whose daughter it seems, was married at Fez, with splendid ceremonial, to the Grand Vizier. It has been determined to stop with him on account of his "*mouna*," for which he has a reputation far and wide throughout Morocco.

The country continues to grow more level and the mountains to vanish in the distance. Nothing but sand and daffodils. Our horizon is gradually transformed into a long straight line, level as the sea, and seems to stretch away to a more and more remote distance.

Toward noon a halt is called for breakfast at the village of this Caid. It resembles all other villages in Morocco. The huts of dried mud are low and thatched with reeds, and surrounded by thorny hedges of bluish cactus. Storks have

built their nests on every roof, and the chirp of
the grasshopper is heard everywhere from the
surrounding fields.

After having breakfasted from the huge pyramids of cous-couss, which almost fill our tent,
we receive an invitation from the Caid to take
tea with him. His dwelling is the only one in
the surrounding country that is built of stone.
It is surrounded like a citadel by a series of low,
very old brick ramparts that have been glazed
with a yellowish wash, and formidable hedges of
cactus further combine to render it almost inaccessible. Three Moorish arcades, whitewashed,
serve as a means of access to an interior garden
that is filled with orange trees. The trees are
all in bloom, and the garden is sweet with a
most delicious perfume. Notwithstanding this,
however, the wild grass that overruns it and its
air of abandonment give it a gloomy aspect,
shut in as it is by the old walls, while the surrounding space is so untrammeled, so vast and
free.

We are received in an apartment opening on
this cheerless garden, where there is but little
furniture ; the walls are whitewashed and there
are some rugs and cushions on the floor. There
is a tesselated pavement with a deep opening
in it where are thrown the rinsings of the tea-

cups and the hot water that is left in the Samovars. In the wall at the lower end of the room there are other openings, like loop-holes, from which the women observe us as we sip our tea.

* * *

We mount again at about two o'clock to continue our march to the Sebou; one of the largest rivers of Morocco and even of western Africa, which it is our expectation to cross this evening.

On the plain in front of us we discern a group of men like supplicants of ancient times, dragging a diminutive ox along by its horns. Just as the minister passes a sword flashes from its scabbard; it requires but two strokes to do the deed; the animal is ham-strung and sinks down in a pool of its own blood, turning full upon us its poor, piteous eyes. What adepts these people must be at chopping off heads! The sacrifice accomplished, the supplicants lay their petition in writing at the feet of the minister; it is an old-time history of great length, running back I can't tell how many years, abounding with family jealousies, with mysterious murders, with all sorts of things incapable of unravelment. It will go to swell the number of complications that will have to be adjusted at Fez with the coöperation of the Grand Vizier.

* * *

The Sebou is invisible until we are close upon it. The stream, wide as the Seine at Rouen, pours its turbid waters along a deep bed between walls of grayish clay, and pursues its winding way through the plain that is as boundless as the sea.

Our camp has continued to move onward during our noonday halt, and is now awaiting us on the opposite bank. We make the passage, which requires several trips, in two boats, to the accompaniment of great uproar. The neighborhood is blockaded by caravans that have been delayed for two hours past by the passage of our tents and baggage, and the spot for the time being has assumed a very animated appearance.

A sharp line of demarcation is drawn by the Sebou between the Morocco which lies on this side of it and that which lies beyond it. As soon as it is crossed there is an impression of being still more widely separated from our own world; of being more deeply buried in the gloomy Moghreb. We are still in the country of the Béni-Malek, but we are fast approaching the lands of the Beni-Hassem, a dangerous tribe of robbers. It is an adage among travelers in Morocco that, the Sebou once crossed, one must keep a sharp eye out and maintain a watchful guard.

On the bank where we now land, the nature of the soil and the vegetation has undergone a complete change; in place of sand and daffodils, we are surprised to find a rich, black soil like that of the plains of Normandy, covered with a thick growth of colza, marigolds and mallows; our horses wade up to their knees through the thick-set, luxuriant mass of verdure.

The sun goes down in a cold, clear light. The landscape is almost like a marine picture, so level are the unbroken horizon lines. A tranquil sea is not smoother than this wild plain, which extends nearly forty miles in breadth. In one direction only does a chain of far-distant mountains, rearing their summits above the grassy waste, stand out against the sky like a wreath of raw, cold blue. The plain beyond is absolutely yellow with flowers, a bright golden yellow, while the heavens, quite free from clouds and reaching, void and empty, toward infinity, are of a pale yellowish green.

And now the wind, which always blows up

cold at the approach of night, rises over these steppes of mallows and marigolds ; it sends a shiver through us after the fierce heat of the day ; it brings a melancholy feeling of winter to us in this place where, for miles and miles around, we could not find a fireside at which to warm ourselves. It is the most disagreeable encampment that we have experienced since we set out. These marigolds and mallows form a deep mass of thicket underneath our tents, which is annoying and troublesome ; it is as if we should lie down and try to sleep in the middle of a flower-bed. It is useless to try to tread them down ; they pretend to allow themselves to be crushed, sending out a penetrating odor, then they resolutely arise and spring up again, bulging out the carpet and the mats. They exhale an excessive humidity. Worst of all, they are the harboring place for bugs, grasshoppers, crickets and snails, which come forth and crawl over us all night long.

XIV.

Thursday, April 11th.

THE dew was heavy over night. The moisture stands in drops on the walls of my tent, which is filled with a thick steam and the acrid odor of the marigolds.

The guard was singing around the camp until daylight in order to keep themselves awake. When the day began to break their voices gave way to those of the quails, calling to each other among the grass. Camp broken at six o'clock, in the saddle at seven.

We at first advance into the great plain under the escort of our friends of yesterday, the Béni-Maleks, to the number of two hundred. The air seems to be warmer here on the southern bank of the river, and the country even more inhospitable. Over the boundless stretches of colzas and marigolds, the sky hangs dark and heavy, with here and there a rift of intense blue. Then we come to a region that is all white, for miles on miles, with camomile flowers, which we crush as we pass over them, and which cause our horses to smell of them all day.

After a two hours' march, we meet the horse-

men of Beni-Hassem, who are awaiting us.
They are a set of thieves, of that there can be no
doubt ; their appearance shows plainly enough
what they are. But they are magnificent thieves ;
the finest bronze features that we have seen
yet, the finest postures, the finest brawny arms,
the finest horses. Locks of long hair escaping
over their ears from under their turbans contri-
bute in giving to their countenances an inde-
scribably alarming expression.

Their chief comes forward with a smile of welcome to offer his hand to the minister. That
we shall be perfectly safe while in his territory
there cannot be the shadow of a doubt ; from the
moment when he assumes the duties of our host
he is answerable before the Sultan for our heads
with his own. Besides, it is always better to be
entrusted to his guard than to be merely camp-
ers in his neighborhood ; the truth of this axiom
is recognized in Morocco.

This old chief of the Beni-Hassems is a free-
booter of a remarkable type. His snow-white
beard, hair and eyebrows are well defined
against his yellow, mummy-like complexion ; his
aquiline profile is of the most-supreme distinction.
He is on a horse that is almost covered by a
housing of peach-colored silk, while the bridle
and harness are of pink silk, the high-peaked sad-

dle is of pink velvet and the stirrups inlaid with
gold. He is attired in complete white, like a
saint, in robes of muslin so thin as to be transparent.   When he extends -his arm to shake
hands, the motion discloses a double sleeve of
singular beauty ; first that of his shirt of white
silken gauze, then that of his under-robe, also of
silk and of an exquisite tint of old sea-green.
To give things their relative proportions, one
would expect to see the tapering fingers and old-
time lace ruffles of some dowager *marquise* steal
out from under the bournous of this old high-
wayman.

At a short distance farther on we find the
reserve force of the horsemen, the handsomest
and the richest of them, whom the wily old chief
had posted there for the purpose of producing a
theatrical effect by letting them loose on us like
a hurricane at the lower end of the plain.   They
come down on us at top speed, with fierce shouts;
admirable as seen thus from their front amid the
smoke of their musketry, in their intoxication of
sound and speed.   Turbans become unrolled
and stream on the air, harness breaks and guns
are discharged.   The earth crumbles under their
horses' shoes and the black particles are thrown
in every direction like a discharge of grape-shot
from a cannon.

What a number of travellers they must have plundered in order to display such luxury! The bridles and harness are all of silk, of a color harmonizing wonderfully with the housings and with the dress of the horseman; blue, pink, sea green, salmon-colored, amaranth or jonquil-colored. The stirrups are all inlaid with gold. Every horse has upon his chest a sort of long, velvet curtain, richly embroidered in gold and kept in place by a large clasp of chased silver or of precious stones. How we look down now on those poor fantasias of our early days, around Tangier, which seemed to us then so fine!

The old chief's breakfast, too, is a wild one, like his territory, like his tribe. On the bare earth, on the carpet of yellow flowers somewhere in the midst of the broad plain, he offers us a repast of black cous-couss, with sheep roasted whole and served up on great wooden platters. And while we are using our hands to tear strips of meat from these monster roasts, supplicants again come and kill a ram before our minister, and the grass around us is streaming with the animal's blood.

All the afternoon the plain lies before us, level and monotonous, as we toil onward; it becomes more arid, however, toward evening, more African in character, and the colzas and marigolds give way to thorny jujubes and to various kinds of mint. A warm, wan light falls from the sky, where there are no clouds. From time to time the direction of the road is marked by the carcass of a horse or of a camel, which the vultures have disemboweled. And in the occasional little villages which lie hidden among these desert wastes, the round conical hut commences to be seen, the hut of the Soudan, the hut of Sénégal.

We change tribes again about four o'clock, having had only a narrow tongue of the Beni-Hassem territory to traverse. We are now coming among the Cherarbas, who are harmless folks and entirely under control of the Sultan. Their dangerous neighbors, however, who will not be answerable for us, will make our safety among them doubtful.

About six o'clock we encamp, at a point where the roads fork to Fez and Mequinez, near the venerated tomb of Sidi-Gueddar, who was a saint of note among the Moroccans. This tomb, like all the Algerian marabouts and all the "Koubas" of Morocco, is a small square structure, surmounted by a rounded dome. It is extremely ancient, chinked and cracked by the weather. The white flag, mounted on a staff, is flying at its side, to intimate to caravans the meritorious-ness of leaving offerings there ; a mat, kept in place by heavy stones at the corners, is laid upon the ground to receive them, and the coins that are thrown there by pious travellers are guarded by the birds of the air until such time as the priests may come and collect them.

We are politely requested not to approach too closely this burial place of Sidi-Gueddar ; it is so holy that our presence, Christians as we are, would be a sacrilege.

The mountains which this morning were scarcely more than blue wreaths upon the horizon, are now not more than six or eight miles away, and to-morrow we shall cross them ; all to-day they have been climbing higher, higher upon the sky. This evening we are in a region of lucerne, which blooms with an abundance that is peculiar to the flora of Morocco. There are little thatched villages near us ; we hear the barking of dogs there in the twilight, just as in our own farm yards, and the little hooded shepherds are bringing home their flocks of goats and bleating sheep ; the whole gives an air of pastoral innocence and reassuring serenity. Moreover, the Fez road runs close to our camp ; so close indeed, that our tent ropes are stretched across it, and the caravans, which always jog along until night-fall, are obliged to turn out into the lucerne so as not to get their camels' feet entangled in the cords. And the pathway is so well beaten, just here, and the plain so perfectly level, that one might call it a real road, easy to walk on, and tempting one to a promenade. One must have lived some time in Morocco, where walking is everywhere difficult and even impossible, to understand how seductive is a *road* and how great is our longing to start off and take a stretcher on such a fine, mild evening.

We must not yield to our wishes, however, and least of all, this evening. Strict orders have been issued not to go outside the bounds of the camp. Not only have we for neighbors the tribe of Beni-Hassem, but we are only distant an hour's travel from the mountains where dwell the terrible Zemours—fanatics, robbers, murderers, and for several years past in open rebellion against the government of Fez. Even the Sultan, when he travels with his camp of thirty thousand men, gives this country of the Zemours a wide berth.

As the moon is coming up, after the ceremonial of receiving the *mouna*, double guards are posted around the camp and all the arms are loaded ; orders are given to let no one approach the tents, and to sing and keep the drums beat-

ing until day-break, so as not to fall asleep.
The chief who is responsible for us all seems
nervous and troubled, and does not go to bed.

XV.

Friday, April 12th.

ALL night long the singing and drum-beating
were kept up, and this morning we awake
under a cloudy sky with our heads still on our
shoulders. As an addition to the *mouna* we are
supplied, as we arise from our beds, with fresh
milk in jars and excellent butter.

We have to accomplish ten leagues to-day.
We have scarcely made a start when a fine, cold
rain begins to fall. It will take an hour and a
half yet to get free of the plain, across fields of
barley and colzas, through the lucerne where
countless flocks of sheep are grazing. Beneath
this cloudy sky we should think that we were in
the rich plains of Normandy, were it not for the
pointed huts of the villages and the bournouses
of the shepherds. The fantasias, by which we
continue to be honored, are not nearly so fine as
those of Beni-Hassem ; it is to be seen that these
honest Cherarbas are much less warlike and
much poorer ; besides we tire of everything after
a time, and it becomes a bore at last to have to

turn out at every moment, the rain beating in our faces all the while, to make way for these cavaliers, who come down on us like the wind, fire off their guns in our faces and frighten our horses.

Leaving to our right the dangerous country of the Zemours, we enter the mountainous region which we shall have to traverse with the daylight. The ascent is difficult, through a series of narrow gorges laid down in wheat and barley, where there is no out-look ahead. Following the custom of Morocco, we ruthlessly trample down all this vegetation; there will still remain more than can be harvested. Over slopes that are often precipitous we stumble through the stiff water-soaked clay soil, so tenacious that it collects around our horses' feet and forms great balls; at each step we feel ourselves slipping back; one after another our mules fall with their loads and roll with our tents, our bedding and our baggage in the muddy sink-holes, in these newly formed torrents, which are rapidly swelling in every direction beneath the pouring rain.

The Caid of the Cherarbas left us at the boundary of the tribe's territory, and, what is very extraordinary, the chief of the region where we now are has not come to meet us. For the

first time we are alone, without an escort. With our sinking mules and our men and horses mired in the heavy soil, our column now extends in a confused line at least a league long. What are we to do? Where are we to stop? Where obtain quarters for ourselves and our beasts? Where are we to look for a shelter of any kind in this country where there are no houses, no trees, where there is not even a hut where the people would take us in?

As we plod wearily on under these conditions, we meet a column at least as numerous as our own; first a squad of horsemen, and behind, camels loaded with baggage and a large number of veiled women. It seems that it is the train of a chief of a distant province, who is returning from a visit to the Sultan. These people, too, like us, are inconvenienced by the heavy, slippery condition of the road.

At last the tardy chief appears, accompanied by his band. He excuses himself profusely; says he was in pursuit of three robber Zemours who have been the terror of the country. He has captured them and has them now in his own house, safely bound, from whence they will be taken to Fez to undergo the "*punishment of the salt,*" as the law enjoins.

As we continue our upward course through

these fearful little ravines that are like walls of gray clay, slipping and stumbling through the rain with many a stumble and fall, I make enquiry about this "*punishment of the salt*," which goes back to very ancient times.

It is the Sultan's barber who has the responsibility of administering it. The guilty one is brought before him in some public place, preferably the market place, securely bound with cords. Taking a razor, he makes four deep incisions, reaching down to the bones and corresponding with them in direction, in the palm of each hand, then forcing back the fingers and separating as widely as possible the lips of the bleeding orifices, he stuffs them full of salt. Then he closes the mutilated hand and places the end of each finger within the corresponding one of the gaping wounds, and that this barbarous arrangement may remain intact until death comes to release the sufferer, he tightly sews over all a sort of close fitting glove of wet cowskin, which will shrink and harden as it dries. When this is done, the criminal is returned to his dungeon, where he is generally supplied with food, in order that the torture may be protracted as long as possible. From the first moment of the punishment, to say nothing of the unspeakable physical agony, he knows that this horrible glove will never be taken off, that his fingers will grow into the wound and stiffen there and never come forth, that there will be no living being to say a word of consolation to him, that neither day nor night will bring relief to his torments or end his shrieks of anguish. But the worst of all, it seems, does not happen for some days, until the nails, growing within the hand, cut their way deeper and deeper into the mutilated flesh. Then the end is close at hand; some die of tetanus, others succeed in dashing out their brains against the wall.

And here I must beg that those who sit by their fireside and receive their humanitarian theories all ready-made to suit their tastes, will not cry out against Moroccan barbarity. In the first place, I will say to them that here, in the Moghreb, we are still in the darkness of the middle-ages, and God knows how fertile was our European middle-age imagination in inventing punishments. Then again, the Moroccans, as is the case with all peoples who have not advanced beyond their primitive state, are far inferior to us in nervous susceptibility, and as they also look upon death with the utmost contempt, it follows that our guillotine would be an anodyne in their eyes, as much as a punishment, and would have no deterrent effect upon any one.

In a country where the distances are so great,
and the roads entirely unguarded, one cannot
feel very angry with this people for having put
into their code some provisions that may give
their mountain robbers a little food for reflection.

* * *

After a weary climb we reach the summit of
the range, and looking down from a clearing between two peaks, we catch a glimpse of the plain
lying far below us, not so extensive as that of
the Sebou, but well cultivated and marvellously
fertile ; a sort of circle within a circle, with a
border of distant mountains, where we shall
have to camp to-morrow night, and which are
much higher than those which we have just
crossed. Half-way down the descent which we
are about to undertake, a village is perched; a
hundred or so of thatched huts with enclosures
of cactus, grouped around an old Moorish
structure, which answers at the same time as
citadel and as the dwelling of the chief. Trees
are as scarce as ever in this other region ; there
are some olive and orange trees in the mysterious garden which is enclosed within the
walls of the little fortress. Looking from above
down into the village, we of course obtain a

birdseye view of it, and the terrace on the roof of the chief's house has the appearance of a public square, where veiled women in robes of pink or white are enjoying the evening air; these raise their heads to observe us as we approach.

After a steep and dangerous descent among the fallen rocks and stones, we halt for the night near the walls of this garden, in a spot somewhat like a fair-ground, which is made use of by all the passing caravans. The tall, coarse grass has been trodden down into the mud; it is infested with vermin, and is polluted by the refuse of the chickens and the cous-couss that have been devoured there, while here and there great black circles mark the spots where the nomads built their fires. We have never experienced such a filthy camping-ground.

Our escort cut the soiled grass with their long swords, which doubtless are more frequently employed in cutting off heads than in work of this kind. Long after us our tents come straggling in one by one, drenched with rain, aud are set up with great difficulty, under a strong wind. The muleteers are forthwith treated to a taste of the stick, for not having got their animals forward with better speed. Last of all the eatables came up; the poor mules on which they

are loaded have had twenty tumbles, and their
knees are skinned and bleeding ; and so, at
three o'clock, almost starving with hunger, we
make a cold breakfast on fare that has been
soaked in rain. All the children of the village,
in their comical little bournouses and queer
hoods, come and frisk about our quarters,
overwhelming us with maledictions and insults.
We make a demand for wood to dry our clothes,
but there is none to be had in all the country;
we are supplied with bundles of dried thistles
and grapevine shoots, which give out abundance of flame and smoke, but little heat.

From our camp half-way up the mountain
side, separated by a hedge of aloes from the per-
pendicular precipice that overhangs the plain
below, we see at our feet the interminable Fez
road, which stretches onward, ever onward,
through these new fields of barley and these
other plains, and rises to be lost among the hills
that face us. It is more and more plainly traced
by the constant tread of caravans, it appears
more and more like a road ; it also assumes an
appearance of greater animation as we approach
the holy city. Between showers, in the great
transparency of the atmosphere, we perceive beneath us, as if from the summit of a watch tower,
the long processions of bournous-clad footmen

and horsemen, of camels and mules with their loads of merchandise, the whole infinitely small, like a procession of marionettes seen far away, deep down in empty bluish space. Fez is not only the religious capital of the land of the setting sun, after Mecca the holiest of the cities of Islam, where priests resort to pursue their studies from all parts of Africa; it is also the commercial centre of the West, which has communication with Europe through the northern sea-ports, and by way of Tafilet and the desert with the black Soudan as far as Timbuctoo and Senegambia. And all this activity has nothing at all in common with ours; it goes on as it went on a thousand years ago, by means which are altogether foreign to the means employed by us, over routes which to us are entirely unknown.

XVI.

SATURDAY, APRIL 13th.

IT rained heavily all night and the wind blew down half our tents. Upon leaving our damp beds we put on our wet clothes and our boots filled with water, and resume our journey under a sky that has the appearance of being shrouded in black crape. We cross the plain to enter the defiles of these other mountains. The thought that we shall have to go over this ground again in order to get out of this gloomy country oppresses us a little now and then. We are sustained, however, by the hope that to-morrow we shall be within sight of the holy city, like those crusaders and pilgrims of old, who after many weary days and nights of travel, were consoled by the promise that they were soon to see their Jerusalem or their Mecca.

Toward noon, when we are among the mountains, the clouds gradually begin to thin, then quickly, at once, they are swept away and reveal the clear, blue sky; we are cheered and warmed by one first timid ray of sunlight, then the true light of Africa is restored to us in his incomparable splendor. In the space of an hour the transformation is complete, the ground is dry, the heavens are blue, the air is scorching. How differently everything appears beneath this radiant sun ! Our course lies through a succession of charming valleys, where the sandy soil is carpeted with fine grass and with flowers. In particular there are gigantic fennels, the flower-clad stalks of which are like yellow trees, and which are festooned by the great white blossoms of the bindweed, such as we see in our gardens. Yellow and pink are the prevailing colors in the Eden through which our path lies to-day. The mountains commence to be clothed with groves of dark-hued olive trees, and their basaltic summits, rising in naked grandeur above the verdure, resemble great organ-pipes; then further, through the clear air, beyond these nearer heights, others are visible, more distant and loftier still, towering gigantic in their height, of a blue like lapis-lazuli. There are no villages to be seen, no houses, no sign of cultivation ; only flowers and the sweet breath of flowers, perfuming this wonderful country.

We meet men and animals in plenty, however ; bands of nearly naked foot-travellers, carrying their clothes folded in bundles on their shoulders ; finely formed women, astride on mules, so closely veiled, even on their travels, that their great eyes are scarcely visible ; flocks of sheep and goats ; notable above all, camels, grave of aspect and slow of movement, bearing their great bales along with a swaying, rolling motion. At intervals we cross a stream of running water, on the bank of which a single isolated palm-tree will be growing. At every ford are old men squatting in front of heaps of oranges ; for a small copper coin one may take and eat as many of them as he pleases.

Toward evening we came to a rapid river, the Oued M'Kez, over which, wonderful to relate ! there is a bridge. A bridge of low, rounded arches, into which plates of green earthenware are let by way of ornament. On the central pier is carved the mystic seal of Solomon : two interwoven triangles ; and on either side mosaic tablets, bordered with green, tell in involved letters the name of the architect who built the bridge and the praise due to the God of Islam from those who cross it. Lapse of years and the sun have combined to give the stonework a warm, almost pink, tint, which harmonizes wonderfully with the dull green of the ornamentation. The situation, too, is peaceful and pastoral, impressed with the melancholy of the past and of neglect.

We have marched through the rain of the cool morning, through the burning heat of mid-day, and now it is the magical, golden hour of sunset. We are coming among the Zerhanas, a mountain tribe, who subsist by their farms and flocks, and on the far side of the bridge we shall encamp in their territory, in a plain of pink anemones, between high wooded hills. Our little nomad camp is already there, spread over the ground, in the fading sunlight, on the fragrant grass.

One by one our tent poles arise, surmounted by their globes of shining copper ; then the great canvas opens out, displaying the black ornaments in arabesque ; the cords which serve to stretch them out and keep them in place are drawn taut, the side walls are placed in position, and it is done ; our houses are built and our camp stands erect, rejoicing to dry itself once more in the grateful warmth.

How cheerful and gay it is, our little camp of Frenchmen, in the bustle of our arrival, in the mellow light of evening ; with its white tents relieved against the verdant landscape, with the brilliant contrasts afforded by the caftans of our Arabs and the carpets of many colors scattered over this meadow of anemones. About us there is an animation which recalls the full, free life of times that are past and gone; fantasias scampering at top speed; half naked shepherds conducting their flocks to the river; the Sultan's boat, which appears in the distance, borne on the shoulders of its forty white-robed bearers; the appearance of the *mouna* (a small ox and twelve sheep dragged along by their horns); finally a messenger from Fez, who comes to seek us, the bearer of words of welcome from the Grand Vizier to the minister.

Now the beautiful golden light begins to fade over it all; the shadows of the horsemen, the quaint shadows of the motionless camels, assume an inordinate length under the rays of the sun which is about to disappear behind the lofty peaks; now he gilds only the tops of our tents— now only the glittering balls on top—now he is gone and we are suddenly lost in a bluish half-light.

Our little camp is even more charming by moonlight. It is one of those tranquil, radiant, luminous nights of benignant Africa, such as are never seen in our northern lands; after the cold and the persistent rains, we are intoxicated with the joy of regaining what we had almost forgotten. The beautiful full moon rides in the midst of a sky bespangled with stars. Our white tents with their black hieroglyphics, have a mysterious

air, ranged as they are in a circle under the blue
light that falls on them from above; their balls
of metal still emit dim gleams; here and there
fires are lighted among the grass, and the little
red flames leap up merrily; around them men
in long white garments are squatted on mats,
and the mournful sound of the guitar arises from
the groups which will soon seek their slumbers.
In the deep outer silence, in the sonorousness of
the night, curlews are calling. The neighboring mountains seem to have drawn nearer, so
clearly can we distinguish their rocks, their hanging woods, their every most secret recess. The
air is filled with sweet, exotic odors, and over all
there reigns a serene tranquility that it is beyond
the power of words to express.

Ah! how fine is the life of the open air, the
noble wandering life! What a pity that to-morrow will end it, that we shall reach our destination!

XVII.

Sunday, April 14th.

OF this country of the Zerhanas there will always remain to me the recollection of the cool morning hours passed on the bank of the Oued M'Kez, among this delightful scenery, on this carpet of pink anemones. A little grove of extremely ancient olive trees near our camp served to give shelter to some shepherds and their flocks. Two or three small hamlets were perched like eagles' nests among the rocks and under-brush of the surrounding mountains. There was nothing African in the landscape, unless it might be the excess and the splendor of the sunlight, and even so, we sometimes see this vividness of verdure in our fields and this clearness of the atmosphere on occasional favored days of the pleasant month of June. The illusion was complete of being in some remote, wild corner of France, and there seemed to be an inconsistency when I saw, in the narrow lanes between the tall flowering grass, the mad fantasias, the Arabs and the camels.

XVIII.

WE get to horse at eight o'clock and forth-with enter the mountains, which imme-diately change their character and become ex-tremely African in appearance, gullied and torn by storms, with ruddy tones of ochre, golden brown, reddish brown. Broad moors, lying hot and waste beneath the sun, pass slowly before our eyes, covered with thorny jujubes and scanty brush. And now and again, far away in the plains that lie consuming in the sunlight, we see *douars* of wandering Bedouins, circles of brown tents with the cattle in the centre; on their lonely eminences, under the all-powerful rays of the burning sun, these little towns describe per-fect circles, in the distance look like rings, or spots of brown so dark as to be almost black. The overheated air everywhere quivers, ruffled like a pool whose surface is disturbed by a light wind.

* * *

After the noon-day halt, we cross a cultivated valley; fields of emerald green barley bright in the sun-light, with red poppies showing their heads among it. As we have met no living being

in the course of the morning, we cast our eyes
about to discern the dwelling place of those who
have sown these fields. We discover their village in an unexpected corner, and can scarcely
regard it as a reality ; three high black rocks,
pointed like gothic spires, stand towering side
by side, most unlikely objects to meet with in
this velvety green plain ; each of them is surmounted by a stork's nest ; a wall of beaten
clay surrounds all the three at their base, and on
their sides, at varying heights, are stuck a dozen
lilliputian huts. There seems to be no one at
home in this queer village, to which the three
storks, motionless on the top of their several
rocks, act as guards ; around there is only
silence and the languor of a summer noon.

*　*　*

At last, at last, about four o'clock in the afternoon, the immense void opens once again before
us : another level sea of vegetation, a sea green
and yellow with barley and with fennel in
bloom—the plain of Fez ! Far in the distance
the great Atlas yields an imposing enclosure of
white peaks, all sparkling with snow.

Two leagues of journey yet—over this plain,
and suddenly, coming from behind a skirt of the
mountain, which draws back as a scene is shifted

in the theatre, the holy city slowly appears before our eyes. At first, it is only a white line, white as the snows on Atlas, that ceaseless mirages transform and twist as if it were a thing of no consistency. It is, we are told, the great whitewashed aqueducts, which bring the water into the gardens of the Sultan.

Then, the skirt of the mountain moving back still further, affords us a view of the great gray walls and the great gray towers surmounting them. It is a surprise to us to see Fez so dark of tint and standing in a plain so green, when we had imagined it as white, standing among the sands. It is true that it has a striking air of melancholy, but seen from such a distance and surrounded by such fresh verdure, it is difficult to believe that it is the impenetrable holy city, and our expectations of it are deceived. Still, little by little, the calm tranquility of its surroundings produces its effect; there is a feeling that a strange sleep broods over this city, so lofty and so great, which has at its gates neither railroads, nor wheeled carriage, nor even a roadway; nothing but grass-grown paths over which the slow caravans pass silently.

We camp for the last time in a place called Ansala-Faradji, at half an hour's march from the great crenellated walls. To-morrow morning

we are to make our entry with all due ceremony;
all the music, the troops, the entire population,
women included, have received orders to go forth
to welcome us.

XIX.

MONDAY, APRIL 15th.

ONCE again we awake beneath a lowering
sky, presage of the deluges, the torrents of
rain that hang suspended above our heads.

The last morning in camp is a more busy one
than usual.   The ceremony so soon to take place
requires great preparations ; we have to unpack
our holiday uniforms, our crosses and decorations, and our chasseurs d'Afrique have to fur-
bish up our arms and our horses' trappings. The
order of march, drawn up yesterday evening in
the minister's tent, is communicated to us at
breakfast ; it is a matter of course that we are
not to straggle in confusion any longer, each according to his own sweet will, but that the march
is to be orderly, a front of four horsemen formed
four deep, correctly aligned as if for a review.

Mindful of the request which we received last
evening on the part of the Sultan, we mount our

horses at ten o'clock precisely, so as neither to trouble certain religous observances of the morning by arriving too early, nor to interfere with the great prayers of noon-day by arriving too late. We have about three quarters of an hour in which to reach the gates of Fez, proceeding slowly, either at a walk or at the slow trot used on parade.

After advancing ten minutes, the city, of which we have hitherto seen only a portion, appears before us in its entirety. It is really very large and very imposing behind its great gray-black walls, which overtop all the ancient towers of the mosques. There is a break above us in the veil of dark clouds; it permits us to see the snows of Atlas, to which the stormy sky communicates changing hues, now coppery, now livid. A collection of white objects outside the walls is discovered to be a group of two or three hundred tents. Over the whole plain, over all the green barley-fields, thousands upon thousands of minute points are moving to and fro, and these are evidently human heads underneath their hoods, the human multitudes that have come forth to witness our entry.

These white tents outside the city are the camp of the " tholbas " (students), who are now out in the fields holding their great annual fête.

But this word *student* is ill-fitted to designate
these correct and reserved young men ; when I
shall have occasion to mention them in the
future, I shall retain the name *tholba*, which is
untranslatable. (It is well known that Fez contains the most celebrated of the Mussulman uni-
versities ; that two or three thousand scholars
resort there from all the points of northern
Africa to follow the course of study of the great
mosque of Karaouïn, one of the most venerated
sanctuaries of Islam.) These tholbas are having
their vacation just now, and they doubtless con-
tribute their numbers to swell the immense crowd
which surrounds us.

Never was there a sky more threatening or
more unnaturally dark, nor lighted from beneath
by more cheerless gleams. The plain over which
stretches this depressing dome is immured, so to
speak, among lofty mountains whose summits
are lost in the darkness of the clouds. Before
us, and closing our horizon, the strange old city
where our journey is to end presents to our eyes
its irregular silhouette just beneath that fantastic
rift in the clouds through which Atlas displays
his glittering snows. A network of little parallel
paths, which the whim of the camel drivers has
traced in the grass, is almost like a road ; besides
the ground is so level that our party can march

anywhere, maintaining good order even, if desirable.

We are commencing to get among the crowd; garments of gray wool, as usual; gray bournouses and hoods lowered. They content themselves with observing us, and as we advance they put themselves in motion to follow us; the expression of their faces, however, is indifferent and inscrutable; no trace of sympathy nor of hatred is to be observed. Every mouth is tight shut, too; that same slumberous silence prevails to-day which everywhere weighs upon this people, their cities, their whole country, whenever there is not a momentary intoxication of movement and of noise.

We are now at the head of a double line of horsemen, extending as far as the eye can reach, up to the city gates, no doubt, drawn up at the side of our route to do us honor. Superb horsemen they are, all attired in their best, their dress harmonizing with the accoutrements of their horses; pink caftans over green saddles, violet caftans over yellow saddles, blue caftans over orange-colored saddles. And the transparent fabrics of mousseline-de-laine which envelope them in carefully draped folds, soften these shades, and almost give the men the appearance of being clothed in white, so that it is only by

glimpses that the bright color of their under-
garments is discernible.

Their double alignment stretches away before
us to a great distance, forming quite an imposing avenue, a hundred feet or so wide, where
our party is by itself, separated from the throng
in the green fields, which is constantly increasing
in volume on our right hand and on our left.
The heads of the horsemen and of their steeds
are turned in our direction ; they remain motionless, while in their rear, amidst a silence that is
almost oppressive, the gray multitude is stirred
to its depths as by a great wave. It follows us
as we pass forward as if we were drawing it after
us by a magnet, and thus it goes on, becoming
more and more dense and spreading out farther
and farther into the plain. As was the case
when we entered Kazar, some are on foot and
some are mounted ; again you may see three
or four together on an ass or a mule, their legs
dangling to the ground ; there are heads of
families with half a dozen young ones hanging
to the paternal bournous and bestriding his
beast, some on the neck, some on the croup.
The sound of all these footsteps is deadened
by the heavy ploughed ground, and the mouths
remain silent, while the eyes are watchful. The
silence is of a singular sort, too ; beneath it

there is the shuffling, hardly audible, of thousands of feet, the rustling of mantles, the deep breathing of the multitude. Now and then a shower beats down upon our heads for a few seconds, as if we were receiving a sprinkling from a watering-pot; the threathened deluge does not fall, and the sky remains as black as ever. The walls of Fez grow higher and higher upon the sky before us, assuming a formidable aspect and reminding us of Damietta or Stamboul.

Among these thousands of gray bournouses, all equally ragged and filthy; among the thousands of faces persistently turned toward us and which keep following us behind the line of cavalry, I notice a man, whose beard is already white, mounted on a lean mule; he is beautiful among the most beautiful, noble as a God, of supreme distinction, with great flaming eyes. It is the brother of the Sultan, there, among the very dregs of the people, in an old threadbare cloak. This does not appear in any way unnatural in Morocco, where the Sultans, owing to the much married condition of their fathers, have an immense number of brothers and sisters, whom it is not always possible to endow with wealth; moreover, many of these descendants of the Prophet find that the grand dream of their religion suffices to satisfy all the requirements of existence, and so they cheerfully live in poverty, disdainful of the good **things** of this life.

* * *

We reach the end of our white-clad squadron, which is succeeded by one uniformed 'entirely in red, a very bright red, which contrasts strik‧ ingly with the monotonous gray of the multi‧ tude ; it is like a long trail of blood, and extends up to the city gate, of which we can now see the monumental arch, opening to receive us, in the lofty ramparts. These troops are the Sultan's infantry, whom an ex-colonel of the English army, now in the service of Morocco, has uniformed, alas ! upon the model of the East-Indian sepoys. Poor devils are these, recruited the Lord knows how, negroes for the most part and ridiculous in their strange uniforms. Their bare legs protrude like black poles from beneath the folds of their scarlet zouave trousers. After those handsome cavalrymen they present a sorry appearance ; when seen close at hand, they resemble an army of monkeys. Their effect is better, however, when observed in mass ; their long line of red, skirting the deep masses of gray, adds another strange effect to the setting of this singular spectacle.

In the avenue of flesh and blood which lies open before us, resplendent personages gallop up to us, one after another, and increase the numbers of our column, which has great difficulty in maintaining its proper order. The Oriental coloring of their costumes is always softened and toned down by long veils of creamy white, which fall around their forms in folds of inimitable grace and majesty. The first to present himself is the " Lieutenant to the Introducer of Ambassadors," all dressed in green, on a horse with equipments of golden yellow; then comes the old Caïd Belaïl, the court jester, in delicate pink; his broad negro features, repulsive in spite of their drollery, are surmounted by a pyramidal, pear-shaped turban, modeled in form upon the towers of the palace of the Kremlin; these are succeeded by other dignitaries; ministers of state and viziers. They all wear long gold-plated scimetars, of which the hilt is a rhinoceros horn, and their silk belts and tassels present a charming variety of shades.

We are about to pass before a military band, which forms part of the line, incorporated with the regiment of scarlet infantry. Strangely costumed it is, and strange to look upon. The bandsmen are negroes, and their long robes, falling straight from their shoulders to the ground, give them the appearance of immensely tall old women in dressing gowns. The colors which they wear are gaudy in the extreme, unmitigated by the slightest presence of a veil; on the contrary, they are arranged as if with a set purpose to heighten the effect as much as possible by contrasting one with another; for instance, a purple robe besides one of royal blue; an orange-colored robe between a violet and a green one. Seen against the neutral back-ground of the surrounding throng, and near the muslin-veiled cavaliers, they constitute the most grotesquely conspicious group that I ever saw in any country.

They carry huge instruments of shining brass, and as we reach their front, they blow with all their might into their horns, their long trumpets and their monstrous trombones; the result is a sudden cacophony, sufficient almost to terrify one. The first impulse is to laugh, but no; it verges on the absurd, but does not reach it; their music is so mournful, the sky is so dark, the scenery so grand, the place so strange, that we are deeply impressed and remain serious.

It acts, however, as the signal for a great clamor; the charm of silence is broken; from every quarter arises a tumultuous roar of voices. Other bands, too, strike up in different directions, and we hear the squeak of the pipes like the yelping of jackals, the thumping of the tambourines, and drawling voices crying : " Hou ! May Allah grant victory to our Sultan, Sidi Muley-Hassan—Hou !" A sudden noisy madness seems to have seized all this crowd, which still keeps following us, still runs at our heels.

Then the bands cease playing, there is an end to the strange confusion ; a great silence suddenly falls upon us and enwraps all again ; again nothing is heard but the rustling of the garments of these countless, hurrying people, the sound of their thousand foot-falls deadened upon the soft earth.

Here come the banners, arranged in line, to right and left, waving over the heads of the troops ; regimental colors, flags of corporations, banners of trade associations, made of silk of all colors with curious emblems ; several have the two intertwined triangles which form the seal of Solomon.

In advance of the lines forming this human avenue, there awaits us a magnificent individual of colossal size, mounted, and surrounded by other cavaliers who act as his guard of honor. It is "Caid Méchouar," Introducer of Embassadors. At this juncture there is an instant of hesitation, almost of anxiety ; he remains motionless, evidently looking for the French minister to draw rein and anticipate him in making advances, but the minister, careful of the dignity of the embassy, rides proudly by on his white horse without turning his head, as if he had observed nothing. Then the great Caid makes up his mind to give in, and spurs his horse up to us; he and the minister shake hands and the incident having terminated to our satisfaction, we continue our progress toward the gates.

* * *

And now we are on the point of entering the city. The lofty walls rise before us at about a hundred métres distance, apparently penetrating the dark storm-clouds with their pointed battlements. On either side of the high archway that yawns to receive us, on the sloping terraces, we see something that looks like a heap of white pebbles ; it is the heads and faces of many women, rising one above the other. They sit there, crowded to the point of suffocation, uniformly veiled in thick woolen stuffs, motionless and silent as death. Others are perched in small groups on the crest of the ramparts, whence they look down and obtain a birdseye view of the ceremonies. The red, green, yellow banners flutter in the air against the back-ground of the dark walls. A

"holy woman," endowed with the gift of pro-
phesy, draws back her veil, and, mounting a
stone, gives utterance to her foreboding in a low
voice ; her eyes are wild, her face is daubed
with vermillion, she holds in her hand a bouquet
of orange flowers and marigolds. Under the
great, gray, sullen archway, we can see at a certain distance another gate of the same immense
dimensions, but to which its bordering of mosaics and pink and blue arabesques imparts an
appearance of freshness and cheerfulness ; like
the entrance to some enchanted palace that lies
concealed among all this ruin.

And all this striking tableau, this multitude
silently awaiting our entry, this display of banners, is distinctly middle-age in character ; it
carries us back to the grandeur, the rudeness,
the sombre naïveté of the fifteenth century.

We enter; then comes the astonishment and
the awe of being among ruins and empty space.

It is evident that all the people must have
been outside the gates, for there is scarcely a
soul to be seen here on the streets where we pass.
And then this gate of the pink and blue arabesques, which appeared so fairy-like from a
distance, loses greatly when seen near by ; it is

huge in size, but is only a coarse recent imitation of ancient splendor. It gives access to the quarters of the Sultan, which of themselves occupy almost the whole of the space of "Fez-Djedid" (Fez the New), whose walls we are now skirting, almost as high and forbidding as the walls of the city. At the foot of these enclosures of the palace, in a cesspool, is a place for throwing the dead bodies of animals, the carcasses of horses and camels, and the air is filled with a disagreeable corpse-like odor. We pass on beyond these horrid seraglio walls, crumbling away in their antiquity, which seem to pierce the heavens with their towers, and surround and enclose the one the other in their excess of distrustful jealousy.

Soon we are among the waste lands which separate New Fez from "Fez-Bâli" (Fez the Old), where our dwelling place is to be. Our way lies over great uneven boulders and the surface of rocks that have been rounded and worn for centuries by the feet of men and the hoofs of beasts. We pursue our course among quagmires, caverns, burying-places, old as Islam; among low elevations covered with cactus and aloes; among *Koubas* (the mortuary chapels of the holy men) surmounted by domes and adorned by inscriptions in mosaic on black plates.

One of those Koubas, almost like a mosque in extent and height, stands on the summit of a great rock ; there are women stationed on its ancient walls, like birds perching among ruins, and looking down upon us through openings in their veils ; every painted eye is turned on us ; higher still, from the top of the dome, a great motionless stork watches us intently and puts the finishing touch to the extraordinary structure. Behind the Kouba two palm trees rise erect and unbending, like plants of metal ; their bunches of yellowish plumes at the top of their lofty stems, stand out in clear relief against the threatening sky. As we ride by a sharp, quick volley of "You ! you ! you ! yous !" salutes us from the top of this Kouba, the women removing their veils from their mouths so as to be heard more distinctly, and as we lift our heads to look at them, our horses shy violently—at some dead animal in the road-way, as we think. But no ; directly in front of them, in the middle of the road and unprotected by fence or railing is a great yawning chasm, large enough to swallow horses and riders, and affording access to those immense subterranean chambers which are excavated in Morocco for the purpose of stowing away grain in case of war or famine, and which are known as *silos.* Now I can understand that

Moroccan expression—" To fall into a silo,"—
the meaning of which is to be caught in a difficulty from whence it is impossible to extricate
one's self.

* * *

Old Fez lies before us; the same grim walls,
seamed with cracks from top to bottom, the same
decaying battlements.   A triple gate of ogival
form, deep set in the wall, warped and thick, exactly similar in every respect to that of the fortress of the Alhambra, gives us admission to this
infinitely ancient and infinitely holy city.   At
first we traverse an ill-looking street, between
ruinous and blackened walls of great height,
without a window to relieve their severe aspect ;
at considerable distances only there are grated
openings, from which we are furtively observed
by female eyes.   Then we pass through a corner
of the covered bazaar, which, even at this distance, is typical of the bazaars of the barbarous
Soudan.   Then suddenly, without warning, we
turn a corner and find ourselves in a region of
gardens.

Here the same melancholy reigns, though in
another form.   We pass in Indian file through a
labyrinth of narrow lanes, which twist in every
direction and return upon themselves, so narrow

that as we pass our knees knock against the walls to right and left. Little, old, low walls of hardened clay, seamed and cracked by the sun and embroidered with yellow lichens, over which are seen palm trees and charming branches of orange trees covered with flowers. The Sultan's red troops, who will insist on doing escort duty and will not be dissuaded, are trodden upon and crowded to the wall by our horses, which go splashing through the mud as black and tenacious as that of Kazar-el-Kébir. There are a few little grated and bolted openings at long intervals, along this labyrinth of narrow lanes, and one has difficulty in explaining to himself how people get into these gardens and how, once in, they get out.

At length our guide stops before the oldest, narrowest and lowest of these gates, set in the most ancient of the walls; one might be pardoned for thinking it the entrance to a rabbit hutch, and even then they must be very poor rabbits to live in such a place; here it is, however, that the French ambassador and his suite are to be lodged.

(I truly regret that I have to make such frequent use of the word "old," and I apologize. In the same way, I remember that when I was writing of Japan, the word "little" recurred at every line in spite of me. Here the dominant impression produced by the surroundings is that of extreme *oldness*, an oldness of decay and death ; it must be taken for granted, once for all, that every thing that I mention has been trodden by the heel of centuries, that the walls are corroded and eaten away by moss, that the houses are crumbling away and ready to tumble down, that the stones have lost their angles.)

The passage is so narrow that it is not an easy matter to dismount ; it is an operation that must be performed without delay, however. As one leaves the saddle, he must jump with a rapid movement to the little old low gateway and enter at once, so as not to be knocked down by the rider who comes up close behind, who is himself in turn driven onward by the succeeding files. The entry once safely effected, we fall upon the bayonets of a guard of soldiers, under the command of a species of old black janissary, whose orders are to never permit any of his French guests to go out unaccompanied by an armed escort. Such a beginning is not promising, but in Morocco one should never trouble himself about the outside of his house ; the most wretched approaches sometimes lead to fairy palaces.

Once past the guard, we come to a delicious

garden; great orange trees, all white with flowers, are planted in quincunxes among a thicket of roses, jasmines, gilliflowers and southern-wood. Then a flagged avenue conducts to another door, very low also and situated at the bottom of a lofty wall, which opens upon a courtyard like those of the Alhambra, with arched passageways, ornaments of arabesques, inlaid pavements, and fountains spouting in marble basins. Here the ambassador will have to pass the three days of quarantine, of "purification," as it is called, which are always inflicted on foreigners who have been granted the favor of entering Fez.

* * *

In all the confusion of our arrival, I approach the minister with my request that I may be allowed to go and live in another quarter, by myself, in a house that a friend whom I providentially met has placed at my disposal.

The minister smiles, suspecting, perhaps, some half-formed project on my part of not *purifying* myself, a black design of escaping supervision and of commencing at once explorations which are not permitted. But he graciously gives his consent, so I mount my horse again, in the fine rain which is now coming down persistently, and proceed in search of my own particular abiding place.

XX.

WRITTEN on this same day of my arrival, at nine or ten o'clock at night in the solitude of my own dwelling.

Of all the shelters which have covered my head during the course of my life, there was never one more forbidding than this, nor less commonplace in its means of approach. Never, too, was there a more complete impression of entire separation from my country, of myself being changed to some other person, of a quite different world and of a long gone time.

Around me lies the sombre city of the saints, upon which the cold darkness of night has fallen, intensified by a wintry rain. At sunset Fez closed the gates of her long embattled ramparts, and then afterwards all the old interior gates which divide the city into many quarters, which at night have no communication with each other.

My habitation is in one of the quarters of Fez-Bâli (old Fez), thus named in contradistinction to Fez-Djedid (new Fez), new Fez itself being a nest of owls that dates back some six or eight centuries. Old Fez is a network of dark covered

anes, which twist and turn in unimaginable
onfusion among great blackish walls. In all
he tall fronts of these inaccessible houses, there
s scarcely a window to be seen; only narrow
lits, which are always carefully barred. As to
he doors, deep set in their embrasures, they are
o low that one must bend almost double to gain
n entrance, and then they are always strapped
vith heavy iron bands and furnished with bolts
nd locks, with great nails and spikes, and with
umbrous knockers worn by the contact of many
ands; all distorted, rusted, warped, and twist-
d—thousands of years old.

Of all this multitude of little narrow criss-cross
treets, I think that the narrowest and the black-
st is mine. It is reached by a low archway, and
t midday it is almost as dark as night; it is
trewn with garbage of all sorts, with dead mice
nd dead dogs; the earth is excavated from the
niddle of it so as to make a gutter and the ped-
strian plunges almost knee-deep into liquid
lth. It is exactly one métre in width, and when
wo persons chance to meet there, wrapped in
heir heavy cloaks or shrouded, like phantoms,
n their veils of white woolen stuff, they must
orcibly squeeze each other against the wall;
hen I go by on horseback, people coming in an
pposite direction must retreat before me or else

seek the shelter of the doorways, for my stirrups scrape against the walls on either side. Higher up the street becomes narrower yet, like a rat-trap ; the tottering walls approach each other, scarcely allowing a pale light to glimmer between them here and there, a light such as is seen from the bottom of a well.

My door, which I have never succeeded in passing in the darkness without bumping my head, gives access to a place where there is even less light than in the street, a staircase, to wit, which you meet as soon as you open the door, and which goes winding in spirals up the little tower.   It is so narrow that one's shoulders graze the walls on both sides ; it is steep as a ladder ; its inlaid stone steps have been worn away by Arab papooches ; its walls are black with the filth of many succeeding human generations, worn by the rubbing of many hands and rough as those of a cavern.   As one ascends, he comes from time to time on bolted doors, which open on all sorts of holes and corners full of rubbish, spider-webs and dust.   At last, about as high up as an ordinary second story, a corridor is reached, intersected by two iron-bound doors, which, from its direction, would seem to run at right angles with the street ; it is not a matter of any importance, however, since there are no windows and the street is as dark as pitch. It is impossible to decipher the plan of a house in Fez ; they are all tangled up together, interwoven, one running into another ; thus the basement, and perhaps the first story, of my house constitute part of another of which I shall never know anything.

At the end of the corridor, we at length meet the light and the cold wind from out-doors ; we reach a large room with naked, cracked and dirty walls. The floor is inlaid, and the lofty ceiling of cedar, ornamented with carved arabesques, is cut in the centre in a great square, which looks out on the gray sky ; through this opening the cold rain falls continually upon the stone floor, with a sound like the plashing of a brook ; that way came down a subdued light when it was day, and that way comes down now the chilly night.

Two high doors of cedar, facing each other, and each with two leaves, open on this interior court. They lead to two symmetrical apartments, very lofty of ceiling, with walls full of chinks and crevices. One of these rooms is mine, the other will be occupied to-morrow by Selim and Mohammed, my attendants.

This same disposition is met with in all Morocco habitations, these same great double-leaved doors on each side of a court open to the sky, through which comes all the light that the dwelling receives. These doors are never shut until after nightfall, for as soon as they are closed, the apartments, which commonly have no windows, are left in darkness. Again, as the doors are massive and require considerable exertion to open ôr shut, an egress is managed in each of the leaves by means of a very small ogival door, like a sort of human cat's-hole, prettily bordered with arabesques. And so it is everywhere, in the palace of the Sultan, as well as in the hovel of the meanest of his subjects.

* * *

As is the custom at the close of day, I have fastened the great doors of my bedroom with a bar of iron a métre in length. Then taking a lantern in my hand, I make my exit through one of my ornamented cat-holes and proceed to make a tour of exploration of my house that I am so little acquainted with. My first care is to descend the staircase in the little turret and prudently secure the low entrance-way which communicates with the street; then, passing to the stories above, my discoveries give me a shock; other little corridors, other dilapidated rooms of irregular shape, filled with rubbish, with lumber, old saddles, pack-saddles for mules, chickens dead and chickens alive !

It is a very exceptional circumstance that an European should thus be living in a private house in the holy city of Fez. In the first place, there are never any visitors except those connected with an embassy, and in such case quarters are always provided for all in some palace designated by the Sultan, which it is not permitted any one to leave unless with a guard. Admitting that a " Nazarene " (as the Arabs call us) should succeed in reaching here unattended, he would stand a good chance of starving to death in the streets, for no Mussulman, for any money, would consent to rent him a place to lay his head or to prepare anything for him to eat. But there is in Fez a permanent French establishment; three officers for the instruction of troops and a military surgeon, Doctor L., whose name I shall no doubt have frequent occasion to mention. These, with the English ex-Colonel whom I have spoken of, and an Italian, superintendent of an arms factory, constitute the entire European colony of the city. Under the protection of the Sultan they are not interfered with, and by observing certain precautions they can circulate in the streets with almost perfect freedom. By imperial order, the chiefs of quarters compelled the inhabitants, who were sulky over it, to hire each one of them a house, and Doctor L., through some circumstances to me unknown, happening at the present time to have two, has placed one of them at my disposal ; so that it is owing to his kindness that I shall live in Fez under very exceptional conditions of freedom.

And now, locked in for good and all for the night, my two cat-holes closed, I am alone in my room, shivering with cold in spite of my bournous ; I hear the sound of the falling rain, the dripping gutters, the wind blowing as it does in winter ; now and then, too, a religious chant reaches my ears from some distant mosque. Very dilapidated and very cheerless is my great bedroom, with its naked walls, cracked from top to bottom, white with the lime that was applied hundreds of years ago, and ornamented with hangings of spider-webs. In two of the corners little half-hidden doors lead to dark garrets. To-morrow, when I shall have had the inlaid stone floor washed and swept of its thick coat of dust, perhaps it will be the only pretty thing that my dwelling will afford.

My entire furnishing consists of a great R'bat carpet of antique design and dull colors, a camp mattress laid upon this carpet and covered with a Moroccan blanket, a small table and a tall brass candle-stick. I have adopted the Arab dress from head to foot, and caftans and bournouses, which a Jew brought for sale this evening, are hanging from their hooks, all ready for to-morrow's prohibited explorations. The only European things near me are the pen and paper which I am using to write with. The poor ''tholbas,'' pursuing their studies at Karaouïn, must be equipped somewhat like me when they are at home.

I review the rapid succession of circumstances which has brought me to this queer dwelling place, as if I were a puppet moved by wires. First the suddenness of my unexpected departure for Morocco; then our twelve days' journey on horseback, during which a little of France remained with me still : the meeting of pleasant companions under the great tent at meal-times and their cheerful talk about the things of to-day, almost to the exclusion of all thought of the sombre land in which we are burying ourselves; then our extraordinary entrance into Fez this morning, to the sound of pipes and tambourines ; finally, my sudden separation from the rest of the embassy, my coming in the rain to this ruinous abode, and the absolute solitude in which I have spent my evening.

This utter abandonment of home and country,

these entire transformations of self and surroundings, have always been my favorite amusement and my great resource against the monotony of life, and so, this evening, I endeavor to
amuse myself with my Arab costumes, and,
especially, by the reflection that I am living in
an inaccessible house in the very depths of the
holy city. But no ; in spite of all reasoning, the
dominant feeling is that of a deep-seated melancholy which I had not looked for ; a yearning
for France, the country of my home ; an almost
childish regret, spoiling all the charm of this
strange novelty ; the sentiment of the shroud of
Islam, falling upon me and enveloping me in its
heavy folds, with not a corner raised to afford
me a breath of outer air, and much more oppressive to bear than I could have thought it. Perhaps, too, the aspect of death which pervades
this house has something to do with producing
this feeling, and the drops which fall from the
ceiling with such a doleful sound, and the
voices chanting in a minor key from the summit
of the minarets, into the darkness of the night.
But really, the impression of the first few days
is one of suffocation ; the being buried in the
labyrinth of these little narrow streets ; the
proximity of all these people who either hate
you or despise you, and who only tolerate you

in their city because they are compelled to, and would be glad to let you die like a dog in their streets; and all these tight-shut interior gates of the different quarters—and tightly shut, too, the great gates of the ramparts, imprisoning the whole; and outside and beyond it all, the black darkness of the wild, fierce country, even more inhospitable than the city, where there are no roads for us to fly by and where dwell savage tribes that delight in murder.

XXI.

Tuesday, April 16th.

THE first night spent in this house was dismal enough; perpetually the same sounds; the rain, the wind, the chanting of prayers in the distance. About two o'clock in the morning, the old doors of the staircase and the corridor were rattled so, there was such a clashing of iron, that I thought some one was trying to get in, so I took my lantern and made a thorough tour of inspection. But there was no one; it was only the wind, and the bolts were all undisturbed.

I went to sleep again and was only awakened by the light penetrating through the chinks of my great cedar doors. I went barefooted over the carpet which covers my stone floor, and opening one of the little cat-holes, looked through the yawning opening in the roof out upon the sky ; a fine, drizzling rain was still falling from the same wintry sky and a cold wind, like that of northern climes, blew upon my face. In the pitiless light, at once bright and wan, which fell from above together with the rain, the antiquity, the desolateness, the dilapidation of my house appeared even more utter than they had done before. The mosaics of the inlaid floor, which the rain had washed clean, could alone boast any freshness of color.

* * *

The morning is spent in trying on costumes for full dress. A certain Edriss, an Algerine Mussulman, whom Doctor L. has procured for me as a guide, has brought me for selection caftans of pink, yellow, brown and dark blue cloth, as well as belts, turbans and great silken girdles to hold the poniard and the alms-bag in which every believer should carry a little manuscript commentary on the holy writings ; finally long veils of transparent woolen stuff to wear over the dress and tone down its colors. He teaches me also the difficult art of enfolding one's self gracefully in these veils, which are wrapped two or three times about the body from the head down, and to the proper arrangement of which the remainder of the toilette is subordinated. To say nothing of the romance of this disguise, it is certain that the Arab dress is indispensable at Fez to one who wishes to go about with freedom and inspect men and things closely.

* * *

Three O'clock of the Afternoon.

There is a knock ; I know who it is and go down stairs to open the door, clad in a very plain Arab dress of white woolen, slightly soiled, such as is seen on the people passing in the streets. At the door I find three mules standing with their heads turned in the direction which we are to follow, on account of the impossibility of turning between these high walls, which are so close together that they almost touch. One of the three mules is held by a groom, and notwithstanding it is a day of *purification* and retreat, I swing myself into the high-peaked saddle, covered with red cloth. The other two are mounted by persons wrapped in long bournouses, one of whom is Edriss, and the other, whom no one could distinguish from a real Bedouin, is Captain H. de V., one of the members of the embassy, who does not care more than I do to purify himself to-day ; he is my habitual companion in all excursions and all his impressions upon this country coincide with mine. Without a word said, the three of us move forward, as if the object of our journey was understood beforehand. The drizzle of rain is still falling from the low-hanging clouds.

For a long time we proceed in Indian file in this persistent rain which makes the dark little streets more dismal still. For the greater part of the time the water or liquid mud is up to the knees of our animals, which slide on the stones, sink into holes, and twenty times come near going down. We often have to bend down to the saddle to avoid breaking our heads as we pass under some low archway. We momentarily have to stop and seek the protection of a gateway, or else back out into another street, so as to afford passage to loaded mules, or perhaps to horses or asses.

We pass through the covered bazaar, where a kind of semi-twilight prevails continually ; here we are elbowed by all sorts of people and things; we crowd the by-passers up against the houses and we are all the time scraping the old walls with our stirrups.

At length we arrive at our destination : a great evil-looking court-yard, old and tumble-down, like everything else at Fez, and surrounded by

massive entrances which give it the appearance of the exercising ground of a prison; it is the slave market, which Christians are not permitted to see.

The market is empty to-day ; we had been incorrectly informed ; there have doubtless been no arrivals from the Soudan, for we are told that there will be no sales for two or three days to come. Following Edriss, then, we pursue our way, in strict silence always, among the entanglement of streets, which seem to us to grow even darker and narrower as we advance.

Now a great murmur of human voices reaches us, voices praying and chanting at the same time in one unvarying rhythm, with a fervid piety that is immense. At the the same time we are aware of a white light in the midst of the black labyrinth ; it proceeds from a great ogival doorway, in front of which our guide, Edriss, who has reduced his mule's gait to the slowest walk, turns in his saddle and looks at us. We question him by an imperceptible sign : " That is *it*, is it not?" In the same manner, by a movement of the eyelids, he answers : "Yes." And we proceed at the slowest possible rate of speed, so that we may see the more.

" It " is Karaouïn, the holy mosque, the Mecca of all the Moghreb, whence war on the infidels has been preached for a thousand years, and from whence emanate those fierce expounders of the faith who year by year spread themselves over the wastes of Morocco, Algeria and Egypt, even to the remotest parts of the Sahara and the black Soudan. By day and by night its vaulted roof is resounding, without any intermission, to this same confused sound of song and prayer; it may be able to contain twenty-thousand people, its size is that of a city. For centuries wealth of every sort has been accumulating there, and mysterious deeds are done within its walls. Through the great ogive of the doorway we can see the pillars and arcades stretching away into the dimness of the distance, all exquisite in form, carved and ornamented with the wonderful art of the Arabs. Thousands of lights are suspended from the vaulted roof, and everything is snowy-white; the half-shadows of the outer corridors are penetrated by the white light. The race of the faithful lie prostrate on the ground in their bournouses, on the inlaid pavement with its bright colors; and the murmur of hymns ascends, unceasing and monotonous as the sound of the sea.

We dare not speak, nor stop, nor even look too inquisitively, for fear of being detected in our violation of quarantine. We will ride around the immense mosque, however, with its twenty entrances, and will see how it looks under other

aspects. There is a sort of narrow circular road
surrounding it, which we follow, our animals
sinking at every step into the mud, filth and decaying animal and vegetable matter. There is
nothing to be seen from the outside except the
lofty black walls, dilapidated and ready to fall,
against which lean the old houses, its neighbors. Whenever we pass one of the doors, we
check our mules with a vague sentiment of awe
and veneration; then for an instant we catch
the white light of the sanctuary and the sound
of prayerful voices. It is of so great an extent
that we are not very successful in deciphering
the main plan on which it is laid out; its arcades
are infinitely varied, some being lofty, light and
graceful beyond expression, ornamented with indescribable wreaths and garlands and with clusters of stalactites; others having the forms of
many-leaved trefoils, elongated arches and ogives.
Wherever our sight penetrates, there, prostrate
on the stone floor, is the multitude of bournouses,
murmuring their never ceasing prayers.

We shall doubtless see Karaouïn frequently
during our stay at Fez, but I do not think that
we shall ever have a more profound impression
of it than that produced by this first glimpse,
furtively snatched on that day when it was for-
bidden us.

XXII.

WEDNESDAY, APRIL 17th.

THIS morning we are to be presented to the Sultan, one day of our quarantine having been graciously remitted to us. At half past eight we are all assembled in full uniform in the Moorish court-yard of the house occupied by the minister and his suite. Then comes the *Caïd Introducer of Ambassadors*, a gigantic, bull-necked mulatto, carrying an enormous staff of some cheap metal. (To perform the duties of this office one of the largest men of the empire is always selected.) Four persons in long white robes enter in his suite and remain standing motionless behind him, all of them furnished with staves like his, which they hold in front of them at arm's length, just as a drum-major holds his cane. Their duty is simply to keep our road clear of people.

When we are ready to mount, we pass through the orange grove, where that same fine wintry rain is falling that has accompanied us so faithfully thus far on our journey, and direct our steps toward the low gateway which gives access to the street ; here the horses are brought up, one by one. The street is so narrow that the animals cannot turn about in it nor proceed two abreast ; we accordingly mount them as they come up, hap-hazard, hastily and without order.

From here to the palace it is quite a long distance, and we have to pass through the same quarters that we did in coming here day before yesterday. In front of us, the sticks play here and there upon the backs of people who are obstructing the way, and we are surrounded by a file of terrified, red-uniformed soldiers who are constantly getting under our horses' heels, and whose bayonets, reaching to the height of our eyes, are a constant menace to us in the confusion of our rapid movements. As on the day of our entry, we cross the waste lands which lie between Old Fez and New Fez, with their rocks, aloe trees, caves, tombs, ruins, and the heaps of decaying animals above which the birds of prey are wheeling. At length we arrive before the first enclosure of the palace, and make our entry into the court of the Ambassadors through a great ogival gateway.

This court-yard is of such immense extent that I know of no city in the world that possesses one of similar dimensions. It is surrounded by those lofty and forbidding walls that I have spoken of before, flanked by solid square bastions—in the same manner as are the walls of Stamboul and Damietta—with something about them still more dilapidated, more threatening, more awe-inspiring; the place is covered with coarse grass, and in the centre is a marsh where the frogs are piping. The sky is black, filled with angry clouds; birds leave their niches in the towers and wheel in circles in the air.

Notwithstanding the thousands of men who are standing in dense array around its four sides under the old walls, the place seems empty. The spectators are the same as ever, the same colors also prevail; on one side, a white multitude in cloaks and cowls, on the other a red multitude, the troops of the Sultan, with their band at their head in their robes of orange, green, violet, brown and yellow. The central part of the immense court, where we have taken our position, is completely deserted. And the crowd, far distant from us as it is, and heaped up against the foot of these overpowering battlements, looks like a crowd of Lilliputians.

This place has communication with the inner precincts of the palace through one of its corner bastions. This bastion, in less ruinous condition than the others and newly whitewashed, has two charming great arched gateways, surrounded with pink and blue arabesques, and it is through one of these arches that the Sultan is to make his appearance.

We are requested to dismount, for no one may presume to remain mounted in the presence of the Commander of the Faithful. So our beasts are led away, and here we are, standing in the mud, among the wet grass.

There is a movement among the troops, and the red infantry and their parti-colored band come and form up in two ranks, making a wide avenue from the centre of the court where we are stationed down to the bastion yonder from which the Sultan is to approach, and all eyes are fixed on the gate surrounded with arabesques, awaiting the holy apparition.

The gate is fully two hundred métres away from us, such is the great size of the court yard, and the first ones to approach through the lane of troops are the great officers of state, the viziers : men whose visages are thoughtful and whose beards are growing white ; they, too, are on foot to-day, like ourselves, and walk with slow steps in the dignity of their white veils and floating bournouses. We know almost all these persons from having met them on our arrival day before yesterday, but they presented a prouder appearance then, mounted on their fine horses.

There appears, also, the Caid Belaïl, the black court buffoon, with his indescribable turban shaped like a dome; he advances by himself with a distracting gait, swaying to and fro as if he were hung on wires, supported by an enormous bludgeon-like staff; there is an unspeakable repulsive and scoffing air about him, which seems to tell his consciousness of the favor which he enjoys with his master.

The rain still threatens; storm-clouds, impelled by the high wind, drive through the heavens in company with the flocks of birds, giving an occasional glimpse of that deep blue which alone reminds us that we are in the country of light. The walls, the towers are in every direction bristling with their pointed battlements, rising in the air with the appearance of combs from which part of the teeth have been broken; they loom up gigantic, shutting us in as in a citadel of immense size and fantastic form. Time has endowed them with a golden-gray color that is very striking; they are broken, cracked, ready to fall; they produce upon the mind the impression of an antiquity that is lost in night. Two or three storks are looking down upon the throng from their perches among the battlements; a donkey, too, that has in some way or other succeeded in getting up into one of the towers with his red-covered saddle on his back, surveys the scene from his vantage-ground.

Through the gateway that is bordered with pink and blue arabesques, upon which our attention is more and more closely fixed, there now streams a band of fifty little negro slaves, dressed in red with white surplices, like choir boys. They march awkwardly, huddling together like a flock of sheep.

Then six magnificent white horses are led forth, all saddled and caparisoned in silk, rearing and pawing the ground.

Then a gilded coach, of the time of Louis XV--incongruous with the surroundings, and looking very trifling and ridiculous among all this rude grandeur. It has the distinction of being the only wheeled carriage in existence at Fez, and was the gift of Queen Victoria.

These events are succeeded by a few moments of silent waiting. Then suddenly the long lines of soldiers vibrate under a thrill of religious awe; the band, with its great brasses and its drums, strikes up a deafening, mournful air. The fifty little black slaves run, run as if their lives were at stake, deploying from their base like the sticks of a fan, resembling bees swarming, or a flock of birds. And yonder, in the shadowy light of the ogive, upon which all eyes are turned, there appears a tall, brown-faced mannikin, all veiled in white muslin, mounted on a splendid white horse led in hand by four slaves; over his head is held an umbrella of antique form, such an one as must have protected the Queen of Sheba, and two gigantic negros, one in pink, the other in blue, wave fly-flaps around the person of the sovereign.

While the strange mannikin, or mummy, almost shapeless, but majestic notwithstanding in his robes of snowy white, is advancing toward us, the music, as if exasperated to madness, wails louder and louder, in a shriller key; it strikes up a slow and distressful religious air, the time of which is accentuated by a frightful beating of the bass-drums. The mannikin's horse rears wildly, restrained with difficulty by the four black slaves, and this music, so mournful and so strange to us, affects our nerves with an indescribable agonizing sensation.

Here, at last, drawn up close beside us, stands this last authentic descendant of Mahomet, crossed with Nubian blood. His attire, of the finest *mousseline-de-laine,* is of immaculate whiteness. His charger, too, is entirely white, his great stirrups are of gold, and his saddle and equipments are of a very pale green silk, lightly embroidered in a still paler shade of golden green. The slaves who hold his horse, the one

who carries the great red umbrella, and the two
—the pink and blue ones—who shake napkins in
the monarch's face to drive away imaginary flies,
are all herculean negros whose countenances are
wrinkled into fierce smiles; they are all old men,
and their gray or white beards contrast with the
blackness of their features.   This ceremonial of
a bygone age harmonizes with the wailing music,
could not suit better with the huge walls around
us, which rear their crumbling summits high in
the air.

This man, who thus presents himself before
us with the surroundings which I have described,
is the last faithful exponent of a religion, a civilization that are about to die.   He is the person-
ification, in fact, of ancient Islam ; for it is well
known that pure Mussulmen look upon the Sultan of Stamboul almost in the light of a sacri-
legious usurper and turn their eyes and their
prayers toward the Moghreb, where dwells the
man who is in their eyes the true successor of the
Prophet.

What result can we expect to attain from an
embassy to such a man, who, together with his
people, spends his life torpid and motionless
among ancient dreams of humanity that have almost disappeared from the surface of the earth?
There is not a single point on which we can un-

derstand each other ; the distance between us is
nearly that which would separate us from a Caliph
of Cordova or of Bagdad who should come to
life again after a slumber of a thousand years.
What do we wish to obtain from him, and why
have we brought him forth from his impenetrable
palace?

His brown, parchment-like face in its setting
of white muslin, has regular and noble features ;
dull, expressionless eyes, the whites of which
appear beneath the balls that are half concealed
by the drooping lashes ; his expression is that
of exceeding melancholy, a supreme lassitude, a
supreme *ennui*. He has an appearance of benig-
nity, and is really kind-hearted, according to
what they say who know him. (If the people of
Fez are to be believed, he is even too much so ;
he does not chop off as many heads as he ought
for the holy cause of Islam.) But his kind-heart-
edness, no doubt, is relative in degree, as was
often the case with ourselves in the middle ages;
a mildness which is not over-sensitive in the face
of sheddiug blood when there is a necessity for
it, nor in face of a row of human heads set up in
a row over the fine gateway at the entrance to
the palace. Assuredly he is not cruel ; he could
not be so with that gentle, sad expression. He
punishes with severity sometimes, as his divine

authority gives him the right to do, but it is said that he finds a still keener pleasure in pardoning. He is a priest and a warrior, and carries each of these characters, perhaps, to excess ; feeling as deeply as a prophet the responsibility of his heavenly mission, chaste in the midst of his seraglio, strict in his attention to onerous religious observances and hereditarily very much of a fanatic, he aims to form himself upon Mahomet as perfectly as may be ; all this, moreover, is legible in his eyes, upon his fine countenance, in the upright majesty of his bearing. He is a man whom we can neither understand nor judge in the times we live in, but he is surely a great man, a man of mark.

The minister presents his credentials to the Sultan in a bag of velvet embroidered with gold, which is received by one of the fly-drivers. Then the customary short speeches are exchanged ; that of the minister first, then that of the Sultan in reply, declaring his friendship for the French nation, spoken in a low tone of voice, with a wearied, condescending, extremely gentlemanly manner. Then comes the presentation of individuals, our salutations, which the sovereign acknowledges by a courteous movement of the

head—and it is all over ; the Commander of the
Faithful has displayed himself sufficiently to
Nazarenes such as we are. The handsome
charger with the silken trappings is turned by
the black slaves, the Scheriffian majesty turns
his back on us, looking like a tall phantom in his
cloudy wrappings. The music, which has been
playing softly while the speeches were going on,
bursts into a funereal crescendo ; another band
of pipes and tambourines yelps and squeaks at
the same time on a higher key ; the artillery
commences to thunder close to our ears, startling
the horses ; the Sultan's steed rears and kicks,
endeavoring to rid himself of his white mummy,
who remains impassible ; all the others, the six
beautiful animals that were led in by the bit,
make their escape with furious bounds ; the one
that is harnessed to the state carriage rears upright on his hind legs ; the fifty little black boys
again run madly hither and thither, without any
apparent object to their course ; (this is a bit of
etiquette that is always observed whenever the
Sultan is on horseback).

While the bands maintain their exasperating
crescendo, while the guns continue their deafening racket, the Caliph and his suite retire rapidly, like an apparition driven away by an excess
of noise and stir ; they disappear down yonder

in the shadows of the archway that is bordered with arabesques of pink and blue. We behold one last plunge of the handsome white steed as he tries to the last to shake off his impassible rider, then they all disappear, including the red umbrella and the fifty choir boys, who pour in through the gateway like a wave of the sea. A shower begins to come down, and we have to run through the tall wet grass after our horses, among the red-uniformed negro soldiers, who have broken ranks ; among all this pitiful army of monkeys. A strange riot and disorder succeed the religious awe that but lately prevailed in this gigantic enclosure of ruinous walls and towers.

**
* **

At last we are on horseback again, bound for a visit to the palace gardens in company with the viziers, as is the custom every time that the Sultan receives an embassy. We pass other enclosures walled in with battlements of fearful height, other ancient ogival gateways with iron-bound gates, other walled court-yards where the ground is cut up by sewers and quagmires ; the whole is extremely old and ruinous, but imposing in every case and sinister. The most striking of these courts is a parallelogram, two or three hundred métres long, between battlemented walls of at least fifty feet in height. At the opposite ends of this court, and placed symmetrically in respect to each other, are two great gateways, freshly whitened and enframed in pink and blue arabesques and tiles in mosaic, like all the gates of the palace. Each of these gates is flanked by four enormous battlemented towers, on which has been left, as has been on the ramparts, the sombre colors that have been given them by the centuries, and which rise in steps, the outside towers being much higher than the inner ones. No words can give an idea of the wild aspect of this place, nor of the depressing monotony of these lofty far-stretching walls, of all these battlements standing out against the sky.

Afterward our way lies between two rows of great gray walls, incomplete as yet, which the Sultan is building and carrying up to a great height, in order that his women folk may be able to visit the gardens without being seen from any quarter, either from the terraces or from the surrounding mountains. We are conscious of a sort of solemn chorus emanating from that direction, accompanied from time to time by something that sounds like muffled drums beaten in unison, several at a time. One might think it was the celebration of a funeral service in some one of the mosques—but it is simply laborers at their work, arranged in line on the crest of a wall of beaten earth. They sing a doleful lament in a minor adagio, and at the end of each beat, which lasts some fifteen seconds, they give a blow to their structure, so as to harden the moistened clay, with one of those heavy wooden mallets which are called "demoiselles"; that is all the work they do, and it will go on in the same way until night. They turn to look at us as we ride by, and we, too, look at them with amusement and astonishment. It seems like a wager, a practical joke; but not so; those people are entirely serious. It seems that whenever there is anything to be done for the Sultan by day's work, this solemn dawdling comes in play. Having passed the enclosed space where they are at work, followed by their droning melody, we turn in our saddles to have another look at them, and think that this time we shall be able to catch a rear view. But with a comical concerted movement they too have turned to watch us, and they resume their work to the same cadence, with the same unimaginable deliberateness.

Passing through one last gate, we enter the gardens of the Sultan. Orchards, they should be called rather; great orchards in an abandoned state, enclosed between ruined walls. But orange orchards are they, charming in their melancholy desolation and redolent with the sweetest odors. The avenues are protected by arbors of grape-vine and flagged with marble, with antique well-worn flagstones that have grown green with time. Golden fruit and white blossoms are hanging at the same time from the branches of the ancient trees. Underneath weeds are growing and in spots the ground becomes marshy, like the savannahs of the south. Here and there are old, cheerless kiosques, where the Sultan, it seems, comes with his women to rest. The arabesques have been obliterated from them by a coat of whitewash.

A melancholy like that of a graveyard characterizes the whole place. How many beautiful creatures, selected from among the proudest families in all the Moghreb, must these orange groves have looked down on, as they walked here, wearied, faded away and died!

XXIII.

Thursday, April 18th.

ONE of the complications of existence in this city is that one can never go out unattended, even in Arab dress ; there would be the risk of some unpleasant adventure, and then, above all, it would not be good form, decorum exacting that one should always be preceded by a servant or two, stick in hand, to drive the common people from one's way. It is impossible, also, to go out on foot, from regard for the proprieties in the first place, and then, because one does not care to wade through mud up to the knees, nor to be driven up against the walls of the narrow streets by loaded mules or by dashing horsemen. The result is that one is a prisoner in his own house for three-fourths of the time, owing to the indolence of the servant class, the mount ordered to be saddled ready for a certain specified time not being forthcoming.

I breakfast every morning at the minister's, in company with the other officers of the embassy, but it woud be impossible to dine there at evening, on account of the return after night-fall, and on account of the closing of the gates between the quarters, shutting off all communication.

I have for a neighbor, however, almost at the next door, Dr. L., he who was so kind as to lend me the house which I inhabit, and we dine together every evening. I go to his house on foot, walking with my legs well apart, my papooches touching the walls on either side of the street, so as to steer clear of the black stream in the middle. At his door, which is as low and dark as mine, I generally knock my head against the casing as I enter. After dinner I return, preceded by Selim and Mohammed, my two servants, with lanterns, to barricade myself at eight o'clock in the evening in my house that is a thousand years old. The two servants occupy the apartment opposite to mine, on the other side of my interior court. Behind their cedar doors, like mine in every respect, they make tea for themselves and sing songs to the accompaniment of the guitar all night long. In the morning, when I open my door, they open theirs, say good-day, put on their bournouses and go for a walk. Neither by love nor money, nor by threats, shall I ever succeed in obtaining from them a little better service. They generally leave me entirely alone in the house, and when I hear the distant sound of the heavy knocker on my door,

I myself am obliged to descend my turret staircase and open for my visitor.

If I relate so many trivialities, it is because
they give the measure of the difficulties of life
for an European who is lost in Fez, even when
he is there, as I am, under exceptional conditions
as regards comfort.

* * *

This morning, like yesterday afternoon, is employed in official visits to different personages of
importance. There is still the same fine cold rain,
which has been our almost constant companion,
and which made our visit of yesterday to the
Sultan's gardens such a cheerless one.

At the Vizier's and the minister's mansions
whither we repair on horseback through the dark
and winding lanes, we are received in those court-
yards open to the sky, which invariably constitute the chief luxury of the houses of Fez ; court-
yards with inlaid pavements, richly ornamented
with arabesques and surrounded by arched
passages of complicated design. On other oc-
casions, our reception takes place in the depths
of those delightful gloomy gardens, which are
rather orange groves overrun by weeds, the
avenues of which, flagged with white stone, are
sheltered by grape-vine arbors ; the whole sur-

rounded, of course, by those lofty prison walls which are designed to afford invisibility to the pretty inhabitants of the harem when they choose to take a walk.

The state dinners will not begin until next week ; as yet we have only collations, but they are Pantagruelian collations, such as ours used to be in the times of the middle-ages. Immense bowls of European or Japanese ware are set either on tables or on the ground, filled with pyramids of fruit, of walnuts removed from their shells, of almonds, "gazelle's shoes," sweetmeats, dates, saffron-bonbons. Veils of gaudy colors, with stripes of gold, are thrown over these mountains of goodies, which would suffice for two hundred persons. Blue or pink decorated jugs, loaded down with gilding, contain an abominable muddy, stinking water, which should not be drunk under any circumstances. We are seated on rugs and embroidered cushions, or upon chairs of a style long out of date, that of the Empire or Louis XVI. The service is performed by black slaves, or by a kind of janissaries armed with long curved swords and with pointed *tarboushes* on their heads. Coffee and cigarettes are never served, for the Sultan has prohibited their use. In his edict against tobacco, he even went so far as to compare the depraved taste of a smoker to that of a man who would eat the flesh of a dead horse.

There is only tea and the odoriferous smoke, slightly intoxicating, too, of that costly Indian wood, which is burned before us in chafing-dishes. The high Russian samovars are everywhere, and the same tea, flavored with mint and spice and sweetened to excess. It is counted good manners to take three cups, and the custom is not a pleasant one, for every time that there is a new deal, the cups are interchanged among the guests without being washed, while the dregs which remain in them are mercilessly thrown in the teapot.

During these visits, it is unnecessary to say, we see nothing of the women, but we are constantly observed by them. Every time that we chance to turn our heads, we are certain to see in some trefoil half concealed in the arabesques of the wall, in some narrow peep-hole, or peering over some ledge of the terrace, several pairs of very long, pointed eyes, watching us curiously, which vanish, disappear in the darkness, as soon as our looks meet.

These great Moroccan personages who entertain us all have the air of the world ; beneath the folds of their thin white veils they have great dignity of carriage and movement ; they are possessed of a certain gentlemanly indolence, of a certain indifference to everything. Still it is evident that they are not the equals of the common people, the fierce, bronzed men of the open air. Wealth, the consuming thirst of increasing fortunes that are already large, and the corruption of political life as well, have spoiled them. In these early visits upon our arrival, our minister says nothing as yet of the affairs that require adjustment, but it is easy to see that they will not be settled quickly by nothing but noting these airs of cunning and mistrust, and the feline half-smiles of these white-veiled men, who answer questions with gracious circumlocution, who seem never to be busy and never to be sincere.

The son of the Grand Vizier is about to be married, and since yesterday all Fez is in an uproar over the wedding. Interminable processions go and come in the dark lanes, preceded by tam-tams, ear-splitting pipes and discharges of musketry. We encountered one this morning of at least three hundred persons, who were firing blank cartridges in the darkness of the narrow vaulted passages, shaking the old walls; those at the head of the line were carrying gifts upon their heads; they were bulky objects, wrapped in stuffs of silk figured with gold.

The Vizier's mansion, as we saw in the course of our visit yesterday afternoon, is magnificently decorated for the grand fête. In the court-yard, all mosaics and laced arabesques, were hung innumerable chandeliers, so close together as actually to touch, absolutely concealing the clouded vault of the sky; all the fine carvings on the walls had been picked out afresh with gold, blue, pink and green, and magnificent hangings of red velvet, embroidered with gold *in-relievo*, were suspended everywhere, reaching up as high as the first story; they were those Arab hangings, the designs on which represent series of arches and wreaths, like the doors of the mosques.

In the apartments opening on this court of honor, there was a display, a wonderful profusion, of rich carpets, hangings and cushions of brilliant or rare colors, where golden yellows and golden greens were intermingled in strange, semi-religious designs. The person of the Grand Vizier, entirely white in his simple white muslins, stood out in relief against all these riches; his handsome, feline, shifting, unreliable features encircled in their frame of gray beard.

Our minister requested to be allowed to see,

not the bride, be it understood, since she was still invisible even for her spouse, but the bridegroom and the young men of his suite. The Vizier consented with a smile, and conducted us across a garden to the house prepared for the new family ; a house quite new, not finished yet, but constructed after the immutable fashion of Granada or Cordova, where an army of workmen were patiently at work carving the arabesques.

There, seated on divans around a great bare room some young men were having a good time with tea, sweetmeats and the smoke of burning perfumes. The gilded youth of Fez, the rising generation, the future Caids and the future Viziers, who will perhaps be called on some day to witness the downfall of old Moghreb. Very young, all of them were, but pale, emaciated, dejected, sunk deep into their cushions. The son of the Grand Vizier, dressed in green (which is always the color of a groom), was apart in a corner, the most glóomy and dejected of them all, with an air of absolute stupidity, completely done up with lassitude and ennui. Half way up to the ceiling of the room where these young men were amusing themselves, the smoke of the sweet-smelling Indian wood hung in a gray cloud.

XXIV.

Friday, April 19th, (Good Friday).

IN a few hours, as is always the case in this country, the sky has cleared and the atmosphere is vaporless. In place of the masses of gray clouds, driven hither and thither and obscuring ideas and objects, there is an immensely deep, limpid void, which is this evening of a changing blue, of a blue shading off at the horizon into greenish aqua-marine tints; over all things is the great resplendency, the carnival, the magical display, of light.

At these witching hours of the dying day, I mount to my roof-terrace and seat myself there. The sombre, fanatical old city lies basking in the gold of the exuberant sunshine; lying stretched at my feet over its hills and valleys, it has taken on an aspect of unchanging, radiant peace, an aspect that is almost cheerful, almost peaceful; it is so changed that I do not recognize it; a rosy halo seems to rise from its lifeless ruins. And the air all at once has become so balmy and so soothing, giving illusions of an eternal summer!

In the immediate foreground, the terraced

roofs of the tall adjacent houses surround me in groups ; houses outwardly like blocks of stone placed irregularly here and there, as if they owed their arrangement to chance. There is a void between these terraces and my own ; although their minutest details, the slightest crack in their walls, is distinguished with the utmost clearness, they are separated from me by a sort of luminous haze which makes them indistinct at their foundations and gives them almost an aërial aspect ; they appear as if suspended in the air. Gradually all these lofty promenades are filled with women, who make their appearance, one after the other, rising from the depths below, in the most striking costumes, bonneted with the " hantouze " (a gilded mitre, recalling the *hennin* worn in the late days of our middle-ages).

Beyond these nearer terraces, which belong to houses built, like my own, on the most elevated part of Old Fez—after another void space and another interval of misty light, the more distant objects are seen stretching away to infinity, as if seen through transparencies of gauze. First is all the remainder of Old Fez ; a thousand terraces, grayish-violet in hue, where the fair promenaders seem to be mere points of bright color scattered here and there upon a monotonous succession of ruins. Rising above these stone blocks, so uniform in shape, are seen some tall and slender palm trees ; and, as well, all the old square towers of the mosques, with their insertions of green and yellow tiles that have been baked and rebaked by the suns of centuries, with their small cupolas, surmounted each by a gilded ball.

Of New Fez, which is more distant, there can only be distinguished the forbidding walls which enclose the seraglios, the palaces and the courtyards of the Sultan. And a belt of verdant gardens, in the freshest green of Spring, surrounds the great city ; its old ramparts, its old bastions, its formidable old towers, are all drowned, as it were, in this ocean of fresh verdure.

The atmosphere is clear, surprisingly clear. Notwithstanding this illusory haze, which is of a bluish tint on the low grounds and of a golden pink upon the summits, distant objects are discernible as if they had been brought near by a glass, or as if the faculty of sight had been endowed this evening with unaccustomed penetration.

Down below us are Karaouïn and Mouley-Driss, the two great holy mosques, which only to name, before my coming here, caused me to shudder as at the mention of some great mysteries. I look down upon their minarets, upon

their roofs covered with green tiles like the roofs
of the Alhambra ; seen thus, in full daylight, in
the calm of this beautiful evening, they no longer
seem to be objects of dread, they no longer seem
to be the awful sanctuaries that they are, and,
in the same way, all this great city, standing in
its enclosure of verdurous gardens, so peaceful
under the softening influence of this pure golden
pink light, ceases to impress us as being, as it
really is, the city of savage religious gloom ;
makes us forget all the mysteriously immutable
things that are contained within its precincts.
It is difficult to realize that this can be the
walled-in heart of Islam, the lonely Mecca of the
Moghreb, without roads to communicate with
the outside world.

Still farther beyond, beyond the ramparts and
the gardens, the gigantic amphitheatre of the
mountains is also basking in the light ; the
smallest valleys, the slightest folds can be
counted this evening ; everything that is going
on there can be seen as if through a telescope.
Here and there caravans, infinitely small in the
distance, are journeying to the Soudan or toward
Europe. Toward the east, in the direction
where the last rays of the sun strike full, there is
a region of burying-grounds and ruins ; the first
slopes adjacent to the city are covered with the

rubbish of fallen walls, with " koubas " of holy men, with innumerable tombs, and as it is Friday (the Mahometan Sunday), the day set apart for paying pious visits to the dead, these cemeteries are filled with people ; the visitors, in gray bournouses, as they move about among the stones, when seen from so great a distance, seem to be other stones endowed with the faculty of movement. High up, the summits are of a bright rose color, with folds of shadow that are absolutely blue. Towering higher still and still more far away, the Great Atlas, wrapped in its glittering snows, of still another shade of rose, paler and more transparent, boldly projects its back against the clear yellow tones which are beginning to trench upon and replace the vanishing blue of the sky.

To the west, and quite near us, a lofty mountain rises like a serrated screen between us and the sun, casting its shadow upon a portion of the city. It is intersected by valleys running obliquely from its summit to its base, and with its sharply defined crest, is not unlike an enormous wave of the sea that has been arrested there in its advance upon the city. We feel that on its far slope we would still be in the full splendor of the sunlight ; its profile is made more distinct by a bordering of light.

Flocks of dark-colored birds are wheeling in the air above the terraces, and great storks also float by with easy flight in the golden-green sky.

*　*　*

It is Good Friday; a season when, in our country, the fickle Spring generally hides her face in clouds, so that the expression is often used; "Good Friday weather," to express a cloudy, windy day. But the city in which I am does not put on those Christian weeds, nor recognize the cause for which Christians mourn on that day, and this evening she is voluptuously basking in the calm warm air, beneath a sky lighted up as if for a fête.

Then again Friday in Mahometan countries is for the people, as Sunday is with us, a day of rest, a day for the display of their best attire, and so the women, more numerous and more gayly dressed than usual, make their appearance at the little doors of the belvederes which protect the tops of the staircases of their dwellings, and come forth upon the roofs, shaking their plumes like birds, and everywhere enamelling the old gray terraces with their brilliant costumes.

Gray are they, all these terraces, or rather devoid of color; of a dead, neutral shade, changing constantly under the influence of the

weather and the sky. They have been white-washed again and again from time immemorial, until they have lost their original shape beneath the repeated coatings ; baking in the sunlight, calcining under the scorching heat, guttered by the rains, until they have become almost of a blackish hue. They are not very cheerful, these elevated places where the women resort. Everywhere, on my terrace as well as on those of my pretty neighbors, the little old low walls on which we lean our elbows and which serve as parapets to keep us from falling into the gulf, are crowned with lichens, saxifrage and small yellow flowers.

The women collect in groups, or seat themselves and chat upon the ledges of the walls, with their legs overhanging the court-yards or the streets, or else throw themselves back and stretch out in careless attitudes with their fingers interlaced behind their heads. They climb from house to house to exchange visits, sometimes by the assistance of small ladders, or of a bridge improvised from a plank. The negresses are sculpturesque in form ; they wear great silver rings in their ears, are dressed in white or pink, and their black faces are surrounded by kerchiefs of silk ; their gaiety has something monkeyish about it, and their cheer-

ful voices are shrill and creaking as a child's
rattle. Their mistresses, the white Arab ladies,
wear tunics of silk figured with gold, the colors
of which are softened with embroidery of tulle;
their long wide sleeves expose their fine arms
which are encircled with bracelets; their busts
are sustained by wide belts of silk worked with
gold, as stiff as bands of cardboard; on the
forehead there is a head-dress composed of a
double row of gold sequins, or of pearls, or of
other precious stones, and surmounting all is
the "hantouze," or tall mitre, around which are
always wreathed handkerchiefs of golden gauze,
the ends of which hang down behind the back
and mingle with the masses of the loosened
hair. Their open lips disclose rows of white
teeth, and they walk with a voluptuously slow
motion, with their head thrown proudly back
and with somewhat of a swing. Their eyes,
very black and already sufficiently large, are
brought nearer together and prolonged in the
direction of the temples by the use of antimony;
many of them are painted, not carmine, but
pure vermillion, as if they were trying to see
how unnatural they could make themselves;
their cheeks seem to have been coated with a
thick paste of red-led, and their arms and foreheads are tatooed in blue.

All this luxury obligingly exposes itself up here to the daylight, which, as often as business or pleasure demands a promenade in the narrow muddy streets, veils itself in grayish white and assumes the appearance of a mysterious phantom. The city, which appears so black and sullen to one who traverses it with eyes cast down, displays all the elegance of its feminine life on the house-tops at these golden hours at the close of day. Mistresses and slaves associate together without distinction of caste, with an appearance of perfect equality, laughing and joking together and frequently walking arm in arm. Those visages which are so carefully concealed in the street, are never veiled here, and as a consequence men are never allowed upon the terraces of Fez. I am committing a great breach of etiquette by remaining seated upon mine..... But then I am a foreigner, and I can make believe that I did not know any better.

However, the gold is losing its brightness, is everywhere fading ; that rosy limpidity which was just now illuminating the religious city is ascending by degrees toward the upper regions of the atmosphere ; the summits of the towers alone, and the most elevated terraces continue to reflect the light ; a violet shadow commences to spread over the distant places, in the valleys and low-lying grounds.   Soon the hour will strike for the fifth and last prayer of the day, the holy hour, the hour of the Moghreb...And all the womens' heads are turned in the direction of the venerable mosque of Mouley-Driss, as if waiting for some pious signal.

There is for me a magic, and an irresistible charm simply in the sound of that word: the Moghreb. Moghreb means at the same time the west, the setting sun, and the moment when the great luminary ends his diurnal existence. It also signifies the Empire of Morocco, which is the most western of all the lands of Islam, where the great impulse which Mahomet imparted to the Arabs faded out and died. Above all else, it signifies that last prayer which, from one end of the Mussulman world to the other, is recited at this hour of the evening—a prayer which has its beginning at Mecca and spreads, like a slowly burning train of powder, with universal prostration, across the whole of Africa, as the sun slowly sinks below the horizon—to cease only when it confronts the ocean, among the utmost sand-hills of the Sahara, where Africa itself ends.

*　*　*

Everywhere the gold begins to grow dull.
Fez is already sunk in the shadow of its great
mountains ; nearer Fez is drowning in this violet
mist which has risen little by little, like a rising
tide—and the more distant Fez is scarcely distinguishable. The snows on the summits of Atlas
alone preserve, for one last fleeting moment,
their rosy brightness. Then a white flag is run
up to the top of the minaret of Mouley-Driss.
In instantaneous response, other white flags are
displayed from all the minarets of the other
mosques :

—"Allah Akbar !" A great cry of unques-
tioning faith runs through the great city.

—"Allah Akbar !" To your knees, every
believer ! To your knees, in the streets, in the
mosques, on your door-steps, in the fields : it is
the holy hour of the Moghreb !

—"Allah Akbar.....!" From all the minarets the muezzins, placing their hands to their
mouth, repeated the long-drawn wailing cry to
the four points of the compass, their shrill voices
dying mournfully away, like the howling of
wolves.

All is quiet ; the sun has set. A vapor of
deeper violet makes the void space between the
houses still more conspicuous; they seem to withdraw from each other, to draw away from me

with their groups of women who no longer move about. . . . .Silence falls upon the city after that great prayer.

* * *

It is night, the stars are shining. Nothing is any longer visible. Only higher up, on the terrace which overlooks mine, there is a woman standing at the corner of the roof, a shadow faintly relieved against the darkness of the sky, planted firmly on her feet, with her hands behind her back, contemplating, I know not what, in the dark gulf below.

XXV.

Saturday, April 20th.

THERE was a fight last night in the camp which is forming outside the walls for the Sultan's approaching expedition. The subject of dispute was a mule to which two squadrons laid claim. There was firing from midnight until one o'clock, and there were twenty wounded and four killed, whom we saw carried off in a heap on a litter.

The splendid weather and the festival of light still continue. The sky is of a pure indigo blue, and the heat is increasing, delightful odors, whiffs from the orange-flowers in the gardens, mingle with the bad smells of the city. I am becoming accustomed to my little house, and it is ceasing to have a sinister aspect in my eyes. In the portion which I inhabit, I have caused the tiled floors to be washed and have had the walls whitewashed anew. (I have discovered more little doors in out of the way corners, leading to passage-ways, obscure nooks and dungeons; this would be an excellent place in case there was a person that one wanted to get rid of.) My little low door, with its iron-work of the year one thousand, seems very natural to me now, and I have ceased to wonder at my dark narrow street; I am becoming acquainted with my quarter, and my neighbors, also, are beginning to know me and do not observe me so closely. Although it is not the correct thing to do, and is annoying to the pretty ladies of the neighborhood, I am commencing to spend more of my time upon my terrace, especially at the holy hour of the Moghreb, when the white flags are hoisted on the mosques, when the muezzins appear on the minarets to chant the prayer and the great mountains drape themselves in their evening shades of violet and pink.

I have learned who that neighbor is whose house is so tangled up with mine. He is a very wealthy personage, an *amin*, something like a pay-master-general in the army of the Sultan. I have heard the noise of pounding in his house every morning and evening, so regularly continuous that it puzzled me vastly; I have discovered that it was sugar and cinnamon, being crushed to make candy for his children, who are very numerous. The restricted life of this country has aspects of great patriarchal amiability when it can be viewed close by. In the evening the voices of the wives and children of this *amin* reach me through the walls and keep me company.

I am becoming accustomed to my long Arab robes, and am learning the correct manner of holding my hands in my veils and draping my bournous. And very often I return to the vicinity of the mosque of Karaouïn, dragging my slippers through the labyrinth of the bazaar, which has assumed such a different aspect, under this bright sun, from that under which we regarded it in the first days of our arrival.

* * *

This evening, accompanied by my usual companion, Captain H. de V , both of us dressed as Arabs, I took my way to the slave market. The desolate courtyard was untenanted. To our enquiry as to whether there would be any business done this evening (for it is generally at nightfall, after the hour of the Moghreb, that the slaves and the buyers and sellers resort to this place), the answer was returned: " We do not know ; *but there is still that negro woman in the corner there, who is for sale.*"

The negress was seated at the edge of one of those recesses which are excavated in the thickness of the old walls, like dens of animals ; her attitude was one of great dread and terror, her head, enveloped in its grayish veil, and her closely covered face falling forward upon her breast ; as she saw us approaching, fearful, no doubt, that we were coming to buy her, she seemed to try to make herself smaller still. We made her arise so that we might look at her, as it is the custom to do with this kind of merchandise. We found that she was a little girl, sixteen to eighteen years old, whose tearful eyes bore an expression of resignation in the midst of a limitless despair ; she was twisting her veil in her hands and kept her eyes directed toward the ground. What a pitiful sight it was, this poor little creature, who had meekly arisen to allow us to examine her and who was awaiting her fate in this gloomy place. Beside her, seated in the same recess, was an elderly lady, her face carefully concealed in her veil, who, notwithstanding her unpretending dress, was evidently of the upper class. This was the mistress, who had brought the girl here for sale. We enquired the price: five hundred francs. And the poor old lady, with tears in her eyes and an expression almost as sad as that of her slave, explained to us how she had bought the child when very young and brought her up, but that now, being reduced to poverty by the death of her husband, she could no longer support her and was obliged to part with her. And thus it was that the two women were here waiting to find a purchaser, with a shrinking, humiliated air, both equally disconsolate. It was like a mother offering her daughter for sale.

At Fez, it is unnecessary to say, one never goes out at night unless compelled to. It is always blackest night in the little narrow, overhung streets as soon as it is eight o'clock, and one would run the risk of tumbling into the sewers, or the wells, or the old dungeons whose openings yawn here and there.

This evening, however, we are all to go to the palace, and orders have been given to leave the gates between the quarters open for our passage.

The time of our departure is fixed for half-past eight, from the residence of the minister. We are mounted on restive mules, and accompanied by the inevitable red infantry with fixed bayonets and carrying great lanterns, the panels of which are cut out in ogives, like the doors of the mosques.

Our way at first lies through the quarter of gardens, zig-zagging in the dark among the low walls, over which protrude branches of orange trees with their loads of perfumed blossoms; then we traverse a corner of the covered bazaar; then through streets with break-neck pavement, where a few lights are burning yet in the sleepy little shops. Then a wide dark street between long ruinous walls. Arabs, wrapped for the night in their bournouses, are sleeping on the ground along with the dogs, and we are near riding over them. At last the gates of the first enclosure of the palace are before us, guarded by soldiers with drawn swords; the massive doors, strengthened by heavy iron-work, have been left open for our benefit. By the light of the lanterns, we pass through the immense courts that are already familiar to us; those solitary spots, where are cesspools and quagmires, lying between the gigantic walls which point their battlements toward the starry sky, like rows of black combs. Everywhere in these wild precincts guards are stationed, sword in hand. We fcel that there is not an excessive hospitality in the place which we are visiting.

At last we reach the courtyard of the Ambassadors, the most extensive of all. Here the space is greater, consequently the darkness is not so intense. The frogs, accompanied by some katydids, are having a noisy concert. Down yonder in the distance we descry other lanterns moving about, and we direct our steps in their direction. By their light we are able to discern the grave personages who are awaiting us: high officers of the palace, viziers and cadis. They are to witness some experiments which we are to make with gifts that we have brought with us for the ladies of the seraglio ; bouquets of electr'c flowers, electric trinkets, stars and cresents to be worn in the hair of these invisible beauties. We are told that the Sultan himself is roaming about, concealed by the gloom which envelopes us all, so as to see without being seen ; that perhaps he will even go so far as to show himself if the experiments interest him. We keep a close watch on the scattered lights which are moving to and fro in the distance of the court, hoping every moment for the holy apparition. But no ; the Caliph, no doubt, does not find himself sufficiently interested to break through his reserve.

The batteries are a long time getting ready ;

they seem to be ill-natured toward the display.
The little nineteenth-century toys are at last
lighted up, after considerable difficulty, glittering like fire-flies in the darkness of their immemorial surroundings.

Sunday, April 21st, (Easter Sunday).

The weather bright and splendid, growing
warmer; the perfumed breath of the orange
trees and the odor of dead animals hang more
heavily in the air. It is delightfully pleasant in
the garden of our minister's house, and we remain seated there for a long time every day after
breakfast, in front of the old pavilion, of which
the arabesques have been obliterated by coats of
whitewash; the great orange trees, with their
white flowers and golden fruit, stand out boldly
above our heads against the blue of the sky, and
the sound of the water gushing from its marble
basin and running away over the stone floor
gives a voluptuous sensation of coolness.

The day was devoted, in company with H. de
V., both of us in Arab dress, to exploring the bazaar; we mingle more and more with these
crowded assemblages, where the people now

scarcely pay us any attention, so correct and natural is our attire in all details. We do not experience so much difficulty as we did in finding our way in this bazaar, among this labyrinth of lanes covered over with hurdles of reeds and trellises of grape-vines, where the white-cowled purchasers circulate among the dark little shops in which is the glitter of arms, of silk and of gold.

At evening, in the twilight of the holy hour of the Moghreb, a whole band of young negresses is brought to the slave market. They were captured recently in the Soudan, and their hair still retains its plastering of sticky gum, and they wear on their necks and arms the rude ornaments of their distant country. Old men, white as snow, whose dress shows that they are of the wealthy class, examine them, feel of them, stretch their arms and open their mouths to look at their teeth. They find no one to buy them, and the merchant marches them back home, a melancholy troop with hanging heads. They gaze at me as they pass, and merely by their touch and by their odor they recall to my mind Senegal, and with it a whole flood of memories that were dead.

*   *   *   *   *   *

By the fading light of day, I behold from my housetop great storm-clouds slowly creeping up the sky, the presage of the end of our fine weather. They are of a dull copper color, under which the thousands of terraces take on tints of cold gray, almost blue.

How quickly the view has familiarized itself to me that is to be had from here over the old city —from whence arises no sound of rolling vehicles or clanking machinery—only a confused murmuring of human voices, the neighing of horses, and the din of ancient industries ; the weaving of cloth or the hammering of brass.

I have come to know by heart all the ins and outs of this life on the housetops at eventide. I know all my fair neighbors who come forth from their little doorways, one after another, seat themselves, and remain there, queer little splashes of bright color against the monotony of gray back ground, until the twilight hour when the green tiles of the mosques themselves become gray, and everything is confounded and swallowed up in shadow. There is a certain beautiful lady, generally dressed in a blue robe with a yellow *hennin,* who makes her appearance followed by a negress in an orange-colored dress, bearing a small ladder, by the aid of which the mistress climbs to the adjacent roof where she disappears.

There is another, down in the direction of Karaouïn, who does her climbing unassisted, raising
her feet very high and crossing a street with a
single stride, in order to reach a house higher
than her own and visit her friends, of whom there
are ten or so, black as well as white. I know
where the storks' nests are, who stand motionless
on their long legs and clash their bills together.
I am even acquainted with the different cats of
the vicinity, who exchange visits just as the
ladies do, climbing the terrace-walls and jumping
across the streets. Finally, too, those flocks of
black, yellow-beaked birds are not unknown to
me, like blackbirds they are, which wheel in
swift pursuit of each other in eddying circles as
long as daylight lasts, just as the martins do in
our country.

* * *

A " Tholba " of the mosque of Karaouïn, a
very pleasant sort of a tholba who condescends
to interest himself as to European matters, is my
occasional companion when I loiter upon the
terraces ; but as he is a Mussulman and a citizen
of Fez, he conceals himself behind a wall so that
he may not be seen by the ladies. This evening
he made me climb a roof in order to show me
my street, which I had never seen from such an

elevation ; at the point to which we ascended it was only some eight inches in width, so closely do the houses approach each other at the top. It would have been perfectly easy to step across it to go and pay a visit to the ladies of the neighborhood ; it seemed nothing more than a cleft, a black fissure, at the bottom of which, as in a well, people, who looked like ghosts, were dragging their papooches through the filth.   In strong contrast, here on the roofs, all was light, brilliant toilettes, merry chatter of women, careless enjoyment, space and pure air.

This *tholba* is really quite modern in his ideas, very much of a *student* (according to our ideas of students) in his manner of looking at youth, in his prepossession for women and pleasure. He is evidently an exceptional person among the tholbas, and thanks to him, I shall soon have a very faithful impression of the fast life of this country.

I should never have imagined that, in all Africa, Fez was the city in which it is most possible to lead a life of this description.   The reason is that, in addition to so many holy personages, there is a great number of merchants of all sorts ; a certain feverish desire for wealth,

though very different from that which afflicts
our people, rages within these walls; men
who have grown rich too suddenly—for instance, at the return from the Soudan of a caravan that has turned out well—make haste to
enjoy life, and marry several young girls; the
next year they are ruined, and divorcing themselves, they clear out, leaving their wives to
take care of themselves. In this way Fez is
filled with divorced wives, who live as best they
may. Some of them live apart, tolerated by
the caids of the several quarters, and become
élégantes of equivocal reputation, wearing a tall
gilt tiara. Others, fallen to a lower depth,
associate themselves together under the pat-
ronage of some elderly matron ; but the houses
of this latter class are always dangerous resorts,
and their location is confined to the farther
bank of the Oued-Fez (the stream which supplies the fountains and flushes the gutters, running for almost its entire length underground).
This river, which in its later course waters the
Sultan's orange trees, so frequently brings down
corpses on its current, thanks to these ladies,
that it has been found necessary to stretch a
strong network of wire across it before it reaches
the royal gardens.

It seems that the irresistible manner—to say

nothing of its being traditional and almost obligatory—of getting into the good graces of a handsome divorced woman, is to present her with a loaf of sugar. No one can imagine what a sweet tooth the people of Morocco—men and women—have. If, then, a mysterious gentleman is seen slinking along the walls at night-fall, trying to conceal a loaf of sugar beneath his bournous, there is very good reason to doubt the purity of his intentions.

Who would believe that such pitiable, droll little things could occur in such a city as this?

XXVI.

Monday, April 22nd.

THE vizier Minister of War, Si-Mohammed-ben-el-Arbi, has invited us to breakfast. It rained in torrents all night, and it is raining still as we plod slowly along on horseback, scraping the walls with our knees at every step in the narrow lanes, and crowding the foot passengers in their gray woolen hoods into the doorways. We pursue our way for half an hour through the windings of the labyrinth, which has again assumed its desolate, rainy-day look, escorted by soldiers, and every now and then obliged to bend down upon our horses' neck when we come to some dark low archway. Again we distribute about us in showers that sticky, foul-smelling mud of which there is always a fresh supply in Fez as soon as rain falls.

We dismount in a puddle of water in front of a wretched little narrow doorway, which forms the entrance for this vizier. The first passage-ways of his dwelling, as we enter, paved with white and green tiles, wind in and out, in order that the interior may not be seen from the gate-way. But there is a large gate at the end of the passage, which, when thrown open, offers to our eyes an unexpected spectacle of magnificence; a great courtyard of imposing dimensions, with ornamental porticos, with delicate carvings of which the effect is enhanced by gilding and bright colors; a strange, slow, solemn music, played and sung by an unseen orchestra and choir; people in costumes of fairy-land, coming toward us over the marble flagging of the floor.

When the Alhambra was inhabited and teem-ing with life and color, I think that scenes like this might have been witnessed there. Perhaps the colors here, the gold, the blues, the reds, are a little too bright, because the house, for a won-der, is new, but notwithstanding that, the gen-eral effect is perfectly harmonious. We see such scenery and such costumes at the theatre ; what astonishes us is that such things should form part of actual life at the present day.

The courtyard is a long, very extensive parallelogram ; it is enclosed by lofty walls of immaculate whiteness, at the top of which, in their entire length, runs a frieze of blue and pink arabesques and a row of tiles in green earthenware ; in the centre a fountain springs from a circular basin, and the splashing of the water, as it falls in a thin cascade, mingles with the unseen solemn music. A kind of awning, constructed of cedar-wood and projecting far into the court, extends the entire length of both the two longer sides of the parallelogram ; the bright red in which they are painted contrasts strikingly with the white walls, and they are ornamented with great rosettes of blue and gold of an extremely involved pattern. They serve to shelter a number of ogive doors, the glass in which is covered on the inside by muslin curtains, behind which we can hear the whispering of the women who are watching us from their hiding-place.

In the middle of the two narrower sides of the rectangle, those which are naturally most remote the one from the other, are monumental doors, which are wonders of form and color. The lower arch is festooned with stalactites of snowy white, which hang down in clusters and seem to depend from each other in an entanglement like that of crystals of hoar-frost. Above their long pendants there is a second lance-shaped arch, picked out in red, blue, and gold, and higher still, an inde-cribable piece of work crowns the whole and rises to the very summit of the wall; it is composed of fine arabesques in polychrome, inwoven with gold; it is an expanse, towering high aloft, of that marvellous lace-work which was formerly woven in pink stucco at Granada, on the walls of the Alhambra. The two leaves of these tall doors are opened to their full width; they are covered as to their entire sur-face with painted and gilded rosettes of kaleido-scopic hues, like an unfolded peacock's tail, their dominant color being a metallic green.

These two great doors face each other at the opposite ends of the courtyard; they have long curtains, divided in the middle, of pale blue and light red cloth, bordered with gold, upon which the fretwork of the stalactites stands out whiter still. These curtains are raised and permit us to see within the customary luxury of carpets, cushions and gold-embroidered silks.

Of the persons who come forward to welcome us in this magnificent courtyard, the first are the Vizier of War, with a face like an Egyptian sphinx, and the principal heads of the army. Behind them come black slaves, male and female, tricked out with necklaces and great earrings and finger-rings. The whole company glide noiselessly over the marble floor in their slippers, to the slow rhythm of the music, which is accompanied by iron castanets.

Passing under the stalactites of the farther of the two doors, we enter with our hosts an apartment furnished in European style, but furnished so quaintly ; high-post bedsteads with draperies of pink and peacock blue brocade, gilded arm-chairs covered with figured stuffs, and on the walls whitewash and arabesques. On silver salvers, lying on the floor, are Spanish boxes in the form of Gothic shrines, filled with bon-bons.

The music is in an adjoining apartment, quite near us. The singers, as usual, use very high falsetto tones, which bring to mind the religious offices that are sung in the Sistine chapel ; the stringed orchestra produces powerful effects of sound. The same motives are constantly recurred to, taken up again and again with a sort of graduated and increasing exaltation.

Among these great white-draped Arabs there is an extraordinary little object, clad in a great profusion of colors, who seems to be the object

of a great deal of flattery.   It is a child of seven
or eight years, the favorite son of the Vizier by
one of his black slaves. (In Morocco, such children have the same position in the family as those
of the white wives, and this is one of the causes
of the deterioration of the Arab race, as it becomes more and more mixed with Nubian blood.)
He is dressed in a robe of pale yellow, over
which is a surplice of white gauze and a bournous of pale blue ; a wide green belt sustains a
small Koran in a bag of network ; his feet are
protected by orange-colored slippers worked in
violet and gold.   He has a charming funny little
face, half Arab, half negro, and the pupils of his
eyes in their setting of bluish white are in constant rapid motion.

The musicians in the adjoining room, some
twenty in number, are seated on cushions upon
the ground and are all in their holiday attire of
many colors.   Each of them plays and sings at
the same time, the head thrown back, the mouths
wide open, in a sort of ecstasy.   Some of them
have great mandolins of inlaid wood, touching the
strings with small pieces of wood; others have
violins inlaid with mother-of-pearl ; they play on
them with very large curved bows, which are
ornamented with designs in mother-of-pearl and
ebony in imitation of serpents' scales.   These

violins are shaped like great calashes, with ends
turned up like the prow of a ship.

The breakfast table is set in the apartment opposite to that in which our reception took place,
behind the other garland of stalactites, at the
other end of the courtyard, through which we
shall have to pass again in the open air. The
meal is a little in European style ; as wine is not
allowed, it is replaced by tea, which the servants
prepare as it is wanted in tall silver samovars.
The dishes are of Japanese ware, the glassware
is decorated and gilded ; the general effect,
which, with us, would be loud and common-
place, is here good, in such a brilliancy of color.

The courses are something like twenty-two in
number. The black slaves lose their wits and
scamper about the courtyard in all directions.
The dishes are so large and bountifully filled
that one man has difficulty in carrying them ;
there are whole quarters of mutton, pyramids of
chickens, fish piled up in mountain-like heaps,
and the cous-couss might suffice for ogres.
They are all brought from the kitchens under
those great indispensable cones of esparto decked
with ornamentation of red, and all these cones
are heaped up on the ground in the court, forming something that looks like a deposit of gigantic Chinese hats. The music continues to play

during the long protracted banquet. As **we** breakfast, our eyes are constantly fixed on the lofty doorway and the handsome marble court, with its fountain, its whitened walls and its multicolored arabesques ; and now the summit of its walls begins to be crowded with women's faces, curious to catch a glimpse of us, even at a distance. They are on the terrace walks, no doubt, concealed behind the walls ; we can only see the tall tiaras that they wear as head-dress, their foreheads and a line of shadowy eyes ; they are like great cats on the lookout. And others of them are continually popping up.

XXVII.

TUESDAY, APRIL 23d.

THERE is a rumor current that the *Sultan of the Tholbas* abandoned his kingdom last night.

He was the king of a day, in his improvised canvas city, a little beyond the walls ; he had a mock battery at the door of his tent, the guns made of wood in imitation of artillery. He was in some respects like our *Pope of the Fools* of the middle-ages, but with more dignity attaching to his office.

In the university of Fez, where everthing re-

mains substantially as it was in the days of
Arabian glory, it is an extremely ancient custom
for the students, every year at the time of the
spring vacation, to hold high carnival for a space
of ten days. They choose themselves a king
(the dignity is put up at auction and goes to the
highest bidder in consideration of many broad
pieces), go into camp with him on the banks of
the river, and then lay the city under contribution in order that they may have a good time
every night with music, singing, cous-couss and
tea. The people join in these amusements with
good grace, cheerfully submissive to the exac-
tions ; they all come to visit the camp of the
Tholbas and bring their presents ; viziers, merchants, and the tradesmen in their associations,
with their banners flying. Finally, about the
eighth day, comes the Sultan in person, the genuine one, to pay homage to the elective monarch
of the students ; the latter receives him as if he
himself were a caliph, on horseback, with an umbrella carried over him, treats with him on a
footing of equality, addressing him as "my
brother."

The Sultan of the Tholbas always comes from
some of the distant tribes, and is one who has
some supreme favor to ask, either for himself or
for his people, and profits by this singular tête-

á-tête with his sovereign to obtain it. As soon
as he has received it, for fear lest it may be taken
away again, as well as from the fear of reprisals
on the part of those whom he has caused to be
soundly beaten while he was enjoying his brief
authority, he silently steals away some fine night,
a thing which is easily done in Morocco ; he
makes tracks for his own country across the deserted fields.

When these merry days are over, the students
return to Fez ; those who have not ended their
studies go back to their cells in those poverty-
stricken cloisters, which are called medercas, and
which are almost holy places, infidels not being
allowed to put foot there ; here the Sultan sends
a loaf of bread to each one of them daily, and
this is almost their entire sustenance. There are
some who also receive the hospitality of private
houses, and it is considered very meritorious to
lodge and board a Tholba. They spend their
entire day in the mosques, more especially in the
immense Karaouïn, squatting on their heels to
follow the courses of learned professors, or kneeling at prayer. Those who, after six or eight
years of study, have obtained their degree of man
of letters and marabout, return to their own
country with great glory. As I have said, these
Tholbas of Karaouïn sometimes come from a

great distance; they have gathered here from the four quarters of Islam, attracted by the fame of this holy mosque, in the library of which, it is said, there are books of priceless value and immense age, which were accumulated in the days of Arab grandeur, brought from Alexandria or taken from the monasteries of Spain. So, when they are back again in the countries from which they came, they become priests with a strong inclination to preach the holy war; they have "taken the rose" in the impenetrable mosque. It is Karaouïn which gives the fierce word of command to all Mussulman Africa; it stands there in the Moghreb as a centre of resistance to all progress, the embodiment of slumber.

Among the sciences taught at Karaouïn are astrology, alchemy and divination. Other studies are the "Talismanic numbers," the influence of the stars and of angels, and many other recondite things which are for the time being abandoned by the rest of the world—until some day, perhaps, when, in another shape, stripped of all that which now seems so marvellous, they shall come forth again in triumph as the ne-plus-ultra of our positive science. The Koran and all its commentators are paraphrased here at great length, and in the same way Aristotle and other of the ancient philosophers. At the same time, too, with all these dry and serious subjects, there is cultivated an astonishing delicacy of style, diction and grammar, and those middle-age subtilities that we can no longer understand— and which are like those pretty and ingenious designs that we see here and there on the massive bastions and great walls of the Arabs.

And while I am on the subject of these old-time elegancies, I will quote the opening words of the letter of a vizier, an old pupil of Karaouïn, in response to a foreign deplomat :

"We have made our illustrious master (whom may God make victorious !) acquainted with the contents of your letter. In reading it we constituted ourselves the interpreters of your sentiments, while artfully emphasizing your words, for the smoothness of a good diction is sweeter than the clearest water, more cunning than the most delicate philter. Dictated by the most affectionate feeling, your letter has appeared to us as agreeable as a refreshing breeze," etc., etc

XXVIII.

Wednesday, April 24th.

IN the course of an early morning walk upon my terraces—which are divided off into little nooks at varying heights—I came upon a new dependency of this aërial domain, separated from the part already known to me by a stretch of wall which it had never entered my head to climb. It forms for me a new loitering place, square in shape and of small dimensions, where I can enjoy the shade during the early hours of the day, while the other situation is so well adapted for watching the sun set upon the receding distances of the lower city.

My view from this new observatory is quite different from the other ; indiscreet glimpses of adjacent houses which overlook mine, rearing their terraces and their bits of wall against the blue sky ; as it is early yet, the good housewives of these dwellings, as is their wont, have hung out on cords exposed to the sunlight and the pure air, their striped coverlets, their variegated cushions, all sorts of articles of bedding which have been in use during the night, the bright

colors of which contrast boldly with the gray of
the old cracked walls; above these things a
distant palm-tree shows its little bunch of plumes,
and, higher still, there rises a shoulder of the
mountain, all blue with its growth of aloes, with
tombs, ruins, the Koubas of holy men; an entire cemetery perching above the city.   I walk
about and keep my eyes open .... But see behind that bit of wall, scarcely two steps from
me, that bit of fluttering ribbon!   It stirs—now
it rises gently, gently, with infinite precaution:
it is a woman's "hantouze!" (One of my neighbors, evidently, who has heard me walking and
has had the curiosity to see what it might be.)   I
am as still as a mouse, as if all at once turned
to stone..... Higher and higher the gilded
head-dress rises, then a frontlet of gold sequins
emerges into view, then the hair, the forehead,
the eyebrows! and two great black eyes that
are turned full upon me!!...... *Coucou!* it is
all over.   The fair one disappears, just like a
marionette in the theatre when the wire is pulled.

I remain where I am, however, feeling confi-
dent that she has not gone very far, and in fact,
here is the "hantouze" again, rising, rising very
slowly, until this time the whole face appears,
the eyes regarding me boldly with a half smile
of guilty curiosity.   My fair neighbor is charm-

ing, thus seen by glimpses in this mysterious way, with her gold head-dress outlined against the background of ruins ; but really we are too near each other and I am wrong in remaining here ; I am conscious of a feeling of embarassment, and, not to protract the interview, I withdraw to my terrace below—where I have other neighbors whom I have been more successful in taming.

It is much less secluded there, moreover ; instead of a few houses with a burying-ground in the distance, I have at my feet the panorama of Fez in its entirety, with its gardens, its walls, and the snow-clad Atlas at the back of the picture ; my indescretion seems more permissible when I look upon the personages that figure in this immense, well-filled scene. When I make my appearance there, the low walls around are generally lined with the heads of idling women, curious to examine the rare species of being that I am in their eyes. Their former wildness, their airs of a frightened gazelle, have been quickly abandoned ; what would be an enormity of imprudence and guilt with a Mussulman seems to them devoid of danger with me, who will never tell of them to any one, and who, besides, am so soon to go away so far, so far, to that strange country of mine. The main point with them is that their husbands know nothing.   And so they look at me, they smile at me and motion to me: Good morning, good morning!   They even approach quite near, and show me various small objects to see how I like them ; ornaments for the neck and arms, or the gold threaded gauze that covers the "hantouze."   My gloves are the subject of the greatest wonder :   "*Oh! did you see*," say the fair ones, "*he has two skins for his hands!*"   The quarter where I live is inhabited by people of wealth, so all these women have nothing to do from morning till night but amuse their husbands, in which occupation they take turns.

One of them, the property of one of my nearest neighbors, acts like a wild beast in a cage. She passes hours at a time, all by herself, on the summit of a wall, her profile sharply drawn against the sky, motionless and indifferent to everything, even to the curiosity of watching me. She is not actually pretty, especially at a casual glance, but slender and admirably modeled, young and of striking appearance, with dark eyes which give one the impression of some wearisome anxiety behind them.   She is at her post this morning, arms bare, legs crossed and bare, too, as far as the knee; her slender ankles are weighted with heavy, common rings, and old wooden slippers suit badly with her exquisite little feet. Her eyes are deeper set than usual, have a harder look, and any one would say that she had been crying. I am certain that it was she that got the bastinado last night! The sound of the blows penetrated through my wall, and I heard sobs and cries of rage for an hour after.

I am conscious of a new face, a tall young brunette, bare-headed, with streaming locks of the most beautiful hair; from whence came this new arrival? Who is my rich neighbor who has purchased that superb form and all that glowing youth? A straight, clean-cut profile; very long, sensual eyes, only half opened; a lofty, untamed air; her arm, which is bare, would itself alone be a wondrous subject for the sculptor's chisel or the painter's brush. After a moment's timidity, she, too, brings herself to look me in the face, seeming to say: "What are you doing there? why do you come and interfere with us women in our dominions among the roofs?

Then I turn and look at the other, the solitary one, who is still nursing her ill-nature and her revolt upon the corner of the wall. Decidedly, she has that irregularity of ugliness, as it seems when beheld for the first time, that sometimes eventually becomes for us the supreme charm. She has those fine-drawn, firmly closed lips, very deeply sunk at the corners, which often constitute the whole attractive and death-dealing beauty of a woman's face. And now the idea that she has been beaten, and will be again, is an extremely painful one to me this morning; I have a sort of feeling of resentment that there are such formidable barriers between us when we are so near and see each other every day; I would wish to be able to dry her tears and prevent her suffering, bring her only a little rest and physical comfort. The pity which I feel, however, is not of a kind for which I can claim any merit, but rather which brings confusion on my head, for I am perfectly conscious that I should feel less uneasiness about her and her troubles were it not for that delicious mouth.

The all-powerful influence of outward charm works upon that class of our feelings which ought to be least subject to such influence— so that we may show more or less kindness toward such and such a creature as its face and shape are prepossessing or the reverse.

It is ten o'clock—time for me to dress to go to breakfast at our minister's at the embassy. One of the fancies that I have taken in my head is to go there in Arab dress; it is a pleasure to me to display my bournous and my caftan there on the inlaid pavement, in the alleys of the orange garden or the court with ornamental arches, and figure myself to be, for a moment, a character out of the Alhambra.

The sun has dried up the mud in the city and brightened up the tints of the old walls; here and there, in the shadows of the narrow passages his long slanting rays fall upon the white veils and bournouses of those who are abroad.

Preceded by one or two servants, as a man of position should be, I leave my house with the sober gravity befitting the place where I am and the dress which I have adopted. When, seizing my heavy knocker, I have with its assistance closed behind me my little iron-studded, iron-strapped door, I insert a key weighing three pounds in the lock that is centuries old. Then I go my way, at first through narrow covered passage-ways, more like blind alleys than streets, and where the indescribable clear transparency of the shadows gives one an idea of what the clear resplendency of light must be outsid·, where the sky is visible. I meet two or three pedestrians, who are walking barefoot, like myself, without producing any noise. As we meet, each of us hugs the wall, drawing in the shoulders as much as possible, and still our veils graze. I turn twice to my right and pass through a small market for fruit and vegetables, which is covered, like the others ; then, to my left, I turn into a wider street where, at last, I have a glimpse of the incomparable blue sky between two ranges of old white walls, which are the walls of mosques ; the side exposed to the sun is dazzling bright, while the side in the shadow is of an ashen blue. Both the mosque to right and the one to left are abandoned and in ruins ; but standing in the middle of their walls that have lost all shape and form beneath repeated coats of whitewash, their gates have remained intact and charming. They have preserved their framing of mosaic-work ; their rosettes of strangely involved pattern or else of the simplicity of large full-blown daisies ; their rows of star-studded designs, the thousand little facets of which are brilliant with colors that are extremely ancient, and, notwithstanding, very bright and very fresh.

A few steps farther on the wall is cracked from top to bottom, then suddenly comes to an end, completely fallen in, exposing to view the holy court where the dead lie sleeping under the inlaid pavement that is overrun with grass and wild poppies. In passing the spot it becomes necessary to turn out into the sunlight in order to avoid a certain stork, who is busily occupied in setting up his household in an immense nest at the top of an exceedingly small minaret, and who showers down upon your head blades of dry grass and bits of plaster. Oh! the all-pervading sunlight, the quiet as of death, the mystery and the charm of it all—how can they be told in words?

This nook, which has become so familiar to me, will perhaps remain imprinted on my memory longer than any other, without my being able to explain why such is the case. I cannot tell how it is that I experience such a feeling of delight in threading this little street every day, under the early sunlight, between these two old mosques. I feel a kind of artistic enjoyment in picturing to myself the inaccessibility of the spot and how far removed it is from the common-place, and in adding by my presence one detail more, which might catch the eye of a painter. I think that it is more than anything else on account of the pleasure of strolling there and looking upon myself and my habiliments of vizier as the genuine article that I am beset by those shifting fancies of pink caftans and light-blue caftans, veiled by white draperies kept in place by silk belts of curious colors. I endeavor to be sufficiently true to my models,

when thus attired, that those whom I meet shall
not turn and look at me, and yesterday I was
greatly flattered when some Berbers from the
mountains, taking me for one of the chief men
of the city, saluted me in Arab fashion. I am
willing to admit that there is a great deal of
childishness in all this ; to those who shall shrug
their shoulders, nevertheless, I shall declare that
it does not seem to me perceptibly more stupid
than to pass one's evening at the club, or in
reading the proclamations of candidates to the
Chamber of Deputies, or in taking pleasure in
the adorable elegance of an English sack-coat.

Turning to the right and leaving this street
of my preference, I soon arrive, through other
narrow passages, at the little low gate of the
minister's dwelling. There, as soon as I have
crossed the sill, I am among the guards, who
are old acquaintances ; the caids and the horsemen who followed us from Tangier, and who
have set up their tents among the blooming rose
trees of the garden, under the orange trees and
the clear blue sky. I know them all, and they
come to meet me with a smile on their faces.
They arrange the folds of my haïk, of my bournous, and strive to initiate me into the little re-
finements of Arab elegance, pleased that I dress
as they do, saying : " It is much prettier, is it

not ?" (Oh yes ! it certainly is). And they go on : "If you should dress in this way when you return to your country, every one would be wanting to have Moroccan costumes." (As for that, I must disagree; I cannot very well picture to myself this mode being generally adopted on the Boulevard.)

Leaving the delightful garden I traverse a corridor where, as soon as I cross the threshold, I hear the sound of falling water, and at last I reach the great inner, two-storied court, which is the marvel of the dwelling. The spray from the fountain brings out the colors of the tesselated pavement with its thousands of little figures in blue, yellow, white and black. Around the sides is a series of Moorish arcades with an ornamentation of fret work, and at the upper story, over these round-headed arches and these arabesques in stone, there is a gallery of cedar-wood carved in open work. A jet of water rises from a basin in the centre, and also from an exquisite mural fountain placed against one of the side-walls. This fountain is in a grand lance-shaped arch of inlaid work where star-shaped designs of rare form and beauty are entangled together ; a bordering of black and white tiles enframes the embroidery of these multi-colored rosettes, and above, crowning the whole, pensile ornaments of snowy white hang from the roof like stalactites in a grotto.

Immense cedar doors give access to the apartments opening on this court ; within, the walls are garnished half-way to the ceiling with hangings of blue and red velvet, embroidered in gold in imitation of great arches.

Here I meet the minister again, with all my other travelling companions, and at his table, served in European style, I find a little of the cheerful gayety of our meals under the tent. For a moment I am again in the world of the moderns ; it seems as if this palace (the property of a Vizier who has surrendered it temporarily for our accommodation) was transmogrified into a little corner of France.

* * *

Then comes the hour devoted to the coffee and the cigarette of the Orient ; we spend this hour in the shade of a colonnaded veranda, facing the ancient, whitewashed kiosk of the garden. From here we have a view of the tranquil little orange-grove in its surrounding of high walls, now filled with Bedouin tents among the rose-trees and the under brush.

XXIX.

MY surroundings are becoming of a more every-day character, and I am almost of a mind to carry my story no further. When I go out, it no longer seems strange to me to descend my dark stairway and find the mule that I have ordered in advance awaiting me at my door with his easy-chair of a saddle on his back, nor to jump into it from the very door-step so as to avoid soiling my long white draperies or my papooches, and ride away hap-hazard through the dark, narrow lanes. I go wherever my fancy leads me, into the lone places or among the crowds, to the bazaar or into the fields.

How can I describe the swarming crowds of the bazaar, the constant, noiseless stir of all those bournouses in the semi-darkness! The little labyrinthine avenues cross each other in every direction, covered with their ancient roofing of wood, or else with trellises of cane, over which grape-vines are trained. Fronting on these passages are the shops, something like holes in a wall as regards size, and in them the turbaned dealers sit squatted, stately and impassible, among their rare knick-knacks. Shops where the same kind of goods are sold are grouped in quarters by themselves. There is the street of the dealers in clothing, where the booths are bright with pink, blue, and orange silks, and with brocades of gold and silver, and where ladies, veiled and draped like phantoms, are posted. There is the street of the leather merchants, where thousands of sets of harness of every conceivable color, for horses, mules and asses, are hanging from the walls ; there are all sorts of objects of strange and ancient fashion for use in the chase or in war : powder-horns inlaid with gold and silver, embroidered belts for sword and musket, travelling bags for caravans and amulets to charm away the dangers of the desert.

Then there is the street of the workers in brass, where from morning till night is heard the sound of hammers at work on the arabesques of vases and plates, the street of the papooch embroiderers, where all the little dens are filled with velvet, pearls and gold, the street of the furniture decorators, that of the naked, grimy blacksmiths, that of the dyers, with purple or indigo-bedaubed arms. Finally, the quarter of the armorers, who make long flint-lock muskets, thin as cane-stalks, the silver inlaid butt of which is made excessively large so as to receive the shoulder. The Moroccans never have the slightest idea of changing the form adopted by their ancestors, and the shape of their musket is as immutable as all things else are in this country; it seems like a dream to see them at this day making such quantities of these old-fashioned arms.

A stifled hum of unceasing activity arises from the mass of people, clad in their gray woolen robes, thus congregated from afar to buy and sell all sorts of queer small objects. There are sorcerers performing their incantations; bands of armed men dancing the war dance, with firing of guns, to the sound of the tambourines and the wailing pipes; beggars exposing their sores; negro slaves wheeling their loads; asses rolling in the dust. The ground, of the same grayish shade as the multitude upon it, is covered with all kinds of filth : animal refuse, chicken feathers, dead mice; and the crowd tread down the revolting mass under their trailing slippers.

How far removed is all this life from ours! The activity of this people is as foreign to us as its stagnation and its slumberousness. An indifference which I cannot explain, a disregard of everything, to us quite unknown, characterize these bournous-clad folk even in their greatest

stir and bustle. The cowled heads of the men
and the veiled heads of the women are occupied
by one unchanging dream, even in the midst of
their bargaining ; five times a day they offer up
their prayer, and their thoughts turn, to the exclusion of all beside, upon eternity and death.
You will see squalid beggars with the eyes of an
inspired man ; ragged fellows, swarming with
vermin, have noble attitudes and faces of prophets.

"Bâleuk ; Bâleuk !"—is the eternal cry of the
Arab masses ("Bâleuk" means something like
" Clear the way !")

It is " Bâleuk " when the little asses are passing in a long string, loaded with bales placed
breadthwise, which catch people and upset
them. " Bâleuk," for the slow-gaited camels,
which move along with a swaying movement to
the sound of their little bells. Bâleuk, for the
galloping, rearing horses of the chiefs, in their
caparisons of wondrous colors. Never does
one return from this bazaar without having come
in contact with some person or something ;
without being run down by a horse or having his
clothing soiled by some small ass with a coat
full of dust.—Bâleuk !

People of all the different tribes meet and
mingle promiscuously among themselves. Negros

from the Soudan and light-colored Arabs ; autochtonous Berbers, Mussulmans without conviction of the faith, whose women veil only their mouths, and the green-turbaned Derkaouas, merciless fanatics, who turn their heads and spit upon the ground at the sight of a Christian. Every day the "Holy woman," with wild eyes and vermillion-painted cheeks, is to be seen prophecying in some public place. And the "Holy man," too, who is incessantly walking, like the wandering Jew, completely naked, without even a strip about his waist, threading his way very rapidly through the throng, always in a hurry and all the while mumbling his prayers. Here and there is a little nook open to the sky, an open square, where there may be a great mulberry tree growing, or perhaps an immense grapevine, hundreds of years old, twisting its branches until they look like knotted snakes. And then there are the "Fondaks," which are a species of caravanserai for the accommodation of the foreign merchants : great courtyards running up several stories high, surrounded by colonnades and galleries in carved open work of cedar-wood, and devoted each to one particular kind of merchandise ; there is the fondak of the dealers in tea and East India wood, that of the merchant who deals in carpets of the western provinces, one for spices and one for silk, one for slaves and one for salt.

All this quarter of the bazaar is considered as not very safe for us, on account of the proximity of the mosques of Karaouïn and Muley-Driss. It is even a fact that the streets leading to Muley-Driss, the smaller but the more holy of the two, are barricaded breast high by great wooden hurdles, such as are put up in the fields to keep cattle from going where they are not wanted ; we must be careful not to pass these barriers or our lives will be in danger. The approaches to this mosque, which is as deeply venerated throughout Islam as the Kasbah at Mecca, are never to be polluted by the foot of a Nazarene or a Jew.

There is a little spot that I particularly affect, close by the entrance of the bazaar, where I leave my mule every day in charge of one of my servants, resuming him again upon my return when I have completed my purchases. At such time of my departure, when I am leaving this labyrinth of shadows, the place of which I speak seems like a bright scene from the Thousand and One Nights. There the dark and narrow street suddenly widens out like a fan, forming a sort of triangular plaza upon which a ray of sunlight falls from the blue sky. The farther end of this little place, where several other mules are wait-

ing along with mine, tied to a very ancient grape-
arbor, is adorned by a handsome fountain ; an
arch of inlaid work, set up against the corner
wall of a projecting house, from which spirt two
jets of water which fall back into a marble basin;
the whole so ancient, so defaced and tumble-down
that there are no words capable of giving an idea
of its aspect of decay.   To the right of the fountain, a wretchedly paved narrow lane ascends a
steep acclivity and loses itself in the darkness
beneath a broken-down, sinister-vaulted passage :
(it is in that direction that I and my mule will
disappear presently when we shall start for our
abode in the precincts of old Fez).   To the left
there is an inimitable monumental gateway, finer
than any of the gates of the city or of the
mosques, but only serving as means of entrance
to a sorry old courtyard.   It is an ogive of immense size, festooned with the rarest arabesques
and the finest mosaic work in polychrome.
Above this entrance-way runs a wide horizontal
band of religious texts, also in mosaics, black
letters on a white ground.   Higher yet is a row
of small ogives, the bases of which all rest on the
same line, and each of which is filled with arabesques of different size, carved in lacework—
first those of a very large pattern, then those of
a very small pattern, and so alternating, thus ac-

centuating still more forcibly the cunning displayed in varying the ornamentation.

Yet higher still, the crown to all, an indescribable arrangement of stalactites projects over the
place below, forming, as it were, a very prominent
cornice, or an overhanging awning. All these
stalactites, absolutely regular and geometrical in
form, fit into each other, cover each other, over-
lay each other, in extremely complicated groups;
in some places they are like nothing so much as the
thousands of cells in a bee-hive; elsewhere, higher
up, they are like icicles. The entire effect of all
these decorations, so elaborately worked out, is
that of a series of arches of charming curvature,
with a marvellous ornamentation. The bright
coloring of the tiles is deadened under a thick
coating of dust, all the fine carvings are broken,
blackened by time, and hung with spiders' webs
and birds' nests; and this fairy-like gateway naturally gives the impression of an extreme antiquity,
as, for the matter of that, do the fountain and
the plaza in which it stands, the pavements, the
rickety houses ; as do the whole city and all its
inhabitants. Moreover, Arabian art is so asso-
ciated in my mind with ideas of dust and death
that my imagination refuses to go back and picture it at the time when it was young and fresh-
colored.   * * *

Outside the bazaar, the winding ways of Fez become darker and more desolate, there are but few streets that are uncovered ; the grape-arbors and the roofing of cane hurdles are replaced by platforms of wood or arches of stone, which span the streets at a distance of two métres or so, surmounted by detached pieces of wall reaching to the top of the houses, stern and forbidding always. It is like travelling at the bottom of a series of wells, connected by arched passages ; the blue or gray sky is seen only by an occasional glimpse, and it is impossible to form an idea of the direction one is taking. Even in those empty and lifeless quarters there are crowds of people; even there the cry "bâleuk " is heard. Bâleuk for the sober, contemplative men who are coming out of the mosques after reciting their prayers ; bâleuk for the restive mules, who have obstinately planted their feet cross-way in the road and refuse to move in either direction ; bâleuk for the herds of cattle passing in single file, their heads menacingly lowered, through the dark little passages, hardly wide enough for their great carcasses.

XXX.

AFTER a few hours of early slumber in my lonely abode, I have a glimpse of moon-light streaming in on me through the cracks of my cedar doors, and in the distance of the silent night I hear the chanting of prayers in unvarying shrill, mournful tones; those cries of burning faith, those wailing laments which seem to express the nothingness of all things earthly. It is two o'clock, and this is the first prayer of another day which the eternal sun will soon come and brighten with his beams. It is an immense, wide-spreading song of praise to Allah, a dreamy canticle, now loud in its fervor, now low and plaintive, but always mournful, so mournful as to send chills through one. The muezzins, like the Arab pipes, seem to have learned to pitch their tones upon those of the jackals. For a long, long time this chant of the mosques hovers above the gray repose of the slumbering city . . . . . . then silence is restored, a silence of death.

The last hours of night wear away. At day-break, in the cool of the early morning, mingling with the crowing of cocks, the voices of these men are again heard, reciting their prayers with increased exaltation ; it is five o'clock and this is the second of the daily offices ; it is also. the hour when the white-robed Sultan in his palace rises to begin his daily austere life of religious observance.

Then the sound of a distant gun announces the day, the hallowed day of Friday ; then the universal hymn arises, the pipes commence to groan, the drums begin to beat ; the sun has risen, night is ended.

While it is yet early morning, I make my way to the bazaar, unattended, in Arab dress and on foot, although that is not considered the correct thing to do, to buy rose-water and the odoriferous Indian wood, with which to perfume my apartment, as is the custom. Never did I carry so far as this morning my amusing illusion of being an inhabitant of Fez. The bazaar, which has but just now opened its thousands of little shops, is quiet and almost deserted ; the bright, gay sunlight sifts through the far-stretching arbors of cane and is tempered by the fresh green of grape-vine leaves. The perfumes which I am after are sold in the same quarter as raw silk and pearls, and this quarter is the most highly colored of the bazaar—in the correct acceptation of the word color. Stretching in a long and narrow perspective down the succession of small passages, thousands of objects of all sorts are attached to the raised coverings of the dens, within which the merchants sit squatting on their heels; there are countless skeins of silk and skeins of gold thread ; there are heaps of pink and gilded pearls ; there are those silken belts and tassels (worn around the neck to sustain the sword or the holy book), which, as I have mentioned, are one of the elegant niceties of the Arab costume. There are very noble and very handsome men in their monkish white *capuchons*, noiselessly walking to and fro, selecting from among all these belts one of a certain shade to harmonize with a certain costume.

Here, before a shop of children's toys, is an old grandmother, veiled like a ghost, but with very kind eyes, who is higgling over the price of a funny little doll for her grand-child, an adorable little youngster four or five years old, with eyes like an Angora cat and finger-nails already dyed with henna . . . . . . I look at everything this morning through the spectacles of tranquillity and naïf simplicity, and then, too, the darkling mystery which at first sight seems to enwrap all things quickly disappears as soon as one becomes familiar with their aspect. I have got to know every corner of the bazaar, and when I pass, some of the merchants bid me good-day, and invite me to come in and be seated.

I involuntarily always find my feet straying to the dark lanes which encircle Karaouïn. There, too, the mystery has faded out, and there is no renewal of the strange feeling which I experienced the first day. I linger before its doors, taking long looks into the interior; it would not require a great deal to induce me to enter; I can scarcely bring myself to believe that it might cost me my life; it would seem quite natural that I should go and kneel at the side of the people whose costume I am wearing.

The aspects of the Karaouïn vary greatly as it is viewed through one entrance or another. I am not surprised that we were unable upon our first view to master the effect of all its details; it is rather a collection of mosques, of different styles and epochs; it is a city of columns and arches of every form known to the Arabs. Here heavy, flat, round-headed arches, springing from low massive pillars, follow each other in endless perspective, with innumerable lamps hanging in the darkness of the ceiling; there are courts flooded with sunlight, vaulted only by the blue of Heaven, and surrounded by tall slender col-

umns and arcades of an infinitely varied ornamentation of never failing rarity and exquisite-
ness of design.   And never has Karaouïn been
so beautiful as to-day beneath this dazzling light
of morning, which, clear and white, penetrates
everywhere and irradiates everything, gilding the
old marbles, the countless mosaics, and the jets
of the fountains.

One of the doorways, in the shadow of which
I always stop in preference to the others, opens
on the largest and most marvellous of these
courts, paved in tiles and marble.   At the sides
are small kiosks, or rather canopies, projecting
into the court, which, though they are finer, recall those of the celebrated Court of the Lions
in the Alhambra; there are the same groupings
of light columns supporting indescribable arcades
of openwork, which seem to have been formed
by a patient superposition of icicles, the whole
effect heightened by a little gold that is
dying under the dust of centuries, by a little blue
and a little pink and I know not what other fading colors.   And on the framing of the doors, in-
tentionally made flat and very rigid, which separate these ornate porticos, there are carvings of
inimitable design and execution, cut to different
degrees of depth ; one might take them for the
old lace of some fairy, of which several thick-

nesses had been fastened up there, one over the other.

All these kiosks have an appearance of lightness, light as little castles built for sylphs among the clouds with facets crystallized from hail and snow. At the same time the unbending rigidity of the principal lines, the employment of combinations of geometrical forms and the absence of all form inspired by nature, animals or men, conspire to give to the whole an effect of austere purity, of immateriality, of *religion*.

The sunlight is falling in floods upon this courtyard, and all the mosaics, all the tiles are glittering with irridescent hues ; the murmuring jet which springs from the fountain in the centre has shifting tints of opal or of iris and stands out deliciously against the background in company with a great inner doorway, which, as well as the kiosks at the sides, is ornamented with the lacework of the Alhambra. As it is Friday, the whole people, in white bournouses, is prostrate on the flags, motionless in prayer.

From the outer dusk, from the darkness as of night which prevails in the circular road, where I am obliged to remain in concealment, but in a security that is only partial, all these things assume to my eyes an aspect of enchantment.

*   *   *

The " Holy woman " is implacable in her pursuit of me this morning. Clad in a ragged dress of yellow silk, her cheeks daubed with vermillion and her eyes wild and dilated, she follows me persistently as I leave the bazaar, uttering in loud tones incomprehensible words which sound to me rather like benedictions ; my costume and my bearing have evidently induced her to believe that I am other than I am. At last, tired of her attendance, I throw her some small coins so that I may be allowed to pursue my way in peace.

* * *

It is an hour later upon the market-place, the most bustling time of the whole day—when the multitude is seething with business.

On the grand plaza, which is a sort of rectangular plain, there is a great stir among the bournouses and the veils, the hooded, masked throng, white or gray in color, to which shepherds in great coats of camel-hair impart patches of brown tones and asses patches of red tones. There are hundreds of women seated on the ground, selling bread, butter and vegetables, their faces invisible, wrapped in muslin. To the rear of the great place and its multitude, there are the walls of Fez, rising dark and gigantic, dwarfing all else, their pointed battlements outlined against the sky. It is only a thing of course that the sound of the pipes and tambourines is heard. Here and there the pointed hoods collect together in a mass, forming a compact circle about some entrancing spectacle; there are the snake-charmers, the men who run a skewer through their tongue, those who gash themselves about the head, those who take one of their eyes from its socket with a wooden spoon and lay it out upon the cheek ; all the rag-tag and bobtail of the town, all Bohemia. To me, who am to leave here day after to-morrow, these things, now so familiar, will soon seem very astonishing, when I shall have returned to our modern world and shall think of them from a distance. At the present moment, I really am a part of an epoch that is past and gone, and it is the most natural thing in the world for me to take my place in this life, exactly similar, I think, in every respect to what life must have been in the people's quarters of Granada or Cordova in the time of the Moors.

To-morrow will be my last day here. The embassy, which is detained at Fez by protracted political business, will remain here, and I shall go on, in company with Captain H. de V., with a small caravan of our own—which will be amusing and not, perhaps, without a spice of danger. Our route will lie in the direction of Mequinez,

another holy city, even more dilapidated and
more dead than this, and from thence toward infidel Tangier, where our dream of Islam and the
past will come to an abrupt ending. I have
scarcely had time to become attached to my Mussulman abode here, which I shall have to aban-
don and forget, as I have already forgotten so
many strange abodes scattered everywhere over
the surface of the globe. Still, I would have
been glad to remain in it a week or two longer.
A few carpets, some arms and ancient hangings
were beginning to make it quite homelike, while
it had lost nothing of its mysterious little airs
and the difficulty of gaining access to it.

XXXI.

SATURDAY, APRIL 27th.

WE were invited to breakfast at the Caid-el-
Méchouar's (the Introducer of Ambassadors), and we wend our way thither on horseback, preceeded by his guards, with their huge
turbans and enormous staves of office, who, by
the Caid's orders, attend us at our doorway.

The great court of his palace is even finer than
that of the Vizier of War. Above all, it is older,
and the kindly touch of many centuries has subdued the gilding and the color where they were
excessive.

There are rows of inner balconies opening upon this court. Their upper galleries of cedarwood are composed of thousands of minute compartments geometrically arranged, producing the effect of the waxen comb which is the product of the patient labor of the bees, but over the general arrangement of all these infinitesimally small details there has presided an indescribable something, in which lies the genius of Arab art and which gives to the whole a harmonious simplicity of effect. All these galleries are filled at our entrance with white-veiled women—in crowds sufficient, one would think, to break down the slender supports—who crane their necks and observe us in silence.

The court, as a matter of course, is paved in tiles and marble, with a fountain playing in the centre. It is pervaded, the whole place vibrates, with passionate music, quick in movement and at the same time solemn; voices pitched on a high key, accompanied by powerful stringed instruments, tambourines and iron castanets. We recognize the orchestra as the same which the Vizier of War had at his house the other day; it belongs to the Sultan, who has loaned it to do us honor.

* * *

Our host, the Caid-el-Méchouar, is an extremely fine looking man. The description of Mâtho in Salâmmbo : " A colossal Libyan, etc.," would exactly suit him. He is of almost superhuman proportions, with admirable eyes and features, while a beard that is already beginning to turn gray and the darkness of his complexion point, notwithstanding the regularity of his profile, to the mixture of negro blood in his veins. Personal beauty, however, is the principal requirement for one seeking to be an Introducer of Ambassadors ; the post is almost always, it seems, bestowed upon the most magnificent person of Morocco.

Like his colleague at the war office, this vizier does not sit at table with us, it being considered improper for a good Mussulman to break bread with Nazarenes. He contents himself with sitting apart, near the room where our board is spread, and seeing that his slaves, who are terribly flurried by our presence, are not remiss in bringing in the mountains of cous-couss and roast meat.

During the meal I sit facing the handsome court, which is visible to me in its whole extent through the lofty arch of the painted gate-way. The Soudanese slaves, adorned with bracelets and great earrings, are incessantly hurrying across it, bearing on their heads dishes of huge size, surmounted by their conical coverings, like the peaked roofs of little turrets. The sunlight flashes on the tile-paved walks. Here and there confused glimpses are caught of women's eyes, flashing from loop-holes that have been cut in the lofty walls, and there is a line of veiled faces watching us from the top of the wall at the bottom of the court, which rises like a screen between us and the sun. And the music is continually repeating the same monotonous phrases, quickening the time more and more, with extreme exaltation, and finally magnetizing and soothing us, producing a sort of mild intoxication.

* * *

It is two o clock of the afternoon, and the sun is at its hottest. As I am to leave to-morrow, I am abroad at this scorching hour, having a thousand things to attend to in the course of this last day. First I have to visit the walled city of the Jews, where horribly dirty old men, repulsive with their cunning and their ugliness, have their squalid hovels stuffed with ancient jewels, rare arms and stuffs that are not to be procured even at the bazaar, which I wish to purchase from them. It is a long way from my house to the quarter of the Jews; it extends in a narrow strip along the southern side of New-Fez, while I live in Old Fez from whence my start will have to be made. I am on horseback, with an escort of the red infantry.

It is two o'clock, and one of the hottest days that we have experienced so far. The old mud-walls seem to be wasting away beneath the devouring sun, the cracks in the old houses seem to grow longer and open wider. The little streets lie deserted between their two rows of lifeless ruins, which bake and split open in the heat. The pavements, the old black boulders polished by the naked feet or the slippers of many generations of Arabs, here and there display their worn surface among the dust and bits of broken straw. There broods over the whole slumberous city that peculiar dejected silence that prevails when the sun puts forth all his energy to dazzle and to scorch.

There is a little shade and coolness as we pass through the thick triple gates of the ramparts. Seated on the ground, in the corners of these gate-ways, barbers are waiting to operate on the wild woolly-haired country people—one of whom, while he is being shaved, is holding two black rams by the horns; and in another corner a practitioner is taking blood from a shepherd.

Bleeding is reputed to be the sovereign remedy for all kinds of ills, as it used to be with us in old times; the operation is performed at the back of the neck, by cutting straight down to the bones of the skull with a razor. I feel more than usually impressed to-day by the wildness of this country about Fez; by its silence and its gloomy aspect of abandonment.

Immediately beyond the gates we come upon a burning desert, where there are no roads, where there is not to-day a human being or a caravan. This is the spot that was so populous and so noisy on the morning of our entry in state, where now there is scarcely to be heard the melancholy little chirp of a grasshopper. The walls of the city and the palace rear themselves toward the sky in confused grandeur, with their battlements and their tapering projections of stone; all alike erect, sullen and dark from foundation to summit, producing an impression of beauty merely by their gigantic size. At their feet, nothing; on this side of the city not a house, nor a tree, nor a tent, nor a group of human beings; only they, the walls, upright and immense in vertical stature. The fierce sun of to-day exaggerates, if possible, their extreme oldness, brings out their cracks and crannies; in spots they are breached and dismantled, and their foundation is sapped.

Other enclosures, completely ruinous and inexpressibly desolate, start from the ramparts, spreading out and prolonging the city into the desert country, and finally melt away among the rocks and bogs and all the chaos of this ancient soil that has been dug over and over for centuries. Time has covered these walls with lichens of a bright yellow color, which stand out on the dark gray of the stonework like spots of gold ; under the deep blue sky, the general effect is that of warm, mellow coloring bedizined with gay stripes.

In the part that has entirely gone to ruin, in those secondary enclosures that I spoke of, which are no longer of use, there are doors, exquisite in form, like all Arab doors, and surrounded by mosaics which are still to be seen under the incrustation of lichens ; they afford access to lonely fields where there is nothing but grass and grasshoppers. As I am pursuing my way among these ruins of the walls, beneath the fierce beating sunlight, my attention is arrested by one of these doors as being the most deliciously Arab object that I have met with, as well as the most singularly melancholy; there it stands, in the middle of a hundred métres of monotonous and forbidding wall, opening its lonely archway, which is set in a framework of mysterious designs, while, beside it, a solitary old date-palm rears aloft its bunch of yellow plumage.

* * *

A hundred métres further, the Sultan's camp appears before me ; its tents strike the eye as a collection of intensely white objects in the midst of the red soil, surrounded by the blue distance ; the snowy walls seem to tremble in the heated air. It is considerably larger than when I was here before. It is said to be six kilométres in circumference, and capable, when completed, of holding thirty thousand men.

The great tent of the Caliph rises high in the centre of the camp. All that can be seen of it is the canvas wall, called " tarabieh," which encircles it and conceals all that is within ; even when he is in the field, the Sultan's dwelling-place must always be concealed from the common eye. Behind this wall, it seems, there is quite a little city ; beside the private quarters of the Sultan and his immediate dependents, there are those of his favorite son, the little Ab-dul-Aziz, as well as those of a certain number of the ladies of the harem, selected to take part in the expedition.

As soon as the Sultan's tent is taken from the

store-rooms of the palace and begins to go up
outside the walls, the intelligence is at once dis-
seminated through the length and breadth of
Morocco by the travelling caravans, and still
more, by those swift messengers who travel night
and day, over streams and mountains, carrying
letters and verbal intelligence, performing the
functions of our postman. Every tribe is soon
informed that the Sultan is about to take the
field, and the rebellious ones prepare for resistance.   The Sultan, naturally nomadic, like his
Arabian ancestors, generally passes six months
out of the twelve under canvas, warring incessantly against the revolting tribes of his own
empire, who only recognize him as religious
Caliph, not always as temporal sovereign, and
some of which (notably the Zemours and the
Riff tribes) have never even been brought to
subjection.

This time the Sultan is to be absent from Fez
for four years.   In the intervals of his raids and
his gathering in his harvests of his heads, he will
take his repose in his other two capitals, Mequinez and Morocco, where he has palaces and
impenetrable gardens, just as he has here.

Those of his women who are not to make part
of his travelling train were sent forward last
week on mules to the walled seraglios of Me-

quinez, to which point they make the journey in three stages.

* * *

I shall have time enough and to spare to spend in this dirty old quarter of the Jews, which was my destination when I started out, and the desire seizes me to take one last look from the mountain which dominates Old Fez. My horse climbs sturdily up through the little rocky paths, with an occasional futile attempt at a gallop. We are quickly at the summit, where we inhale the cooler breezes, which ruffle the carpet of flowers as they pass over it. Here and there are trees in the hollows, and in the little valleys are clumps of olive trees, in the shade of which the Moorish shepherds are singing pastoral ditties to their goats in the depressing silence that reigns about them. Above all, there are tombs—tombs everywhere, of great antiquity, among the greenery and the aloes. There are the " Koubas " of saints, venerated ruins, the well-proportioned porticos of which are tenanted by families of birds. Then there is the historic kiosk, built by a Sultan of former days, which cost him his throne, the men of Fez, grumblers as they always are, taking it ill that he could look down from its summit at evening-tide upon all their women on their terraces.

In fact, all the terraces are visible to me from
here, thousands of grayish promenades, but untenanted now, under this blazing sun.   I overlook the holy city, its long line of dilapidated
walls, its bastions, its green minarets and its infrequent palm trees.   Two or three strings of
mules and a few camels, filing away toward I
know not what country to the south, are the only
things that give any sign of life in this solitary
region.   The whole country is flooded with great
waves of light; there are only a few small, fleecy
clouds here and there, lost in the bottomless blue
of the sky. And not a sound arises from the city,
over which continually broods the same torpor,
the same stagnation.

I tear myself away and turn my steps resolutely toward the Jews' quarter, in my quest after
old hangings and ancient arms.   Like the Jews
of our mediæval Europe, it is they who amass
in their strong-boxes not only wealth and fortunes, but also precious stones, antique trinkets,
and all sorts of old priceless objects that viziers
and caids who have gotten into debt to them are
finally obliged to leave within their clutches.
With all this, they assume an appearance of
deepest misery and want ; they are looked down
upon by the Arabs even more than the Christians, living a furtive life, imprisoned within their

dark and contracted quarter, fearful and constantly on guard to protect their lives.

Descending from the mountain, steeped in light, where, under the flowers, so many saints and dervishes lie sleeping, I wind for a long time along the surprisingly old walls of "New Fez," by paths that are at first bare, but soon become green and shady with mulberry trees, and poplars that still retain their small fresh leaves of April; with clear streams bordered by reeds, iris, and great white lilies.

The ramparts of the Jews are as high and well-battlemented as those of the Arabs, their ogive gateways are as lofty, with the same heavy iron-bound gates. These gates are closed every night at an early hour; Israelite guards with a distrustful aspect are posted in the embrasures, allowing no suspicious person to pass; it is evident enough that life in this den is spent in perpetual fear of their neighbors, Arabs or Berbers.

Directly in front of their gate is the place of deposit for dead animals (which is one way of showing them a politeness). To gain access to them, it is necessary to pick one's way between heaps of dead horses, dead dogs, carcasses of all sorts and descriptions, which lie rotting in the sun, exhaling a nameless odor. They are not permitted to remove this plague-spot, and every night the jackals hold high festival beneath their walls. Neither are they permitted to remove the filth which is thrown from their houses into their narrow streets—streets so narrow that two cannot pass ; bones, skins of vegetables, refuse of every kind, accumulate there for months, until it pleases some Arab ædile, in consideration of a round sum of money, to have the street cleaned. In this dark, damp quarter, there are mouldy stinks in varieties that are not found elsewhere, and all the inhabitants carry around wan faces.

Two or three persons, stationed at the gateway, observe me as I come up, curious to know what I am after there, scrutinizing me with eager, covetous eyes, scenting a bargain to be driven ; long, pinched, white faces ; thin, hooked noses of inordinate length, and long, thin hair, falling in greasy, scattered corkscrew curls, which smear the black robes that hang from their sharp, narrow shoulders.

So much the worse for their costly stuffs and antique arms, I cannot bring myself to put foot within those mouldy hovels, among such repulsive beings, on the eve of my departure, on such a charming evening, while the sun is so gloriously gilding the tranquil old Mussulman city and its grand old walls. Accordingly, I wheel my horse away from the gates and turn his head in the direction of the Sultan's palace; I shall reach there as all the great white-robed personages are coming out after the evening audience, to return to their dwellings in Fez-Bâli, and I shall have one more look at these characters of another age, as they pass upon the scene that is so admirably set with great walled courts and immense ruins.

Again, then, I approach the palace by the well-known ways, through the long lines of walls, so resembling each other in their stern, forbidding height ; I see before me the succession of cheerless courtyards, great and empty as the exercising ground of troops, and which seem almost narrow, so lofty are the walls which close them in ; to get an adequate idea of their size, one must look at the men, the infrequent white ghosts, who traverse them, and whom the contrast reduces to the size of pygmies.

The sun is rapidly sinking as I and my guide enter the first of these enclosures, and the dusk is already beginning to settle down upon it. The tall dark walls, masking everything, like immense screens, all at once make dim the light ; their rows of pointed battlements give them a cruel and menacing aspect. The great ogive which gives access to the inner of these haunts

stands there in the centre of the far wall, flanked
by its four towers, which rise all of a piece, imposing after the fashion of the *donjon* of Vincen-
nes, but more forbidding because of their summits of pointed stone-work.

The surface of this court is strewn with boulders, bones, and refuse of all sorts, and is cut up
by openings in the ground ; two or three camels
are roaming about in search for the infrequent
tufts of grass, looking very small in their immense surroundings ; lost in one of the corners,
also, there is an encampment of white tents
which looks like a pygmy village, and three persons, enfolded in their bournouses, who emerge
from the obscurity of the great gate, appear to
me like inhabitants of Lilliput. The inevitable
storks are flying above our heads, crossing the
square space of sky that is cut out by the jagged
battlements. Thousands upon thousands of
black, shiny birds, too, are clustered in bunches
upon the walls, crowding each other, climbing
over each other, forming dense masses of moving, stirring objects, just as we see swarms of
flies in summer-time settle upon carrion ; and
while I stop to watch these thronging little wings
and claws, the three grave persons who emerged
from the great gateway have drawn near to me ;
they are old men, who smile good-naturedly and

give me some information in Arabic in relation
to the birds, which I fail to understand. (Such
affability for an unknown Nazarene upon a casual encounter is not an usual thing in this country ; it must be my excuse for preserving so trifling an incident.)

I turn my steps towards the gate at the far
end of the court ; it will afford me admission to
the second, and generally more animated, court,
where the white-robed viziers sit every day and
administer justice to the people. Oh ! these
Arab gates, with their infinite variety of mysterious design—how can I express the charm
there is for me simply in beholding them, the religious melancholy, the revery of the past, that
they all inspire within me. Standing alone
among walls that sadden us like the walls of
prisons, possessing in their form, whether round
orogival, a certain indefinable quality which remains always unchanged even in the midst of
the most fanciful diversity ; then always framed
in that fine geometrical ornamentation, the rare
elegance of which has in it something severe and
ideally pure, something that is in the highest degree mystical.

The other court to which this gateway leads
me, after passing through a dark vaulted passage, is as grand and wild and imposing as the

first.   It is filled with people, however, as I had expected it would be, and the approaches are obstructed by horses and mules, with their high-peaked saddles, which grooms are leading by the bridle. The reason for this is that at the far end, under some old arches that form a sort of alcove, the ministers are performing their functions, almost in the open air, with very few clerks and scarcely any papers.

The Vizier of War holds his court under one of these arches, and under the other the Vizier of Justice gives instantaneous decisions from which there is no appeal. Soldiers keep a clear space around him by a free use of their sticks, and plaintiff and defendant, witnesses and prisoners, are hauled up before him, all in the same way, two muscular guards seizing them by the nape of the neck. As this is said to be a rather unsafe neighborhood for Nazarenes, I do not advance beyond the entrance, in order not to bring on a diplomatic complication.

Business is over now, however, as I thought it would be. In turn the Viziers, with the assistance of their attendants, seat themselves on their mules to return home. White-bearded, with long white robes and long white veils, they mount their red-caparisoned white mules, each of which is led by four slaves dressed all in

white with tall red caps. As the crowd rever-
ently parts to let them pass, they move off
quietly at a walk, proud as the prophets of old ;
their veiled eyes beholding only a dream of the
past ; like the snows of Atlas in whiteness ; pic-
tured on the background of their mighty ramparts, their grand ruins. . . . . . . The sun is
about to set, and a cold wind has sprung up, as
it does every night, beneath the sky that has suddenly taken on a yellowish tinge; it roars through
the tall arches and whistles among the stones of
the parapets.

I make my retreat also, following the Viziers.
I desire, for one last time, to behold the wonders
of my terrace at the holy hour of the Moghreb.

There, on the roof of my house, the same enchanting scene greets my eyes that has done so
already so many times ; the city bathing in a
pink or yellow golden light, the nearer terraces
separated from me by a film of bluish vapor, and
the distant terraces, those thousands of stone-
paved squares, of which the changing tints are
slowly fading, stretching away upon the slopes
of the hills until they are merged in the surrounding ramparts and the verdant gardens.
The female slaves are there at their post, with

black, smiling faces, covered with light-colored
kerchiefs, white or pink. There, too, are all my
pretty neighbors in tall hautouze, leaning on
elbows, reclining, or proudly erect, very graceful
in attitude and very showy in color, with their
stiff cardboard belts, their flowing sleeves and
the rich cascade of gold embroidered handkerchiefs and loosened tresses falling down their
backs. And once again, as it has done for centuries and centuries, the great prayer resounds in
mournful, dying tones, while the snows of Atlas
fade upon the pale yellow of the sky.

Dinner over, I make an unwonted excursion
by lantern light, before the doors of the quarters
are closed, for the purpose of saying good-by to
the minister and the embassy; they are to remain here, for how long a time I am unable to say.

Captain de V. and I are to start to-morrow
morning at early daybreak. We have each been
presented on the part of the Sultan with a tent,
a selected mule, and an Arab saddle; we have
also a tent for our attendants, a caid to act as
guide, and eight mules to carry our traps and
our baggage.

I find the embassy in its usual place, seated by
the light of the lanterns under the verandah of

the delightful old kiosk in the perfumed orange grove. The minister has secured for us the letter of "Mouna," duly signed and sealed by the Sultan, authorizing our passage through the several tribes and according us the indispensable right of levying contribution; but notwithstanding the steps he has taken to get them, he has not as yet been able to obtain the letters for the chiefs of the city of Mequinez, nor the permission to visit the gardens of Aguedal. This has assuredly happened not through any want of good-will, but simply from procrastination and inertia; it seems that the Grand Vizier went about the business at such a late hour that he could not obtain the Sultan's signature before prayer time; he promises that everything shall be signed in readiness for us by to-morrow morning, and in case we shall have started, that couriers shall follow us, even as far as Mequinez, if necessary, with the documents, and the gifts that have been prepared for us. But we do not put much faith in it all, and it is a disappointment.

Our travelling companions who are remaining at Fez display some regret at being unable to accompany us. It seems that their detention is likely to be longer than they had anticipated. There are a thousand complicated affairs to be adjusted, which seem to have neither beginning nor end, disputes that date from years back, debts due to Jews that it is impossible to collect. No conclusion can be reached with this people. The Sultan, entrenched within his impenetrable palace, is scarcely ever to be seen, and the Viziers find it convenient to employ procrastination, in which lies the great strength of Mussulman diplomacy. Then the Ramadan is approaching, during which nothing can be done; its influence is already beginning to make itself felt. Again, it is only very early in the morning that our affairs can receive attention, the middle of the day being set apart for prayers and slumber, and the afternoon for the consideration of questions of domestic policy. In addition to all this, one of the principal political personages has just been bitten in the arm by one of his many white wives, who is jealous of one of his many black wives; he has taken to his bed, and there is another delay.

On the eve of our departure, we are charged with many commissions for Tangier, for that modern and living world from which people here are so widely separated. Those who are to remain, it is easily to be seen, have already begun to suffer from that peculiar disease, that *longing to get away*, which is so very well known, which infallibly attacks, as it seems, embassies that

have been a couple of weeks in Fez, and which
is a political force which Arab diplomats are
accustomed to count on. Though I, for my part,
would so willingly remain, I can still understand the feeling, for I have at times been conscious of the oppressiveness of Islam.

XXXII.

SUNDAY, APRIL 28th.

IT is a gray morning that dawns on our departure. Awaking in my old house with the
first glimpse of day-light, I peer anxiously into
the square of darkling sky which shows through
the opening in my roof ; it threatens to rain.

There are no longer any carpets or hangings
about me, no trace of my ephemeral housekeep-
ing ; everything has been removed and packed ;
the aspect of antiquity and wretched dilapidation
reigns again in every direction.

Captain de V. and myself have agreed to travel in bournous, so as to attract less attention
among the tribes by the way, and as my Arab
wardrobe is somewhat limited, I had my long
floating shirts, my long white faradjis, washed
yesterday, so as to be ready for the road, and
they have spent the night stretched out to dry
upon my terrace. I go up to get them, amused

by this petty detail which identifies me for a
moment with the life of an Arab in humble circumstances getting ready for a journey. They
are still quite damp, those faradjis of mine,
and when I put them on they give a disagreeable sensation of cold.

From my roof I can see that the sky is of an
uniform gray over its whole extent. A deep silence, very melancholy and very solemn, broods
at this early hour over the city, which is hardly
visible as yet. I say farewell forever to all the
surrounding terraces in their gloom and desolation, a farewell to all the old ruinous walls
around, behind which my fair neighbors are
slumbering, including the beautiful mutineer, of
whom I shall never hear again.

At five o'clock one of the Sultan's soldiers
brings my mule, ready saddled, to my door. I
am to meet de V., with our muleteers and our
baggage, at the gate by which we leave the city,
at quite a distance from my house. For the last
time, then, I journey along through the network
of the little dark streets of Fez, making my way
among a compact herd of cattle. (The cattle
are brought in at night from fear of robbers and
wild beasts, and sent out to the pastures again
with the first light of morning.)

* * *

Leaving the city by the blackened gates of Old Fez, I am now skirting the ancient walls of New Fez. The depressing gloom of the lofty walls, the quagmires and the ruins, becomes thicker in the gray half-light and silence of the morning ; all that I can hear is the pattering on the ground of the hoofs of the cattle that surround me ; their breath arises from their nostrils in white clouds of steam. The herdsmen who have charge of them wear their capuchons down, are bundled in their rags of earth-colored gray, looking like dead men.

I come to the sombre gateway of the palace ; from it there issues a row of a hundred black slaves, bearing on their heads those conical objects in esparto, each of which serves to cover an enormous dish, and a smell of hot cous-couss is diffused through the cool air as they pass. It seems that to-day is a great Mussulman holiday, the precursor of the austerities of the Ramadan, something like our *Mardi-Gras*, and it is customary on this occasion for the Sultan to send each of the dignitaries of the city a dish prepared in his kitchens.

Captain de V. is punctual at the rendezvous at the gate of New Fez, followed by our small escort with the mules and tents. Nearly all our comrades of the embassy, too, are there on horseback, at this early hour, to accompany us some distance on our way.

Once clear of the walls, we pay a salute to the Sultan's camp and his great enclosed tent as we pass, and then fairly commence our journey under the gray threatening sky, over that irregular network of paths that the tread of many caravans has worn in the turf. Everywhere sombre tints of earth and sky emphasize the desolate grandeur of these approaches to the city. A low hanging mist trails over a great meadow of bright green barley, and the plain seems to merge at every point of its circumference in a confused darkness, in a black opaqueness which rises to meet the sky, and which is really the great mountains in their wrappings of cloud.

Fez fades to the sight upon its surrounding of dark background, and takes on that same sinister aspect which is still fresh in our memory as characterizing it on the morning of our arrival. Turning in our saddles, we can see for a long time yet the little snow-white cones at the foot of the black walls, which constitute the encampment of the most holy Caliph.

On every hand the tinting is gloomy and sad; the infrequent traveller in his woolen wraps, the camels, the asses, everything that goes and comes by this, the only track between the two cities, are of neutral, earth-colored shades, brownish or grayish. Here and there we come upon little Bedouin encampments, their tents of the brown hue of the soil, from which arise curls of smoke that ascend straight into the air on the dark gray of the horizon, and away up, deep in the heavens, the " bright lark," invisible in the mist, is singing in full tones his morning song over the green fields of barley, reminding us of France.

At the first " M'safa," our French friends leave us to return to Fez, with the expression of many good wishes for our safe journey, and we continue our lonely march in company with our Arab escort.

There are thirteen " M'safa," that is to say thirteen stages, between Fez and Mequinez, the position of each of them marked by a well of drinking-water, which yawns, without the slightest pretence of an enclosure, directly in the middle of the path. The trip generally occupies two days, and even three, when there are ladies, but with our selected mules, fresh and in good condition, we expect to get in at an early hour this evening.

There is soon an end of the cultivated fields.

Then commences an immense, wide-stretching plain of fennel, the gigantic African fennel, the flowering stalks of which are two or three métres high and almost as large as trees. It is as if we were entering a forest of yellow verdure, stretching in every direction away to the opaque black distance that shuts us in like prison walls, and which is, in fact, the surrounding mountains with their overhanging clouds. The whole length of our narrow, blind path the fennel brushes against us and our horses, rising above our heads and caressing us with its cool foliage, as fine and curling as marabout plumes ; we are buried in the light yellow and green mass and are quite lost to sight, while we inhale the over-powering odor.

The joyous song of the lark is still heard in the heavens, though the songsters, soaring high above our heads, are invisible in the gray fog; and now and then, a league or so apart, perhaps, a great isolated palm-tree rears its head above the monotony of the vegetation.

For a space of four hours we proceed in this way among the fennel. Sometimes we hear a rustling in front of us, in the pathway that lies hid among this thicket of fine, downy verdure, which does not proceed from our train, and then there emerge from among the leaves herds of cattle, or a band of bournous-clad men coming from Mequinez, or a caravan. It is amusing to meet camels, especially if it is in a narrow place ; you think that they are still some way off with their long straddling legs and their great bodies, when all at once the head, at the end of the swaying, outstretched neck, is directly over you, the eyes examining you point-blank with an expression of disdainful ennui ; they stop in their tracks to gratify their curiosity the better, then, turning their heads again, resume their unvarying slow, silent gait. They exhale a peculiar sweetish, insipid odor, something midway between a perfume and a stench, which lingers behind them long after they have passed.

We are making our return journey on mules—which seems a less imposing way of travelling than was our advent on horseback—but it is the only really practical, the only truly Arab way of travelling in Morocco. By this means we do not lose sight for an instant of our tents and baggage, which follow us at the same gait, on the same species of animals. We are not attended, as at the start, with a great escort, three or four hundred horsemen and guards stationed the entire length of the route. We keep our little column of a dozen men and as many animals well closed up, and we have to watch everything with our own eyes, finding ourselves a little at a loss in the wide extent of desert.

Our saddles with their housings of red, are very capacious and solid, and as our mules get over the ground in their rapid, untiring swing, we quickly learn to make ourselves comfortable, like the Moroccans, by frequent changes of positions ; astride, seated sideways, reclining, or the legs crossed on the animal's neck. Now and then our muleteers spin robber yarns for us, showing us points where travellers have been plundered and killed ; at other times they sing queer little airs in a thin, piping voice, a sort of compromise between that of a bird and a grasshopper, and their monotonous little melodies are in plaintive harmony with the deep silence of the waste places.

After four hours among the fennel, we come to the brink of a great fissure winding through the plain. A gulf, a ravine, in the depths of which rolls a torrent. We ascend it, pursuing our way along the bank until we reach a cascade, beyond which the torrent dwindles to a rapid brook. It is the Oued-Mahouda. Just above the noisy cascade, which falls thirty métres at a single leap, we cross the stream by a deep and dangerous ford, raising our legs on the necks of our mules, which are half submerged in the seething, turbulent water.

This ford is just midway between the two holy cities ; it is much used by Moroccan travellers.

We make a long halt upon the far bank, while one of our Arabs keeps on toward Mequinez so as to notify the Pacha of our coming, that being the proper thing to do for travellers of quality such as we are. Our halting-place is just above the cascade, overlooking on one hand the ford by which caravans are crossing and on the other the pool into which the stream plunges with a sullen roar. The surrounding country is everywhere bright with the fresh verdure of spring, and the walls of the ravine are all pink with hanging garlands of bind-weed. The gray clouds have risen, keeping the sky still veiled, but leaving the distant landscape distinct and clear to our vision.

In addition to the travellers, horsemen and foot-passengers who from time to time pass the ford, there arrives a whole tribe of nomads, people, animals and tents. The women of this *douar*, who are the last to cross, pick up their skirts with naïf immodesty—displaying their fine, statuesque legs, rather tawny and a little tatooed in spots—but keeping their faces chastely veiled.

We make a fresh start. The region that we pass through first is mountainous and stony. Then there comes another ford, set in a strange scene that has a wildness all its own ; it is situated facing a desolate plain of great extent, at the foot of a pile of rocks, on which are seated a number of old men, motionless as statues, who pay us not the slightest attention, who are like mystical hermits engaged in a deep contemplation.

* * *

This is succeeded by four hours of travel through regions that are absolutely wild, wastes of dwarf palms and asphodel, such as we have traversed so many of in coming hither. We frequently turn around to count noses, to see that none of our muleteers or of our bat mules are missing, for we have no great confidence in the faithfulness of our people. In this level plain, where the vegetation does not reach a very great height, it is easy enough to embrace at a single glance our small caravan, moving along in good order, well closed up ; it even appears to us very insignificant, lost and isolated as it is among the vast wastes.

The caid on whose shoulders rests the responsibility for our heads comes first, jogging along with imperturbable gravity : an old man· in a pink cloth caftan beneath a transparent robe of white muslin ; his eyes are dull and without expression ; his harsh, strongly marked features seem to have been chopped out of brown stone with a hatchet, and his white beard is like a lichen growing on a ruined wall ; he holds himself upright, self-contained, majestically mummified upon his white charger, carrying his long copper musket crosswise on his saddle.

*　　*　　*　　*　　*　　*　　*

Mequinez ! . . . . Mequinez appears before us in the lonely plain. But so distant still ! That we can see it at all is only owing to the uninterrupted lines of the country and the great clearness of the air. There is only a little dark strip, the walls, no doubt, above which, scarcely visible, the towers of the mosques arise, seemingly no thicker than threads.

Our advance still continues for a long time, until we reach a point where the view is hidden by old, crumbling walls, which seem to be the boundaries of great parks. It is the suburbs of the city. We make our entrance at a place where the wall is broken down, and find ourselves among olive trees, symmetrically planted in quincunxes on a very close turf of grass and moss, such as is only met with in regions that have·been for a long time undisturbed and untrod by the foot of man ; the trees, moreover, are sapless, covered with a kind of mould, and dying of old age, so that their foliage is quite black, as if it had been smoked. There are other of these enclosures beyond this one, all of them in ruins, in which are seen the same ghosts of trees, stretching away, correctly aligned, in every direction, as far as the eye can reach. They are like a succession of parks that were abandoned centuries ago, or places for the dead to promenade in.

It is rather a strange surprise for us, therefore, to perceive, as we ride by, in one of these funereal alleys, a group of those bright-colored little bournouses—green, orange, blue or red—which are worn by children as a gala dress. Behind them are white veils of women, standing around a thread of smoke which rises from the ground toward the tree-tops. Our Arabs explain to us that to-day is the anniversary of the yearly fête of the school-children of Mequinez, when they come out to have a little feast upon the grass ; so here they are, in their fine clothes, enjoying their outing ; the white veils at the back of the scene stand for the mothers who have come with them ; the smoke is that of the rural repast that has been spread for them on the moss. And now their small feast is ended, and they are getting ready to go to their homes in the city, so as to be in before nightfall.

I think that this children's fête is one of the most unexpected, most charming, and also saddest sights that I have met with in the course of my travels ; the bright display of the Oriental coloring of these little bournouses as they frisk about on the fine smooth turf of this lonely park.

We pass beyond these walls and olive trees, and all at once Mequinez comes in sight again, very near to us and immense in aspect, crowning with its great shadow a range of hills behind which the sun is setting. We are only separated from the city by a verdurous ravine confusedly filled with poplars, mulberry trees, orange trees, trees of all sorts scattered at random, all in their fresh tints of April. High above us, upon the yellow sky, are drawn in profile the lines of the ramparts rising one above another, the innumerable terraces, the towers and minarets of the mosques, the stern crenellated kasbah, and, overtopping the several walls of the citadel, the green-tiled roof of the palace of the Sultan. It is even more imposing and more solemn than

Fez. But it is now only the immense ghost of a city, a collection of ruins, a pile of rubbish, where dwell a bare five or six thousand of human beings, Arabs, Berbers and Jews.

Ever since our long noonday halt our people have been telling us that we would arrive in time for the hour of the Moghreb. In fact, just as we make our appearance, the white flag of prayer goes up on all the minarets; the " Allah Akbar !" resounds in frightful clamor over all the extent of the holy city, even as far as the silent fields that lie around it. And, by reason of these long, mournful cries, this Allah, to whom these men cry aloud, seems to us at the moment so great, so terrible, that we, too, would wish to prostrate ourselves in the dust at the call of the Muezzins, before his dark, terrible eternity.

The horseman whom we sent forward express returns, having seen the Pacha and received instructions as to our camping-ground, to which he is to conduct us; of course, it is outside the walls. Following this guide, we cross the ravine, with its delightful thicket of trees, which separates us from the city. For a long, long time we wind along the outside of the old embattled ramparts; they are fifty or sixty feet high, are all eaten away at their base, crazy and cracked from top to bottom. There is not a soul passing in the circular path on which we are advancing; three or four corpse-like beggars, slinking in corners of the bastions, are the only signs of life we meet; hideous and frightful they are in their rags, lousy fellows covered with bleeding sores, the result of some leprous disease. There are dead animals, half devoured, lying on the ground, mules, horses and camels, their bones exposed in places where the flesh has been eaten away; and, where the jackals have left them, are everywhere other bones, picked clean, and heaps of offal and decaying matter.

At length we are halted on a lonely piece of bare ground, among ruins and fallen stones and open chasms, at about five hundred métres from one of the gates; we have reached the place appointed for our camp. It is at the foot of one of those gigantic walls, which in this place, as well as in Fez, stretch away into the open country as far as the eye can reach, a puzzle to every one as to what can have been the motive that induced their construction. There, in the yellowish twilight, the little canvas houses quickly go up under our direction, while a few drops of rain all at once begin to fall from the great clouds that have overspread the heavens.

The huge wall that backs up our little camp and dwarfs it by its enormous bulk is pierced by a succession of lofty porticos, some of them partially closed up with stone-work and others opening upon the black and treacherous country. This wall, conforming to the upward slope of the ground, reaches to the ramparts of Mequinez at the point where the nearest gateway is, which is one of the main entrances to the city ; it is unnecessary to say that there is no road leading to this gateway ; no one enters, no one comes out by it ; there is no sign of life, and since the great prayer went up a while ago, we have not heard sound or stir, any more than if all around us were only abandoned ruins. The impression of sadness is extreme which characterizes the portion of the ruins that is visible from here, standing, as they do, upon a rising ground with an old minaret towering over them; the great city gate affording us through its pointed arch a glimpse of a bit of yellow sky from which the light has not entirely disappeared.

The arched gate, the minaret and the bit of wall are all that we are to see to-night of Mequinez, the holy city.

*   *   *

Near our camp are two springs set in enclosures of stone, with basins from which the camels

may drink, all of the greatest antiquity. While the darkness is rapidly settling down upon us, we take a lantern and go to secure a supply of cool water from them ; they are charmingly embellished with clusters of arabesques, which are being slowly eaten away by the dust. While we are there the son of the Pacha of the city comes up, mounted on a fine charger and preceded by a great lantern with panels of Moorish openwork. His object is to bid us welcome, and also to excuse the non-appearance of his father, who has been absent for two months, the holy old man, with all his cavalry, fighting the terrible Zemours, who have been laying all the country waste.

He (the son) is very young and very good-natured. He tells us that he is preparing an abundant "mouna" for us, with dishes of couscouss, smoking hot ; also that he will send a guard for our protection during the night. In fulfilment of his promise, he is quickly followed by two little asses, loaded, one with charcoal, the other with branches and twigs, so that we may cook our chickens on the grass. He comes in and takes a seat in our tent and relates bits of history. He cannot give us much information upon the purpose which the wall above our heads served in by-gone times ; he only knows that it was built by Mouley-Ismaïl, "the Cruel Sultan," three hundred years ago. Mequinez, moreover, reached its highest degree of prosperity under this Mouley-Ismaïl, who was the greatest monarch that ever Morocco had.

The young Pacha is succeeded by a Jew, who comes in the now rapidly increasing darkness to pay us a visit, his attendants bearing a great lantern before him. Notwithstanding the simplicity of his brown raiment, he is said to be the wealthiest man in the city. His features, moreover, are regular and distinguished, and expressive of great sweetness of disposition. He received advice of our approach two days ago through one of his co-religionists in Tangier, M. Benchimol, second dragoman to the French embassy, who, during the entire course of our journey, has displayed the most untiring kindness for us all--and so he very courteously comes to see if he can be of service to us. We promise to repay his visit to-morrow, and he departs in haste, fearful lest he may find the gates of the old ramparts closed against him.

The ground about our tents is broken and uneven, as is the case with the approaches to very ancient places ; there are entrances leading to caves and underground passages, and mounds of turf of singular shape, which afford food for reflection. To take two steps beyond the tents in the darkness demands an infinity of precaution. The jackals, the owls, all the wailing, whining, screeching dwellers in the caverns and the old walls make their presence known by some single, unrepeated cry, which sounds like a low death-call. And the rain keeps coming down, as if the surroundings of our camp were not already gloomy enough.

Half-Past Eight—Nine o'Clock.

Our two visitors have been gone for a long time and nothing has yet reached us that was promised—neither "mouna" nor guard. No doubt Mequinez is afraid of foot-pads and has closed her gates and forgotten us, leaving us to the mercy of people and adventures of all kinds. We become doubly conscious of the black silence that reigns around our little canvas abodes, beneath the clouded sky which makes the night darker than ever, so close to the walls of this strange, dead city.

At last there is the light of lanterns shining in the distance, coming, no doubt, from the adjacent gateway cut in the ramparts overhead, and they approach, coming down the uneven, hillocky avenue into which the caverns open ; it is our "mouna" making its appearance with all its wonted gravity and deliberateness'; cous-couss with sugar and milk, a live sheep and several chickens in cages. We would be glad to send back the poor animals, but such a course might have awkward results : we must surrender them to the knife first and afterward to the voracity of our escort.

Then other lanterns appear upon the heights and descend toward us ; a band of armed men marching to the tap of the drum. They are the soldiers who are to guard us until daylight, and judging from their numbers—there are eighty of them at least—we come to the conclusion that either the young Pacha is very prudent or the place has a very bad name. They seat themselves in a circle around our tents, either on the grass or on shapeless black objects, facing each other two by two, and strike up a song to keep themselves awake. They will keep this up until morning ; it is the proper thing for sentinels to do who perform their duty conscientiously, and we must do the best we can about sleeping in the midst of this wild chorus which will never let up. Along toward midnight their music degenerates into a charivari that is truly diabolical. The fact that they have been selected to guard the " Nazarenes " seems to inspire them with ironical mirth. They no longer sing, they imitate all the animals of Morocco, barking dogs, grunting camels, cackling hens, and these failing, they invent preternatural yells and shrieks of their own. I endure it as long as I can, then arise and grope my way to the tent of the old Caid, upon whose shoulders rests the responsibility for all things, and arouse him; together we visit the posts, he bearing a lantern, I a horse-whip, and by dint of threats of immediate punishment, of complaining to the Pacha, of the bastinado, and even of imprisonment, silence is finally restored.

One o'clock in the morning. We are presented with a second "mouna," more imposing than the first; cous-couss again, pyramids of cakes, baskets of oranges, tea and loaves of sugar; the young Pacha insists on doing things in style. Our escort make ready to recommence their noisy feasting and in the end we go to sleep again.

XXXIII.

MEQUINEZ.

Monday Morning, April 29th.

WHEN we open our eyes upon the sombre landscape, we perceive that our encampment is in a burying-ground, probably the potter's-field of the place; there are no tomb-stones, but the mounds of turf scattered about, some recently thrown up, others very old, show that we have been sleeping among the dead.

The approaches to the city are as destitute of movement to-day as they were yesterday; through the archway which opens in the wall up yonder on the rising ground, there is no sign of a living thing, and the cheerless desert begins immediately at the base of the long walls.

About eight o'clock, however, three or four Jews show themselves, easy of recognition at a distance by their black robes; they have emerged from the gateway and here they are, coming down the uneven, grayish, stony path in the direction of our camp. They wish to sell us old-fashioned trinkets and embroideries, which they unpack on the wet grass among the pegs and cords of our tents.

NINE O'CLOCK.

A horseman whose dusty aspect shows that he has ridden at speed reaches us from Fez; he brings us the letters which we were awaiting from the Sultan to the Pacha and the Amins to enable us to enter the holy city; they accord us full permission to go about freely and to visit the mysterious gardens of Aguedal. Thereupon we order out our mules and make our way up through the grayish avenue to the great gateway which last night so attracted our eyes, and at last, passing under the great arch with its setting of tiles and arabesques, we enter Mequinez.

The first things that we meet are quagmires and ruins; other ramparts, other enclosures, other tumble-down gates, the picture of desolation and the extremest old age. A few scattered inhabitants, loitering in the angles of the walls, and draped in bournouses of the same color as the stones, observe our entry with an expression of vague distrust.

The streets are wider and straighter than those of Fez and the aspect of the city more imposing, but even more dilapidated and more tomb-like. There are great gray mosques and tall minarets overlooking the empty squares. On all the terraces, on all the old cracked walls, on the lintels of the doors, grass and wild flowers, mignonette and daisies, are growing in thick clumps or in trailing garlands ; the effect of the ruins is lost in a garden of white and yellow flowers.

Our guides conduct us through steep little vaulted passage ways to the house of the young Pacha, in order that we may give him the Sultan's letter which is to be the "open sesame" affording us access into the city. As we approach his dwelling the walls put off their decrepitude and are covered with an immaculate coat of whitewash, and the roofs are no longer ornamented with wild flowers. There are several persons of sober aspect seated on stones, awaiting an audience ; they are all draped in muslin veils kept in place over their robes of pink or blue cloth by silken cords and tassels.

The young Pacha receives us at the threshold of his house ; he first kisses the Sultan's seal upon the letter which we hand him, murmuring a pious benediction the while ; then he proceeds to read it and places himself at our orders to conduct us to those gardens of Aguedal which may be opened by no other man but he. When do we wish to start?—We answer, " Right away," as we have no time to spare, and at a signal, an attendant runs to bring him a horse. Almost at the same instant two black slaves appear, bringing up the charger at a gallop; restive and superb he is, and knocks the plaster off the walls in the narrow street with his furious kicking. He is white, with long, flowing tail, and the saddle and bridle are of sea-green silk embroidered with gold.

Following our host, we make our way through the dead city among the ruins of Mequinez, which we shall have to traverse in its entire extent, the palace and gardens of the Sultan being far distant in the opposite quarter. The infrequent foot-passengers bow before the young chief or stop to kiss the hem of his mantle. There are other enclosures in every direction, stiff, battlemented walls, succeeded by empty spaces and ruins, of which the ground plan is no longer distinguishable. The ramparts are all undermined at their foundation and it is difficult to understand how they maintain their erect position, but notwithstanding this, they still offer an imposing and forbidding aspect, with their huge proportions and their tall crenellated bastions.

Toward the centre of the place we come to a wall higher than all the others, of immense height and length, the square bastions of which stretch away in perspective, perfectly aligned, like the "seven towers" of Stamboul ; it forms a city within a city, more closely walled, more impenetrable. We are standing on a sort of esplanade, from which we have a view of the sad, peaceful country in the distance, the ranges of dilapidated walls, the lifeless minarets and the empty terraces. In our immediate vicinity, however, there is a little more life ; there are some men in their stone-colored bournouses, and a group of unveiled Jewish women, attired in gold-bespangled robes of blue and red velvet, who stand out against the grayish neutral tints like so many showily dressed dolls. At this moment, too, we see a small band of horsemen filing into a deserted street ; they appear wearied, as if after a long ride, and signal us and shout to us to halt, and finally advance rapidly toward us.

Ah ! It is our presents, the presents that the Sultan is sending us ! Praise be to Allah ! we had certainly given them up. There is a splendid dapple-gray horse for the governor of Algeria, which will be entrusted to us for delivery, and, for ourselves there is a great tightly nailed box, which constitutes the entire lading of a mule. We send the horsemen back to our camp, where we shall ourselves proceed forthwith to unpack and investigate our treasures. But the tidings of the monarch's gifts have spread, and now the people collect about us and look at us with respectful awe as being great chiefs. In days to come, in the misty twilight of the future when I shall look upon these gifts of the Caliph under my own roof, I wonder if I shall be able to recall all the circumstances of the strange bright scene, in which they appeared before me one day in this plaza of Mequinez, in front of the deserted palace of Mouley-Ismaïl, the Cruel Sultan.

Directing our steps toward the gardens of Aguedal, we continue to skirt the funereal gray wall, its pointed battlements stretching upward into the blue æther. We come to another plaza, the greatest and most central one of Mequinez, surrounded by minarets and windowless old houses covered with whitewash. Here, in the wearisome wall that has kept us company so long, there is a wondrous gateway, all covered with an embroidery of mosaics, opening like a surprise before us and bearing witness to the fact that this place, with its fearful prison-like aspect, was once the abode of a magnificent sovereign, who displayed all the refinement of an artist in his unequalled luxury. In front of this gate, in the midst of the bright sunshine which falls upon the plaza and sharply defines there the black shadows of the battlements, there is a great flutter among a group of fantastic cavaliers, who appear very small of size as they sit in their velvet-covered saddles, whose gay laughter has childish inflections in it, and whose mantles, instead of being white, as is the custom for men, are of all the brightest and lightest shades that are known. It is a party of school-boys, who are keeping up yesterday's fête; they are the " Amins," the " Pachas " of the future, dressed in their fine clothes and mounted on their fathers' parade saddles ; it is a bright cavalcade of children among the ruins, a wonderful display of color in the bright sunshine, relieved against the sombre, crushing background of the palace walls. I think that this bit, surpassing all others, will remain imprinted on my memory as being the most characteristically Oriental of anything I have met with in my travels in the Moghreb. How charming they are, and how odd, these school-boys on horseback ! And what a wondrous and mysteriously marvellous thing is the palace gateway that yawns behind them in those immense ramparts ! There is one little chap who may be five or six years old—not more ; he wears a salmon-colored bournous over a green velvet saddle and is mounted on a tall, neighing, rearing horse, who dashes his flowing mane back

into the face of his rider, but the urchin shows
no sign of fear ; he only smiles, turning his fine
eyes to right and left to see if people are looking
at him ; what a delicious little creature he is, and
what a superb cavalier he will be one of these
days !

This gateway, known as the gate of Sultan
Mouley-Ismaïl, the Cruel, who was contempora-
neous with Louis XIV, is a gigantesque horse-
shoe arch, supported by marble columns and
surrounded by exquisite ornamentation. The
whole of the adjoining wall, as high as the very
summits of the battlements, is covered with tiles
arranged in mosaic patterns as fine and as intri-
cate as a piece of costly embroidery. The two
square bastions which flank the gate to right and
left are covered with similar mosaics and also
rest on marble columns. Rosettes, stars, broken
lines, intermingled in an endless tangle, geometric figures that puzzle the brain that tries to
pursue them, but which all evince the purest and
most original taste, have been lavished upon the
embellishment of this arch, together with my-
riads of little varnished tiles, some in bas-relief,
some in high-relief, so that the total effect, as
seen from a distance, is an illusion of a piece of
stuff that has been embroidered over and over
with priceless thread until it has become daz-

zling with flashing, brilliant color, and then hung out over the old stones to break the stern monotony of the lofty ramparts. Yellow and green are the prevailing tones in this medley of color, but the rain, the sunlight which has baked it all, the succession of many centuries, have worked together to mellow these tints, to bring them into harmony and endue them all impartially with one uniform warm and golden coating. These embroideries are crossed and surrounded by broad dark-colored belts, like mourning ribbons stretched horizontally across their face; these are religious inscriptions, texts from the Koran, in flowing Arabic characters, patiently worked out in mosaics of black tile-work. Along the uppermost of these belts there are iron hooks, such as those we see in butchers' stalls, projecting from the wall to receive, as occasion offers, rows of human heads.

We continue on our way, still in the direction of the gardens of Aguedal; still skirting the interminable wall, we come to more mosaic gateways, more bastions and rows of battlements. As we advance, the surroundings become more and more ruinous and abandoned. There are other immense, deserted plazas, surrounded by walls that seem to be the enclosures of vanished cities; I could not count the number of dismantled

gateways, broken arches, decaying walls. Nowhere any signs of life, except the storks perching among the ruins and surveying from their
height the desolation around them, an aspect of
utter abandonment never witnessed elsewhere.
Wide empty spaces, covered with stones and
rubbish and cut up by deep holes, caverns and
sink-holes. Here and there wheat-fields enclosed by lofty, imposing walls, which in times
gone by must have served to protect so many
hidden treasures. From time to time, deep set
among the foliage of enclosures where we do not
penetrate, great roofs of green tiles, covered
with moss and wild flowers, rise above the monotonous line of the ramparts; palaces of Sultans that have passed away, they are, the doors
of which were closed after their master's death
(it not being customary for the new Sultan to
inhabit the abode of his predecessor), and which
have been abandoned to the slow destruction of
centuries. And overlying all this wilderness of
ruin, which will soon be simmering under the
scorching summer sun, is always and everywhere
the same exuberant profusion of herbs and flowers, actual beds of daisies, anemones and poppies, red, white, and pink; immense natural
gardens, delightful in their melancholy wildness.

We continue to press on under the guidance of the young Pacha, trotting along behind his horse in his equipments of green and gold. We can no longer tell whether we are in the city or in the fields, the limit of the ruins being so indistinctly drawn ; about us are great pieces of wall, unfinished and yet ready to fall from age, caprices of different sovereigns who have succeeded to the throne and then have disappeared in the everlasting gulf before they could finish the work that they had put their hand to. Long lines of battlements stretch away to lose themselves, no one knows where, among the thickets and the verdure in the distance of the desert country.

The gardens of Aguedal ! What a desolate place ! How impressive the unlooked-for sadness of them, even after all the funereal sights that our eyes have witnessed ! First, a broken-down, worm-eaten gate set in the lofty ramparts at the end of a grass-grown path, which swings open with an air of secrecy ; at the summons of the Pacha, a white-bearded keeper draws the bolts on the inside and closes them again when we have passed. A first enclosure, like a burying ground, between walls at least fifty feet high, then

a second bolted door ; a second enclosure, then still another door—and at last the "gardens" are before us. We are impressed by the nudity of what seems to us an immense, limitless meadow, covered with short grass dotted with daisies, where herds of cattle and droves of horses are grazing in the wild state, and bands of ostriches are seen racing in the distance—and where the ground is scattered with bones and carcases of dead animals. As to gardens, there are none here ; a few trees, perhaps, yonder, in an enclosure like an orchard ; that apart, it is only an uncheerful, walled meadow, so extensive, however, that its gray wall appears to run to meet the horizon, seems to be only a slender line encircling the plain where the herds are grazing. The fields beyond, absolutely deserted, lie green beneath a lowering sky ; it is all like some land of the north, in a country destitute of roads and villages, like the park of some manor in a district abandoned by its inhabitants. The horses, the cattle, the little white daisies among the grass, also serve to remind us of our climes, and there are even small pools of water here and there, where the most every-day kind of frogs are croaking. The only thing surprising to us then, the only dissonant note, is this Arab chief riding at our side—and those ostriches, running about on their long, slender legs as if they were at home here. If the place is sad, at least it is not common-place ; for it is no doubt the fact that very few Europeans have ever gained admission to these *gardens* of the Sultan.

Our mules proceed with a certain amount of caution; they are afraid of the carcasses lying there on the grass ; then they shy at a band of ostriches who come up to investigate us, stretching out their long unfeathered necks, and then race away, swaying to and fro on their long legs.

We are curious to learn what has become of three Normandy mares, presented to Mouley-Hassan some four years ago by the French government at the time when a former embassy was here, and we diverge from our route to see if they may be among the drove of horses that we see grazing not far away. We finally recognize the three expatriated Normans standing closely bunched together, apart from their companions, and evidently forming a select society of their own. Each of them has her little foal by her side, the offspring of a foreign father, and it surprises us to see these animals remembering their common origin after their four years of exile and living thus in community, as if they understood that they were strangers in a strange land.

After looking at the horses, we stroll along

under the walls to inspect three or four ancient
edifices which stand backed up against the ramparts, separated from each other by wide intervals; they are garden kiosks, surrounded by a
few dark cypresses. They have verandahs overlooking the Aguedal and supported by rows of
charming old columns; uninhabited for centuries, may be, they exhibit a mortal sadness beneath the thick coats of whitewash which deface
their arabesques. Their gates are shut, bolted,
or even walled up with masonwork. No doubt
the Sultanas, beautiful prisoners invisible to man,
have often come in days of old and seated themselves under the colonnades in front of these
kiosks, and created for themselves a short-lived
illusion of freedom by gazing upon the broad
extent of the daisy-enameled plain; and mysterious love dramas have been enacted here, the
history of which will never be written. Leaving
the gardens of Aguedal, our guide conducts us
back by other ways, through the inner dependencies of the palace, between the inevitable great
battlemented walls, of immense height, which
give to all this locality its character of impenetrable savageness. All the courtyards, avenues
and broad plazas are untenanted and lifeless.
The prevailing color of the ramparts and the
ruins is an earthy yellow with streaks of a red-

dish brown ; the lime used at Mequinez is generally mixed with ochre ; and then, more than all else, the course of time, the rain, the sunlight and the lichens have endued the whole with the primitive tints of the rocks and the soil. These dependencies of the palace are of immense extent ; in the low grounds, where there are running streams, we pass through abandoned orchards, which are delightful thickets of orange, pomegranate, fig and willow. There is abundant opportunity furnished the pretty captive Sultanas of wandering among the verdure, and they may easily enough delude themselves with the idea that they are roaming in the wild-wood.

The Indian fig grows in all the crevices of the ramparts and attains the size of trees, flaunting in the sunlight its yellow flowers and its rigid bluish leaves. Quantities of storks, standing motionless upon one foot on the very top of the battlements, watch us as we pass by.

The Pacha takes us to see an artificial lake which is used by the ladies of the harem to bathe in, and upon which the Sultan intends to launch the electric boat which we have presented him with. It is a rectangular sheet of water, three or four hundred métres in length. It is surrounded on three sides by a forbidding wall, sixty feet high, which is reflected upside down in the still water, giving a false impression of great depth. The fourth side communicates with the great empty esplanade before the palace by means of a quay flagged with marble. Here we walk about, entirely by ourselves, our vision embracing the whole series of formidable ramparts which rise one above another, twist and double on each other, and shut us in from the world. Above the old cracked walls, now baking in the noonday sun, the grass-grown roofs of the palaces of the older Sultans again raise their heads—concealing, perhaps, still more wonderful rubbishy things that have never seen the light ; and still beyond, a confused distant mass of terraces, mosques, minarets, cracked and tumbling walls ; all Mequinez outlined in solemn desolation against the gloomy sky. The shrilling of the locusts comes from among the old stones, and all the surface of the lake is dotted with small black points, which are the heads of frogs, piping at the top of their small voices among the silence of the ruins.

There is only one building of recent date lifting its roofs above the old walls down yonder; it is the palace of the reigning Sultan, white as snow, roofed with green tiles and furnished with blue awnings. The Sultan is obliged to pass most of his time at Fez or Morocco, his other two capitals, and so is here only a month out of the year, but the palace is now tenanted by a detachment of the ladies of the harem who left Fez last week, and who, as may be well supposed, were scrupulously sequestrated within the walls before we reached the gardens.

Just as we are preparing to take our departure, a group of black slaves, the royal laundresses, wearing great silver rings in their ears, emerge from the palace, carrying on their heads great bundles containing the soiled linen of the invisible beauties, which they nonchalently proceed to wash in the lake to the accompaniment of songs of their country.

I cannot tell how many courts we have to cross in order to get away, how many gateways we have to pass through, nor how many turns we have to make, between the great sun-dried ramparts where cacti are growing. It so chances that we are to make our exit by the wonderful mosaic gate of Mouley-Ismaïl which we admired so much this morning. We pass beneath. the shadow of the great arch, between the marble columns, and here we are, in the great central square of the city, in the bright sunshine. Some groups of Arab bystanders, catching sight of their Pacha between us two foreigners, advance and salute profoundly, bowing almost to the dust.

There must have been scenes like this in the olden time, when Mouley-Ismaïl took his informal walks abroad in the early morning.

Here we thank the Pacha and say farewell, to direct our steps toward the Jewish quarter and pay the visit which we promised to the friend whose acquaintance we made last evening. It will be a change for us after all this dead grandeur.

To reach our destination, we have to traverse the most thickly inhabited quarters; first, that of the jewelers, where, in little shops like boxes along both sides of the street, glittering displays of silver-ware and coral are fantastically exposed upon old tables of common wood ; then a long street of private dwellings, straight and wide as a boulevard and lined with little roofless houses that look like great cubes of stone ; it ascends toward a hill, on the summit of which the painted cupola of a saint's tomb projects its form upon the crude blue of the sky, flanked by two slender palm trees.

The gateway of the Jews is situated at the end of this street. As we pass under it, the entire aspect changes at once, as if we had been taken bodily up from the middle of one country and

dropped into the middle of another one. In
place of silence and immovability, here is an unceasing stir and bustle ; in place of brown men,
walking with slow and majestic step, draped in
white mantles, we have men of pale or pink complexion, their long straggling curls surmounted
by black caps, who go about with down-cast eyes
in close-fitting robes of dark colors ; the women
are unveiled and are very pale and have scanty
eye-brows ; there is a swarm of fresh and ruddy
young Hebrews whose looks are expressive of
fear and cunning ; a population too closely
crowded in this stifling quarter, outside which
the Sultan will not suffer them to live. The
merchants congregate and block the streets, and
the ground is strewn with animal and vegetable
refuse and all uncleanness ; the filth is astounding, even after having seen the Arab cities, and
the nameless stenches, a mixure of the pungent
and the sweetish, are enough to turn one's
stomach.

Our friend of yesterday evening advances to
receive us, advised of our arrival, no doubt, by
the tumult raised by the multitude in our honor.
His countenance still exhibits the same expression of mild good nature, but for a million-
aire his get-up is really very shabby ; an old-
fashioned, smooth, threadbare, faded robe. It is

said to be customary for these rich Jews to affect simplicity when they go about the streets.

The entrance of his house, also, is very unassuming, quite low and narrow, on the brink of a gutter filled with filth. Once inside, however, we remain dazed in the presence of a singular luxury ; we are received and welcomed, in the midst of scenery worthy of the Thousand-and-One-Nights, by a band of smiling women literally covered with gold and precious stones. We are in an interior court, open to the sky, running quite around which are a colonnade and ornamented arcades. The floor is composed of bright colored tiles, and the walls are covered with the same as high as a man's stature ; over these are arabesques of infinitely varied design and astonishing lace work carved in stone, the whole picked out with blue, green, red and gold. The patient artists who decorated this house are the descendants of those who did the carving in the palaces of Grenada, and they have changed nothing, in the course of so many centuries, in the artistic traditions bequeathed them by their fathers ; the same fairy-like embroidery that we admire in the Alhambra beneath its coating of dust, reappears here in all the splendor of its new, fresh coloring.

The women are fairly dazzling in the bright

sunlight ; they wear velvet petticoats, embroidered with gold, chemises of silk striped with gold, and open corsages almost entirely covered with gilding ; there are heavy rings set with precious stones in their ears and on their arms and ankles ; and their small peaked caps are of brilliant colored silks worked in gold thread. They are very pale, of a waxen complexion, their black eyes are painted in deep circles, and their hair, dressed " à la Juive," black also as the raven's wing, falls in smooth bands down their cheeks. The mistress of the house is the only one of this group who is not absolutely young ; the others, who are presented to us as *ladies*, and who, as the luxury of their dress indicates, must be married, are children, whose age, taking the average of them, may be about ten. (Among the Jews of Fez and Mequinez, it is customary for girls to marry at ten and boys at fourteen.)

All these small fairies come up to us and shake hands with pretty smiles ; our reception at the hands of the lady of the house is cordial and not wanting in dignity ; she is magnificent above the others; her petticoat of crimson velvet and her corsage of sky-blue velvet are lost beneath the raised ornamentation of gold, while splendid pearls, and emeralds large as hazel-nuts, are set in her ear-rings. We were never before in the mansion of a rich Jewish family, and all this unknown and unsuspected wealth seems to us like a dream, after the squalor and the stenches of the street.

Notwithstanding our host's insistance, we decline to stay breakfast, but they seem so pleased to receive us that, not to disappoint them, we take a cup of tea.

The tea is to be served in a room of the first story; we ascend a steep and narrow stairway in mosaics, followed by all the little women in their attire of idols; we pass through an upper gallery with decorated walls, enclosed in openwork relieved by gilding, and enter a drawing-room decorated in the style of the Alhambra, where we seat ourselves on the floor upon velvet cushions and marvellous rugs. Our spiced tea, too, is smoking on the ground in silver tea-pots and samovars of rich design.

The windows of this drawing-room are small trefoils, or rosettes, of an exquisite elegance of form; on the walls is the same inlaid work, the same carved lace work of which the Arabs possess the inimitable secret; as for the ceiling, it is an aggregation of small vaulted arches set with stars, in the composition of which it would seem as if the rarest and most difficult geometric combinations must have been exhausted, as well as the most extraordinary blending of colors.

Through the stained glass of the windows the sunlight falls in patches of blue, yellow and red upon the medley of silk and gold and the brilliant colors of the women's attire. From a silver chafing dish in the middle of the room rises in a thin blue cloud the perfumed smoke of burning aloe wood.

After we have swallowed the three indispensable cups of tea, and have been served with little cakes, preserves of watermelon and many little sweets of every description, we make an effort to say good-bye and leave, but our hostess renews her invitation to breakfast with such an urgency of entreaty that we finally are vanquished and say yes. Thereupon an expression of unfeigned pleasure appears upon her face, and all the little married ladies jump for joy. But before taking our places at table, we have to visit all the apartments of the dwelling, of which our host seems to be pardonably proud.

First we ascend to the terraces, otherwise known as roofs, the ordinary exercising place for the family. We can scarcely bring ourselves to step on them, so snowy white is their immaculate coating of white-wash. They are divided into several plots, from which the desolate grandeur of the surroundings presents itself under different aspects. Such is the absence of regularity in the streets of this old city, where for centuries and centuries houses have been built into and on top of the more ancient ruins, that a part of these white terraces are lost beneath the dark, forbidding arch of an old ruinous fortress that was formerly erected on this spot by Mouley-Ismaïl, the Cruel. From this lofty elevation the eye first settles upon the Jewish quarter, with its airless huddle of houses, crowded up against each other as if they had been screwed in a gigantic compress, and emitting all sorts of stifling odors. Beyond is the remainder of Mequinez, the-entire incomprehensible development of walls of fortress and palace, on which, by way of contrast, space and breadth seem to have been lavished *ad libitum*, and in the middle of the highest and the sternest of these enclosures appears the wonderful gate through which we so lately made our exit from the Seraglio, the great mosaic-embroidered arch which was the magnificent Sultan's entrance of honor. Still farther, beyond all these ramparts and ruins, glimpses are obtained of that country where the only law-givers are the brigands. " It has happened more than once," our host tells us, " when the

Sultan was absent with his army toward the south upon some expedition, that it has been necessary to close the gates of Mequinez in bright daylight, so bold and dangerous were the robber Zemmours."

The Israelite's whole family has followed us up here in Indian file along the steep and narrow stairway, to do the honors of their airy retreat ; the velvet and the gold of the women's costumes contrast with the brilliant whitewash of the terrace ; all the little married ladies are here, too. Especially to be noted are two little sisters-in-law, about ten years old, who are always together, arm in arm, and who are entirely quaint and charming, with their great, excessively painted eyes, which have nothing in common with children's eyes ; the splendid rings on their wrists and ankles, which were wedding gifts and which are to be worn by them later when they shall be full-grown, are now too large for their slender limbs and are kept in place by ribbons. In the case of them all, whether young or the reverse, what seems to be their hair, falling from beneath their little caps of gold gauze, is not hair, but an imitation of it in silk ; two stiff, carefully combed plaits of black silk enframe their cheeks of waxy white, and two little " spit-curls," also of black silk, are pasted in front of their delicate ears.

Wherever their true hair may be, it is invisible, concealed no one knows where.

As my eyes survey these terraces and the melancholy horizon, in face of which these women are born and die, their situation flashes upon my mind and a feeling of horror seizes me at the thought of what life can be for these Jews, constrained to obey the law of Moses only with fear and trembling and immured in their narrow quarter, in the midst of this mummified city, apart from the whole world.

The whole house is arranged and decorated in the most exquisite taste, and might be taken for the residence of some fashionable Vizier, were it not for the smallness of its proportions, or still more, for the presence in every room, framed and under glass, of the Tables of the Law, or inscriptions in Hebrew, or the stern face of Moses, or some other indication of this particular obscurity which is not Mussulman obscurity.

Our breakfast is awaiting us. It is served in a room of the ground-floor, opening on the fine courtyard with its ornamentation of lace-work carved in stone and picked out with gold. Its inner walls are embellished with mosaics of surpassing fineness, representing rows of Moorish arches that are fantastically intertwined with rosettes in a series of kaleidoscopic designs. The ceiling is composed of those innumerable little pendents, arranged in complicated, inlaced forms, which I can only compare to those crystallizations of hoar-frost that we see hanging from the trees in winter.

As a mark of politeness toward us, the table is spread with a white cloth and in the European style; the china is French, from Limoges, with decorations in gold, in the style of the Empire. Through what Odysseys have these things passed that they should turn up at last in Mequinez?

Four musicians; two singers, a violin and a drum, are introduced, who seat themselves on the ground at our feet and entertain us with an unceasing succession of squeaking, doleful airs. Our hostess, notwithstanding her pearls and emeralds, cannot be satisfied without superintending in person the kitchen arrangements and bringing the dishes in to us, all which she accomplishes, moreover, with perfect gracefulness and a distinguished manner that is natural to her.

Twenty courses succeed each other in due order, which are washed down by two or three varieties of an extremely good little old red wine

that the Israelites make from grapes that grow on the hill-sides around Mequinez, to the great scandal of the Mussulmans. And while the music is howling and shrieking at our feet and the scented smoke of the wood that is burning before us curls around our breakfast in a bluish cloud, we behold, in the midst of the bright court, the family grouped together in their gold bedizened costumes, and among them the two little sisters-in-law, who pass and repass, arm in arm, their childish airs contrasting with their heavy trinkets and their clothes like those of grown women.

When the time comes for us to take our departure, we do not know how to thank these kindly people, whom we shall never meet again, and to whom we would like, nevertheless, to offer hospitality, if, which is impossible, they should ever visit our country.

When we go forth into the squalid street to mount our mules again, we find quite an assemblage of people who have collected there in their curiosity to have a look at us ; the whole quarter is on foot, and we make our way through a dense crowd until, the gate of the Jews once passed, we again reach the solitude of the Arab city. The roasting two o'clock sun is beating upon the stillness of the ruins amid the hum of thousands of locusts. We leave the precincts of the ramparts to descend to our camp.

There the horsemen are awaiting us who came from Fez, bearing our gifts. Before dismissing them, we wish to verify the contents of the boxes, lest they may have been broken into and robbed during the night while they were in transit, and at the announcement that they are to be opened, our muleteers form a close circle around us with eyes distended by curiosity; the people of a small caravan, who have pitched their tents beside ours while we were away, also draw near, attracted by the spectacle, and soon we have some thirty Arabs, of equivocal appearance and draped in majestic rags, pressing close about us in silent impatience to admire the presents of the Caliph. We open the first case; it contains the green velvet saddle, richly embroidered in gold, which we are commissioned to transmit to the Governor of Algeria, together with his steed of dapple-gray; its appearance in the sunlight is greeted with the admiring murmurs of the crowd.

Now let us open the long box which contains our personal gifts. For each one of us there is a musket of "souss" in its red case, an old-fashioned arm with a barrel five feet long and silver-plated in its whole length. For each one of us there is also a great Moroccan Pacha's sword in an enameled scabbard, with a belt of silk and gold, the hilt of rhinoceros horn, the blade and guard damascened with gold. It glitters in the sunlight, and the bystanders utter expressions of feverish delight. A camel-driver is so carried away by his enthusiasm for a Caliph who can make such presents as to shout ; " May Allah grant victory to our Sultan Mouley-Hassan ! May Allah prolong his days, *even at the cost of my own life !* " We conclude that we were imprudent in having aroused such desires about us.

We mount our mules again, and, preceded by the old Caid who is answerable for us, make our way up to the city, this time with the intention of wandering about haphazard in quest of rugs and arms until the sun goes down.

The bazaar, much smaller, darker and more gloomy than that of Fez, is completely deserted when we reach it ; all the little lids to the merchants' dens along the walls are tightly closed. We are told that every one is at the mosque, but that they will very soon return ; we had, in fact, forgotten that it is half-past three, the hour of the fourth prayer of the day.

One by one the merchants return from their

devotions, with measured steps, veiled in their transparent muslins, white like ghosts in the dusk of the little vaulted passageways. Abstracted in their dream, careless or disdainful of our presence, they open their niches, raise the lids and seat themselves within, holding their chaplets between their fingers, without condescending to look at us. Still we are the only buyers on hand—and one is tempted to ask one's self, what is the use of a bazaar in this necropolis? The goods offered for sale are chiefly bournouses and clothing, leather work, and horse equipments enameled in gold and silver, together with those bed-coverings of outlandish design, woven by the tribes-women of the south by their tent-doors in the evening—among the Beni-M'guil or the Touaregs.

For a long time we roam among the deserted and funereal precincts; always in the gloom of the covered streets, we pass before several immense mosques, where we catch furtive glimpes of rows of mysterious arches and columns. Finally we reach the jeweler's quarter, where there is a little more activity.

What queer old jewelry finds a market in Mequinez! When could the things have ever been new?—There is not one which has not an air of extreme antiquity; old rings for wrists or ankles, worn smooth by centuries of rubbing against human flesh ; great clasps for fastening veils ; little old silver bottles with coral pendants, to hold the black dye with which the eyes are painted, with hooks to fasten them at the belt ; boxes to enclose Korans, carved in arabesques and bearing Solomon's seal ; old necklaces of gold sequins, defaced by wear on the necks of women long since dead ; and quantities of those large trefoils in hammered silver, enclosing a green stone, which are hung about the neck to avert the bad effect of the evil-eye. These things are all spread out on little, dirty, worm-eaten tables, in front of the squatting merchants, in the little dens in the old walls.

The bazaar is near the Jewish quarter, and several of that race, knowing us to be here, come and offer us trinkets, bracelets, quaint old rings and emerald earrings, things which they take from the pockets of their black robes with furtive airs, after having cast distrustful looks around.

We are also approached by the dealers in the fine woolen rugs and carpets of R'bat, which they throw upon the ground, among the dust, refuse and bones, to show us the rare designs and splendid colors of their wares.

* * *

The sun is getting low ; its rays are already beginning to stretch in long golden bands across the ruins. It is time for us to end our bargaining, which has not been conducted without some wrangling, and to leave the sacred city which we are to behold no more, and betake ourselves to our tents.

Before passing the last gate of the enclosure, we halt in a sort of small bazaar, of the existence of which we were not previously aware. It is that of the bric-a-brac merchants, and the Lord only knows what queer old oddities shops of this kind in Mequinez can display. These dealings are carried on near a gate which opens on the wilderness of the fields, at the base of the tall ramparts and in the shade of some old mulberry trees that are just now bright in their tender young April foliage. Ancient arms constitute the principal stock in trade of the dealers in this quarter, rusty yataghans, long Souss muskets ; then old leather amulets for war or for the chase, ridiculous powder-horns, and also musical instruments ; guitars covered with snake-skin, pipes and tambourines. To keep the rubbish which they are selling in countenance, no doubt, the dealers are mostly all broken-down, worn-out, used up old men.

Beggars, who have selected their dwelling-places among the crevices in the rocks by this entrance to the city, are attentive listeners to our bargaining ; a one-armed man covered with sores, a leprous cripple, and several men, who, in place of eyes, have only two bleeding cavities swarming with flies ; these latter are thieves whose eyes, as the law provides, have been burned out with a red-hot iron.

No doubt the people in this bazaar are very poor and have great need to sell their goods, for they crowd around us and press us with their wares. We make several surprising bargains. As the sky grows yellow and the cold breeze of sunset springs up, we are still there, near the lonely gate, beneath the branches of the old trees, surrounded by some fifty wild, ragged forms, Berbers, Arabs and Soudanese.

XXXIV.

TUESDAY, APRIL 30th.

AT the first bright rays of the sun we break camp, leaving what remains of our feasts to the dogs and the vultures. Quickly the holy city disappears behind us, shut in by the wild hills.

Mountain passes, carpets of flowers. Great blooms of pink bind-weed among the bluish aloes, in such profusion that it is as if one had taken great handfuls of pink ribbon and thrown them among the pale, ashy foliage of the aloes. And so it is for leagues on leagues. Then come belts of blue bind-weed, so blue that they resemble pools in which is reflected the beautiful deep coloring of the sky.

It will be to-morrow before we turn into the direct Tangier road which we followed in our journey hither; to-day we are traversing a region still less frequented, and which is quite strange to us, a very solitary region. It is growing warmer, the African odor is more marked among the fields, and there is a greater abundance of flowers and more of the vibrating hum of insects, in a deeper silence.

We are to proceed by forced marches, about sixty kilométres a day ; our camping places, which have been discussed and fixed by us in connection with the Caid who is conducting us, have been marked off at such distances. This evening we are in hopes of camping on the far side of these lower ranges of the Atlas, at the opening of the great plain where winds the Sebu.

Our manner of travelling is quite different, this time, from what it was before, and the country through which we passed as if on a holiday excursion, where all the horsemen of the

different tribes collected to do us honor, appears
to us now in its true aspect, in its sullen quiet,
with all its boundless untenanted space. With
no disparagement toward our comrades of the
embassy at Fez—of whom we retain the kindest
remembrance—we prefer to return in this manner, like a brave band of Moors, avoiding the
curiosity of passing caravans, forming a not in-
harmonious speck in the vast solitudes where we
are journeying, disguised as we are in our bournouses and blackened by the sun; we feel ten
times more African, gossiping with our muleteers, listening to their songs and stories, ini-
tiated into a thousand small details of Moroccan
life that we had never dreamed of in our cere-
monious inward march.

The old Caid who solicited the honor—and
the profit—of bringing us back to Tangier is an
inhabitant of Mequinez, where he is said to possess a harem of young white women; he requested permission yesterday to spend the night
at his home. He was promptly on hand at the
camp at daylight this morning, faithful to his
promise. To-day, however, though always erect
in his saddle, he looks like a corpse that has been
sun-dried, and in place of taking the head of the
line, he follows painfully in the rear; too proud
to own up that he is tired, spurring up his ani-

mal with a heart breaking spitefulness each time that he sees us drawing rein to wait for him.

All day long, we meet neither village, nor house, nor cultivated field. At considerable distances from each other, there are a few *douars* of wandering bands, generally stationed away from the road, but whose watch-dogs, scenting us in spite of the distance, howl in the silence of the fields as we pass. Their yellowish or brownish tents are always arranged in a circle—like the mushrooms which they resemble so closely— with their cattle grazing in the middle, and there is in the plain, beside each *douar*, two or three great circular spots, covered with filth and where no grass grows—which are the sites of former camps, abandoned on account of the herbage being exhausted. We are told that the tents are inhabited by the women only, all the able-bodied men having been drafted by the Pacha of Mequinez for his expedition against the Zemours.

Toward noon, as we are passing a ford, we meet a Berber tribe on its travels, the men breasting the rapid stream with robes tucked up high above the water. According to Berber custom, the women wear very scanty veils, and some of the younger ones among them are very pretty. The cattle make the passage with great lowing and bellowing, kept in order by dogs that seem to have their hands full. Little girls carry lambs in their bosoms, and from one of those large baskets called *chouari* that the mules carry on their backs, there looks out wondering-ly a little new-born foal that has been placed there for safe transportation, who seems to find his quarters comfortable.

At last, about four o'clock, from the top of the last peak of this range of the Atlas, the plain of the Sebu, which we shall have to cross to-morrow, appears before us like a shining sea. In the fore-ground it is striped and variegated with yellow, pink and violet, according to the predominance of the different kinds of flowers that have never been disturbed by foot of man. Far away in the distance, where the horizon lies in a clearly defined circle, all these bright tints are confused and blended in an uniform blue, like that of the real sea. Descending a steep declivity, we encamp for the night in the plain, at an hour's march beyond the foot of the mountains, near the holy tomb of Sidi-Kassem and close to a small cluster of thatched hovels that are supposed to be under the protection of this marabout.

That is always a delightful hour, when, the

long day's march ended and the camp pitched, we seat ourselves voluptuously outside our tent on a carpet of fresh wild flowers which are always different, always changing. Around us on every side is boundless space. The air smells sweet, is filled with that perfume which it has in our country, although in less degree and more ephemeral, at hay-making time; our Arab clothes are light and easy, increasing the restful sensation that we experience as we lie stretched out under the cool evening sky ; and that deep limpidity which pervades the whole scene, which is a feast to the eye, it seems as if we breathe *that* in also, that we receive a physical sensation of taste from it when we fill our lungs with air. The stability of the old Arab ground on which we are to repose seems infinitely pleasant after so many hours spent in rocking to and fro to accommodate ourselves to the short step of the mules ; and then we are very hungry, too, and are not sorry to think that the hour of cous-couss is approaching, nor do we look scornfully on the preparations that our muleteers are making for us yonder ; sheep and chickens roasting on the grass.

Our location here is near the Beni-Hassen, whose territory we shall cross to-morrow without a halt, so as to put the stream of the Sebu between us and our next encampment; the Zemours are not far away, too, but it is difficult to imagine a danger near us in this delightfully calm and flower-decked spot.

The lowing herds are returning to the adjoining little village, driven by hooded children. We are quickly furnished with a supply of warm milk in earthen vessels, and the old chief, who is to supply our guard for the night, comes to have a chat with us. After all sorts of questions and answers have been exchanged between us, we make inquiries about the three robbers who were captured hereabouts the day we first passed this way. "Ah!" says he, "the three robbers!.... this is the fifth or sixth day that *their hands are in salt!*"

XXXV.

Wednesday Morning, May 1st.

THERE was firing all night long about our camp, in our very ears. It proceeded from our sentinels, who were greatly exercised and very alert. We could hear them say to each other: "It is a robber."—"No, it is a jackal." And then they would discuss the shape of what they thought they had seen approaching in the darkness: "They were men, I tell you, but stooping, stooping, crawling along on all fours——."

* *

At half-past four in the morning, with the first glimpse of day, we are called, according to orders, to break camp and be off; we want to be clear of the territory of the Beni-Hassem and to have crossed the big river before nightfall.

As we awake in our small canvas house—which is always the same, where the mats and the rugs are always arranged in one unvarying fashion— it often happens that we do not well remember the aspect of the country about us, which, on the contrary, is constantly changing; which is it? a great lifeless city, a deserted plain or a mountain that gives us a view of the surrounding region?

As I step from my tent this morning, still dazed with sleep, I see before me a wide expanse of country, a mass of pink mallows and violet-colored lucerne, lying beneath a black sky; an unimaginable profusion of flowers in a flat, boundless waste, which has something to remind one of both the Garden of Eden and the Desert. It is scarcely light yet, and the thick clouds, which seem to touch the ground, make the vault of heaven darker than the earth beneath. At the far end of the plain, however, just where the clouded sky comes down to meet the earth, the golden sun reveals his presence by the long, level rays with which he penetrates the thick darkness in which we are enveloped; his presence is rather felt than seen, and, for an instant, the contrast makes the regions which adjoin the luminous shafts that emanate from him, darker than before. The mysterious sunrise reminds me forcibly of those which I used to be familiar with on the coasts of Britanny, or in the southern seas during the foggy season. But while I am thus at a loss and undecided where I am, as I watch the far, pale rent in the sky, great beasts pass in single file between me and the sun ; slow-moving, swaying beasts, whose long legs project upon the plain shadows that seem to have no end : the caravan for Africa. Only then do I fully grasp again the idea of my situation, which had three-fourths escaped me.

The clouds are absorbed, disappear, no one can say where. The blue appears again in all quarters simultaneously, then becomes uniform over all the dome of heaven.

For seven hours we journey without a halt over the broad plain, in a magnificent desert of daisies, marigolds, lucerne and mallows, now and then meeting trains of camels or heavily loaded mules ; all the traffic coming and going between Tangier and Fez—between Europe and the Soudan. Finally we weary of so many flowers, a'l of the same kind and seen through half-closed eyes, for the rocking motion of our mules and the fierce heat of the sun together induce a state of semi-somnolence.

About two o'clock, we come to a halt in a spot of which this picture remains fixed upon my memory; the same limitless plain, decked with flowers as was never any garden, and apart, by himself, the old Caid, completely done up, on his knees in prayer. It is a belt of white daisies, interspersed with red poppies; the old man kneels at the far end, with his complexion of the color of clay, his long white beard like moss, clothed in the bright colors of the daisies and poppies around him, his pink caftan visible beneath his white veils; his white horse with the red saddle grazes beside him, his head buried to the ears in the long grass; and himself, half buried among these pink and white flowers, in the midst of the immense flowery plain that stretches, an infinite desert, beneath the deep blue of the summer sky; prostrate upon the ground where he will soon find a resting-place, and beseeching the mercy of Allah with that fervor of prayer that is inspired by the knowledge that death is not far off.

* * *

We passed the Sebu at four o'clock, and encamped near a village of the Beni-Malek, on the north bank of the stream.

XXXVI.

Thursday, May 2nd.

NEW recruits are added to our little band : some Arabs that we met by the way, travelling unprotected, who requested permission to join us from fear of robbers. We have also with us two of those persons called Rakkas, members of an important corporation at Fez under the command of an Amin, whose business it is to carry letters across Morocco, travelling night and day when necessary, according to the price paid them, and making up for it afterward by a week's sleep.

Four hours of the cool morning are spent in traversing these sandy wastes, carpeted with ferns and small rare flowers; a region with which we had already formed acquaintance, but which seems strange to us—more forbidding, more melancholy, more extensive, too—now that we have to pass through it without our noisy ambassadorial escort, who were constantly firing their guns in the air. The air, no longer defiled by the smoke of powder nor disturbed by the thunder of the fantasias, is surprisingly calm, pure, sweet and vivifying. The light, too, is so fine ! Beyond the grand lines of the plain, the mountains which we are to enter to-morrow are drawn against the bright void of the sky as if with firm, clean-cut strokes of the pencil in colors of startling intensity. Now and then a stork, motionless on his stilts, watches us as we pass, or sails above us in the air, his great black and white, fan-like wings flapping over our heads. And that is all the life there is in this lonely land, where the sense of living is still so keen.

Toward noon, among hills that are violet with lavender. the penetrating odor of which is intensified by the heat of the sun, we perceive a shallow ravine where there chances to be a tree, an actual tree of some size, an old wild fig-tree, knotted and twisted like an Indian banyan. It is a thing so seldom met with in this naked country, where there is no other shade than the fugitive clouds, and offers such strong temptation, that we dismount and make our way down into the hollow for our noonday halt. The advantages of the spot have already been discerned by a dozen bulls who have taken up their quarters there, keeping close together for the sake of company and well concealed amid the dense foliage, seemingly contented in their cool, moist retreat, while everything outside is baking and broiling. They do not contest the point, however, but give way to us and retire in affright, and we take possession as masters of the little oasis.

Judging from its great size and the fantastic shapes into which its branches are twisted, this fig tree must be centuries old. A little stream runs murmuring over black pebbles at its roots, between banks covered with cresses, blue myositis, and all those water-plants that are to be seen in our French brooks. Behind the dense mass of foliage, an overhanging rock forms an arched entrance to a grotto, a second small room, more sheltered and retired, carpeted with fine moss and from which trickles the outlet of a spring. As we enter, we experience a delicious sensation of coolness and shade, after the oppressiveness of the burning light out on the hills of lavender. We stretch ourselves out lazily among the roots of the tree, as if in easy chairs, our bare feet dangling in the water of the brook. There is nothing of Africa, nothing foreign in our surroundings ; we seem to be in some wild nook of France, a France of other days, in the full splendor of June, in the cloudless noontide. The living things, too, that have never been abused by man, are not afraid of us ; the water turtles come shyly up in their black shells to feed among the rushes on the crumbs of our bread, and the little green tree-frogs hop over us and allow us to catch and stroke them.

XXXVII.

SATURDAY, MAY 3d.

TO-MORROW we shall be in Tangier the White, the extremity of Europe, and shall renew our acquaintance with the men and things of the present century.

This penultimate day of our journey is a long and harassing one, and the sun grows hotter. Our old Caid, who is breaking down under the fasts of the Ramadan, fails to recognize the road. Our muleteers, who have also given up food, are slower and sleepier than usual. They fall behind, and our little column stretches out in a manner that causes us great anxiety ; it is now strung out over two or three kilométres of hot, deserted road. Sometimes our mules are quite lost to sight, together with the muleteers, who are following us with our baggage and the Sultan's gifts ; those famous, long wished-for gifts ; then, ourselves a little under the influence of the Ramadan and lacking courage to turn and re-trace our steps in the broiling heat, we throw ourselves down on the ground to wait for them to come up, anywhere, but inevitably in the sun, since there is nowhere any shade : anywhere, on the old, baked, burning Arab ground, covering our heads with our white cowls as shepherds do when they compose themselves for their siesta.

About three o'clock we have quite lost our way among the wastes of ferns, lentiscus and lavender. There is not a sign of our tents and baggage, which must have taken another road. Our old Caid, whom we would be justified in being very angry with, only excites our pity in the state to which his fatigue has reduced him.

But when we have once found our road and night comes on, the last one of our encampments seemed designed expressly to increase our regret that this is to be the end of our wandering life in this primitive land of flowers. In a spot that has no name, on the slope of a lofty hill and facing a peaceful landscape, it is a little circular plateau, or small terrace, surrounded by a dense growth of dwarf palms, like a garden plot within a hedge. Allah, for our sake, has laid upon this plateau a carpet of white, blue and pink, of virgin freshness, whereon no man has ever planted his foot : daisies, mallows and gentians, so close set that the plain seems to be embroidered with them ; the short, thin stalks, growing from a sandy soil, make a soft bed and invite us to repose. The pure air is loaded with sweet, health-giving odors. There is, a thing seldom met with, an olive grove crowning the height above us. A network of small fleecy clouds floats like a veil in the blue sky, which is beginning to pale, to change to a clear green tint. There is no sign of man to be seen in any direction ; it is the sweetest, the most peaceful nook that we have met as yet in the course of our journey, and all these delights are our's alone, the flowers, the music of the insects, the resplendency of the colors and of the atmosphere. The peace of Eden rules over this May evening on this wild plateau ; it is what the vernal evenings must have been in prehistoric times, before man inflicted ugliness upon the earth.

XXXVIII.

Sunday, May 4th.

AFTER another long day's march under a. burning sun, toward evening we behold Tangier the White rising before us; above it, the blue line of the Mediterranean, and higher still, the vaporous, indented outline which we know to be the coast of Europe.

As we pass among the European villas of the suburbs, the first impression which we experience is one of embarrassment, almost of surprise, and our embarrassment is changed to consternation when, as we enter the garden of the hotel in our bournouses, with our black faces and bare legs, with all our bales and packages, attended by our muleteers and the rag-tag of nomadic Arabs, we fall plump into a bevy of young English *misses* getting ready to play lawn-tennis.

Really, Tangier appears to us to be the acme of civilization—of modern refinement. A hotel where we can eat without having to show a letter of *mouna* with the Sultan's signature; black-coated, white-tied waiters at the table d'hote to bring us our cous-couss, wearing little scanty caftans, stopping in front at the waist, as if the price of cloth was too high, and floating in two ridiculous tails down behind the back, like the divided wings of a June beetle. Things ugly and convenient. The city everywhere open to us, and safe to travel about in ; no more need for a guard when we want to walk in the streets, no necessity for guarding one's person ; to sum up, we are forced to admit that material existence is vastly simplified, is more comfortable, and is made easy to all with very little money. In our first moments of relaxation, we are conscious how oppressive, notwithstanding its charm, was the plunge which we have just taken into former times.

Our preferences and regrets, however, are still for the land whose gate has just closed behind us. For ourselves, it is too late; assuredly we could never be acclimated there, but the life of those who were born there seems to us less wretched and less perverted than ours. Personally, I confess that I would rather be the most holy Caliph than president of the most parliamentary, most literary, most industrious, of republics. The lowest of camel-drivers, even, who, his courses in the desert ended, lies down and dies in the bright sunlight some fine day, extending his confiding hands in prayer to Allah, seems to me to have had by far the better part than the laborer in the great European workshop, be he diplomat or be he stoker, who ends his martyrdom of toil and covetousness in blaspheming upon his bed.

Rest, then, dark Moghreb, many years yet, immured, impenetrable to the things that are new. Turn thy back on Europe and strengthen thyself in holding to the things that are past. Let thy sleep be the sleep of centuries, and so continue thy ancient dream. So that at least there may be one land where man may pray.

And may Allah preserve to the Sultan his unsubdued territories and his waste places carpeted with flowers, his deserts of asphodel and iris, there in free space to exercise the agility of his horsemen and the sinews of steel of his horses, there to do battle as in old times the paladins, and gather in his harvests of rebel heads. May Allah preserve to the Arab race its mystic dreams, its immutability, scornful of all things, and its gray rags! May he preserve to the Bedouin pipes their mournful tones which make us shiver; to the old mosques their inviolable mystery; and their shroud of whitewash to the ruins.

FINIS.

9 783742 819901